Stephen U'Ren was raised in Arizona by two public school teachers, both of whom read whenever they had time and that was passed down to their four children. Mr. U'Ren attended Northern Arizona University and then he studied law at the University of Arizona. He first practiced legal aid in Juneau, Alaska and then Legal aid in El Mirage Arizona followed by a solo practice until retirement allowed more handball, multiple seasons as a volunteer ranger at Yellowstone National Park and hiking at Grand Canyon while writing in Arizona and Montana. Mr. U'Ren is married with two children and four grandchildren. He is working on a novel and a series of short stories. *The Salt Shack Dweller* is his first published book.

I would like to dedicate this book to my great friend, Bill Ott. Bill indirectly encouraged me to do things that I might have been talking about doing but had not started. Bill did not talk about doing something, he did it.

Stephen U'Ren

THE SALT SHACK DWELLER

AUSTIN MACAULEY PUBLISHERS™

LONDON • CAMBRIDGE • NEW YORK • SHARJAH

Ordering Information
Quantity sales: Special discounts are available on quantity purchases by corporations, associations, and others. For details, contact the publisher at the address below.

Publisher's Cataloging-in-Publication data
U'Ren, Stephen
The Salt Shack Dweller

ISBN 9798891556935 (Paperback)
ISBN 9798891556942 (Hardback)
ISBN 9798891556966 (ePub e-book)
ISBN 9798891556959 (Audiobook)

Library of Congress Control Number: 2024913171

www.austinmacauley.com/us

First Published 2024
Austin Macauley Publishers LLC®
40 Wall Street, 33rd Floor, Suite 3302
New York, NY 10005
USA

mail-usa@austinmacauley.com
+1 (646) 5125767

I want to acknowledge my wife, Marcia Melton, for her encouragement and her joy in the creation of fiction. I would also like to acknowledge Dr. Colin Flint for reading and commenting on the manuscript and assisting me in the publication process.

1

After he survived the Vietnam war, the Salt Shack Dweller swore that he would never again subject himself to anyone else's moral compass or lack thereof. He enrolled in a microbiology program where science and facts controlled where he wasn't ordered to shoot strange little people, or be shot at, 8500 miles from home. Strange little people who had never done anything to him or anyone he knew. He had heard what Mohammed Ali said.

But when he witnessed his plant pathology professor falsify test results by insisting that lab students use samples he had mishandled; samples that had been entrusted to him (along with a hefty payment for his services by the government of a poverty rich African nation), the Salt Shack Dweller did three things. He reported the malfeasance to deaf ears. He removed his lab coat. He departed from the university lab, never to return.

He walked down Mill Avenue, crossed the dry riverbed of the Salt River, and built a shack from discarded everything and nothings that littered the riverbed. His sole mission was to right the major misdeeds of the world he inhabited. First, on his list was to restore life to the Salt River, a river that once ran across Arizona from the New Mexico border in the east, joining the Gila and then the Colorado, headed for the Gulf of California in the southwest, with little or no water to offer, none left over for Mexico. Poor pitiful me could be heard from deep into Mexico.

The only way to restore the river was to remove the dams: Roosevelt, Horse Mesa, Mormon Flat, Stewart Mountain and Granite Reef, so that the river could once again run free, instead of being sucked up in its entirety. The only way to remove the dams was to instigate a massive flood that ripped it all out of existence. The only way to inspire a massive flood was to unleash rain such as the desert had not seen since white people arrived and started damming the river. And the only way to unleash that much rain was the old way, the native way, the sorcerer's way.

Capturing a hawk was essential to create a flood that would wash away the dams that imprisoned the river out of existence. Fortune favored the Salt Shack Dweller. He saw a red-tailed hawk circling above his abode for two days. He took a shovel 300 feet from his shack and started digging a pit at a sustained pace, his sweat dripping into the deepening pit. He stopped only to drink from a gourd that he found and turned into a water vessel. He needed the pit to be deep enough to accommodate his tall and lanky body. He next constructed a camouflage covering for the pit. For hawk bait, he captured a cooperative little rabbit.

Almost ready now, the Salt Shack Dweller summoned the hawk. Steady patience paid off. Before dark, he saw the hawk circling, lower and closer. He was in the pit with the camouflage cover pulled over it. The furry volunteer was wailing in severe protest, now that the sweet bunny understood the true nature of things. The hawk started down, focused on its prey. The Salt Shack Dweller prepared himself. He set his body so there wouldn't be the slightest movement from him. He set his mind so there would be no hesitation on his part.

The hawk dove with such blinding speed that all would have been lost if the bunny had not been tied down. The hawk struggled to lift off, enabling the Salt Shack Dweller to reach through the camouflage and grab hawk's both talons, yanking the raptor into the hot, dark pit. Momentarily, he lost control of one talon, and before he could crush the bird's head with his knee, the talon claw ripped a four-inch gash on his arm. But soon it was over. The beautiful bird was dead, but highly honored for sacrificing itself for the reincarnation of the Salt River.

Cecilia, a 27-year-old ER doctor at the county hospital, first met the Salt Shack Dweller when he presented himself at the ER wearing shorts that were too short, a cotton T-shirt and wing tip shoes, all courtesy of Goodwill Enterprises. The condition that he reported to the doctor was that he'd been bitten by a mongrel quadruped that seemed a bit out of sorts. Since the bite, he wasn't feeling so good. Cecilia asked him if he meant a dog bit him. Yes, he did. She asked why he hadn't come to the ER earlier. He said he didn't think he was going to die until a dream whispered that he could die. She asked, if that was his usual way of making decisions. He said, it usually was.

Because the mongrel quadruped could not be located to be tested, Cecilia administered the full range of rabies shots. By the time his treatment was finished, he was quite certain that he should invite her to his abode for locally sourced smoked quail and home-grown squash. She accepted. She found him to be an apple with sufficient worm holes to be unpredictably interesting. She was bored with predictable. She would bring wine, Rioja from Spain. He gave her detailed (too much detailed) directions to find his abode. She smiled and said she could find it.

A month later, Cecilia sat on a wooden crate that served as a chair inside the dark shack. She removed and cleaned each feather point from the hawk, first by scraping them in alcohol to sterilize them. She had already cleaned, stitched, and bandaged the nasty cut that hawk had inflicted on the Salt Shack Dweller in the death pit. Her beauty and calm competence were easily accentuated by the atmosphere under candle light and the weird unknown quality of the mysterious endeavor. Her heritage, many generations back, was pure Castilian, fresh skinned, dark hair and dark eyed, willowy, and athletically built. Cecilia's beauty and sense of order looked somewhat out of place in the shack, but she felt right at home. She was happy to be part of it, whatever it was supposed to be, and anxious to see what would come of it all.

Octavio Pedroza De Jesus sat next to the American doctor on another wooden crate. As Cecilia handed him the beautiful feathers, Octavio carved the quills into arrows, sharp points with his pocketknife sharpened by a small piece of whetstone. Never in his wildest dreams did he believe that he, a humble peasant from Central Mexico, would find himself occupying a seat next to a beautiful young doctor sharing a fine Spanish wine. But he had become accustomed to the strange and the unexpected since he started his annual journeys to the United States to work in the citrus fields of Arizona, in order to earn money to send to his sick mother back in Mexico. The Salt Shack Dweller had commented more than once that Mexico had more sick mothers and honorable sons than the rest of the world combined. Octavio nodded solemnly that it was, of course, true. Since Octavio's pilgrimages were not politely welcomed by the host country, he was forced to travel the back ways where he hoped not to be noticed and it was along such a route, the Salt Riverbed, where Octavio passed the shack and made the acquaintance with the Salt Shack Dweller. Now, it was common for him to stay a few days when he came and went, and where he was often entertained beyond that which a Catholic peasant from Central Mexico was supposed to experience or could resist.

Octavio's appearance and dress was dictated by his origin. He was a small man with black hair, dark eyes, and a quick, innocent smile. He wore a white cotton shirt, burlap pants, rough leather sandals, and a straw hat. Once he finished sharpening the quills he passed them (and the wine) to the rough-skinned man to his right.

Raymond, a Yavapai Indian from the Fort McDowell Indian reservation, had the courage of Ira Hayes, and the concentration of a surgeon as he prepared the Salt Shack Dweller for the supernatural undertaking that was soon to begin. Lying calmly and quietly, stripped to the waste, his arms outstretched like a Christ figure, the Salt Shack Dweller waited for Raymond to start his work. A candle, the only light in the shack, illuminated Raymond's work and also his hot, sweaty face. His job was to take the sharpened, sterilized feather quills, and insert them into the Salt Shack Dweller's arms, piercing the skin, each about two inches apart, so that the length of the Salt Shack Dweller's long thin arms might be transformed, for a brief time, into the wings of a hawk capable of lifting him to the moisture filled clouds.

After a feather had been inserted, it was secured by Cecilia wrapping the remaining exposed quill with strips of leather taken from the hide of a coyote. This assured that none of the powerful feathers would come loose in the middle of his upward flight into the clouds to trigger a massive rain; a deluge impossible for any dam to withstand.

Raymond was a trained sorcerer. He was the apprentice and heir apparent to his grandfather, the most powerful and accomplished sorcerer in the land. But Raymond's grandfather moved slowly, heard less, saw more, and rarely agreed to engage with anyone seeking the power of a sorcerer, especially a non-native. Raymond knew not to even speak with his grandfather about the effort. He explained to the Salt Shack Dweller that sorcery sometimes failed for reasons not evident. But Raymond believed strongly in the admirable goal of bringing the Salt River back to a full life and existence. He agreed to use all of the powers he had.

There were times when Raymond's long hours of study, practice, and struggle under his grandfather proved useless. In the modern world, some of his own people weren't even interested. With nothing else to do, he began frequenting the Jefferson St. bars and sleeping in Library Park or the Deuce Hotel. One day, after drinking for about a week, Raymond was trying to make his way back to the reservation, perhaps to die, perhaps to recover his strength for a future of serving and saving his people. The only way he knew to reach the reservation from downtown, without encountering the police, was to follow the Salt Riverbed until he reached the reservation again. But well before he got home Raymond literally ran into the Salt Shack Dweller, who just happened to have some locally grown native food and an idea for a plan to bring the Salt River to life again. If the plan worked, the river would run right through the reservation again. Praise be to God.

The piercing-of-the-skin ritual was merely the last stop in preparation for the ceremony that was about to begin. Earlier, with Raymond's help, the Salt Shack Dweller had fashioned a simple headdress out of a curved hawk bone in which he set four of the bird's finest feathers standing straight up. This was to give him the mental quickness and alertness of the hawk. Cecilia was supposed to create thick anklets from the hawk's downy breast feathers for the Salt Shack Dweller to wear, giving him the grasping strength in his feet possessed by a hawk, but lacking in a man. With Cecilia being late, Octavio was happy for the opportunity to make feather anklets, even though he did not fully understand their purpose or even that of the ceremony.

Cecilia's redemption for her unexplained tardiness was complete and immediate. Accompanying her was a large jug of wine, another necessary ingredient for the ceremony. All forms of drugs and narcotics were banned from the shack by edict from the Salt Shack Dweller except, of course, for peyote.

The Salt Shack Dweller lay calmly and passively through the piercing-of-the-skin event. If there was pain, he did not show it. It was as if the Salt Shack Dweller had passed beyond the realm of pain. His anklets were in place. He wore a loincloth, which was actually a cut up tablecloth salvaged from flood waters hung in place by a strip of coyote leather. Now his wings were attached, and he could stand on the dirt floor in the middle of the shack. The simple headdress made the Salt Shack Dweller too tall for the shack's low ceiling, so he had to bend a bit making him resemble a Kokopelli.

Cecilia, Octavio, and even Raymond were startled at just how much the Salt Shack Dweller resembled a hawk now. In addition to the downy anklets, wings, and headdress, there was the Salt Shack Dweller's nose, a thin bone hard protrusion that came out and turned down to a point remarkably like that of the hawk. His sharp round eyes penetrated deeply and darted from one subject to the next with speed and precision. High, small cheekbones set off his nose and eyes leading back to his small ears. The Salt Shack Dweller's head was shaved specifically for the purpose of the upcoming ceremony. That was a man truly transformed into a hawk, felt Cecilia, Octavio, and the proud Raymond. The hawk/man was almost ready to begin. There were two more preparatory tasks to be accomplished.

When the Salt Shack Dweller had dissected the great bird for feathers and bone, he had been careful to capture the bird's blood in a small bowl. The blood was to serve two purposes. A small amount was used to decorate his body by finger painting red streaks across his naked chest. This he did himself, setting aside the rest of the blood for a later use. Also, saved in a small wine filled bowl was the hawk's tiny heart. The Salt Shack Dweller had the talons of the hawk, the wings of the hawk, and the mind of the hawk but all of this was nothing if he did not have the courage of the hawk. To receive this, he now swallowed the hawk heart, and then chased it down with half of the remaining wine in the bowl in which the hawk heart had passed a hot day, just in case he found himself in need of a shot of courage. The Salt Shack Dweller now felt prepared.

The Salt Shack Dweller began the ceremony by dancing in a small circle in the hot, stuffy shack. Raymond beat the drum he had brought to the shack from his grandfather's shack in heartbeat time. Cecilia and Octavio took up the chant and the only pause came when one or the other found it necessary to take medicine from the jug of wine or peyote from the cup of tea. The Salt Shack Dweller was able to take wine and peyote while he continued to dance. He felt this was important, not to interrupt the flow of the dance. He could not exhibit laziness or slovenliness or a lack of concentration—otherwise he could not expect this ceremony to be a success.

The hot dance, the drum beat, and the chant all went on for hours. The heat built up in the shack, the air became thick and difficult to inhale. Sweat poured from the Salt Shack Dweller, flooding his body, and turning the dirt floor into thick mud. As the heat and exhaustion increased, the sounds of the drum and chanting began to fade. The world within the shack grew dark to the Salt Shack Dweller but he kept dancing until he had given away all the moisture on his body, and the light in his eyes, as he began to drift into darkness. This was the time, he knew, to beat his hawk wings and he did so, full of purpose, surrounded by blackness, but still he pounded his weary arm-wings until he saw a spot of light below him.

The first light that he saw was the small candle in the shack just below him and then he passed through the roof of the shack, rising slowly but effortlessly through the hot night air. He saw the lights of Monti's Steakhouse dropping below him, the great lights of the maroon and gold stadium, the endless lights lining the countless boulevards and avenues, and finally a sea of lights, sparkling like a magical sea of jewels from mountain to mountain. These were highly addictive liquid lights, and they were everywhere the eye could see except in a wide, dark swath that cut through the sea of lights where the river had once flowed but was no more. It was taken from its channel and turned into liquid light to chase away the beautiful and harmless hours of darkness, and turned into all manner of citrus: oranges, lemons, grapefruit, tangerines, and even some fruity,

"Minotaur these silly men call tangelos. Mi padre, can you believe it? They've turned our water into lights and fruits and green crops always in season and stolen the night from us for good measure."

The Salt Shack Dweller continued the rise toward cooler air and finally to the underside of the clouds. The liquid salt lights had inspired his anger. He reacted by digging his talon-strong claws into the soft, vulnerable underbelly of the clouds to rip an opening and start the great rain to fall. He sought so great a rain that it would turn the lights back to their liquid form so it could flow on, released from the trap and the prison known as the Salt River Valley. He dug and tore with such unrestrained violence that the rain did began, in soft warm drops. Excited, the Salt Shack Dweller turned downward, and dove like a hawk that has prey in its eye and on its mind. He raced down toward the sea of lights, the grillwork of corridor lights, the massive stadium lights, and the lights of Monti's until he had a soft candle flame in view. His speed became so great that he wasn't able to stop himself from crashing into the dirt floor of the shack in a heap of feathers, anklets, headdress, and mud. It was all necessary if he was to turn the soft rain into a deluge that would wash away the artificial civilization that surrounded him. One final ceremonial event remained.

The Salt Shack Dweller picked himself up from the mud, retrieved the small bowl of hot blood, and with Cecilia, hurried outside. Tossing the hot blood into the air to mingle with the soft rain was the formula to turn a gentle summer sprinkle into a deluge and flood.

Quickly, Cecilia chanted the words, "Let the deluge begin."

The Salt Shack Dweller tossed the bowl of hawk blood into the air. Upon being released from the bowl, the blood separated into ten thousand drops, but instead of finding raindrops to mingle and multiply with, the hot blood drops found only static charged air. 10,000 black moths on a downward fall. 10,000 black moths that flew off to be sucked into the 10,000 bright lights of the Mill Avenue bridge.

There was no deluge. There wasn't even a soft summer sprinkle. The rain the Salt Shack Dweller unleashed in the clouds had evaporated in the hot nightmare long before it could possibly reach the ground. Since there was no rain and definitely no great deluge, the liquid lights continued to burn, sucking up more water, throwing off their heat into the already scorching night. Without a word, the Salt Shack Dweller and Cecilia turned back to the shack. Overhead, level with the cut banks of the dry riverbed, rays from the Palo Verde nuclear power plant filled the sky. The topographical depression, known as the Salt Riverbed, was below the altitude of the poisoned rays which was why the Salt Shack Dweller had built his shack on the river bottom despite the fact that there was no sweeping view from the bottom land. The rays came from the west, like driving at night into a blizzard. Being below the rays enabled the Salt Shack Dweller to observe that, unlike screaming snow, the rays had uniform length, like countless spears unleashed by a relentless enemy each night. Some nights the rays were thicker, some less. The rays did not yet flow into the daylight.

Overhead were high-tension power lines that crossed the river bottom carrying old-fashioned liquid electricity. Though this power was contained within the thick wires and was less dangerous to his physical well-being, the Salt Shack Dweller still held the high voltage lines in contempt since the power within the lines was nothing more than the water that used to fill the river, stolen, converted, and forced to march within copper wire rather than flow through sand and rock channels.

To add insult to injury, the high-tension power lines gave off an extremely irritating buzzing sound when the Salt Shack Dweller was trying to sleep. As he watched the endless rays march through the night skies and listened to the constant buzzing of the high-tension wires, the Salt Shack Dweller counted the cars passing over the bridge—100 per minute and the jets that used the river bottom as their private causeway—one every three minutes. A very busy night all the way around, soon to be changed.

Octavio sat on the coil spring bed frame and Raymond sat on the old fruit crate. Cecilia sat on the floor, leaning against the wall. The Salt Shack Dweller took his seat, a broken-down chair that he had liberated from the river bottom. The silence from the failure to instigate a massive 100 years rain storm that would bring forth a 150 years flood filled the shack. The wine jug made several passes before Octavio, in the English he'd learned so well, nervously attempted to break the silence.

"Was the journey a great distance?"

"To the clouds," answered Raymond.

"Did it seem to you that the man/hawk traveled no further than the dirt in front of your feet?" continued Octavio.

"No, it's only that I could not see him once he became the hawk," answered Raymond.

"It was a successful endeavor," said Cecilia. "A lot was learned that will be useful in the future."

"Yes, you are correct." Octavio nodded to the educated woman.

"Do not men turn into hawks in your village in Mexico, Octavio," asked Raymond, betraying a touch of irritation, not at Octavio, but at the lack of one hundred percent success.

"Yes, but usually it is the women who change into birds. Usually ravens, not hawks,"

This fact interested Cecilia. "Can you tell when a raven is really a woman in disguise?"

"Not before it is too late."

"Is there a ceremony that helps them change from a woman to a raven?" asked Raymond.

"No, they just do it."

Raymond nodded his firm belief. "They haven't lost the touch, those people haven't."

Octavio said, "There's one thing I do not understand. What was the reason for this sorcery tonight?"

"That wasn't sorcery," said Raymond. "This was a ceremony in which we used just a tiny bit of sorcery."

"But there must still be a reason for it."

"To bring rain" answered Cecilia.

This answer satisfied Octavio. He smiled and made his half nod after pulling on the wine jug another time.

"Yes, we could use a little rain in this heat," he said.

"Not a little rain, Octavio," said the Salt Shack Dweller from his dark corner of the shack, his first words since his failure to produce a flood and unleash the imprisoned water of Eastern Arizona. "But a great rain to bring on a great flood."

2

The Salt Shack Dweller built his shack secured against one of the concrete piers of a condemned bridge across the riverbed. Building materials were easy to come by. There was something about the fact that the river usually had no water in it that encouraged people to view the river bottom as a dump.

Consequently, all up, and down the river bottom were piles of junk that once cluttered some poor soul's garage and couldn't be pawned off at a ubiquitous weekend garage sale. Heaps of junk littered the river bottom.

Much of this junk was easily accessible to the Salt Shack Dweller since it was neatly stacked in piles that had not been flushed out of the river bottom. It had been years since the last good flood, leaving most of the flotsam to be flushed down and deposited against one of the piers of the bridges or train trestles that crossed the dry riverbed. In its own way, the river still provided.

One of the concrete bunkers for the bridge served as a back wall to the shack. The remaining three walls and roof were constructed from cardboard, old plywood, tires, pieces of chain link fence, corrugated sheet metal, hunks of plastic, and one very valuable, classic campaign sign that the Salt Shack Dweller had found mostly buried in the silt: AuH20 for President.

After constructing the walls and setting the AuH20 sign in a prominent place, a roof was put on. The roof was flat, in the traditional style, and would have leaked had it not been for the fact that the entire shack sat under the bridge. When the roof was on the Salt Shack Dweller piled old brush and tumbleweed on top of the shack to insulate and camouflage it.

There was a doorway but no door, only an old army blanket tacked up over the small entryway. Lizards, black widows, and scorpions had no difficulty finding their way into the shack to browse around and they were welcomed to do so even though the Salt Shack Dweller occasionally captured them in a glass box.

Great entertainment was to set up a contest between a black widow and a scorpion, or a tarantula and a praying mantis. Such events would be held when there was a decent group of people to participate and to place wagers, such as when Octavio and his friends were present at the same time as Raymond and his friends. Then there would be an air of excitement, campfires all around, much gambling, wine drinking, and choosing up sides.

Invariably Octavio's camp would come to an agreement after much argument and discussion on which creature to bet their collective fortune on. The same would occur with Raymond's group except that the discussion and arguments were secretive, silent, and private. It would be late in the evening before all of the bets were settled and all of the pre-fight partying had been concluded.

More often than not the battle would turn out to be inconclusive or the creatures refused to fight, being, as they were, not trained to fight to the death as cocks were. But once in a while the contests would get out of hand for some reason, the wine would remove all good sense, tempers would flair, and a flashing knife would appear.

Usually, the Salt Shack Dweller could put a stop to the proposed violence by threatening to call the border patrol from the telephone on the back desk in the shack. Few (only Cecilia) knew the phone was connected to nothing.

One of the Salt Shack Dweller's biggest goals was to capture a healthy road runner and a healthy rattlesnake, and to stage a great contest between these two masters of the mythical desert. Perhaps he would charge admission and take a percentage of the bet for that event.

Perhaps he would invite the state's politicians to show them real sport— forget the canines and the cocks. He had read legends about great battles between the bird and the snake, but he had always wondered if the legends were true, the road runner would be the victor at the end of a fierce battle. Only Ira Hayes would know for sure.

The shack's interior was simple, one room construction: not up to suburban code. It had a dirt floor and was furnished with a small steel frame cot; several wooden-orange crates, a broken-down chair, from which much of the stuffing was missing and a small table piled high in confusion with the books and papers of the Salt Shack Dweller.

The interior walls were undecorated except for one wall which was devoted to a display of crass advertisements by those who the Salt Shack Dweller considered to be his enemies, and therefore, enemies of the people. The advertisements tacked to his wall served as wanted posters. Unlike the FBI's wanted list, the Salt Shack Dweller established his list in no particular order.

This allowed him to have a different enemy #1 every day, Acme air conditioning sales and repair, Arizona land Developers Association, Arizona Public Service, Salt River Project, Palo Verde Nuclear Plant, Phoenix Zoo, Maricopa County Citrus Growers.

The Salt Shack Dweller did not consider his shack as his permanent dwelling unit. Already, in his spare time, which some considered to be all of his time, he was at work on a massive pueblo, built out of the river bottom on the floodplain, using mud, straw, and sand for building materials. The plan for the structure was occasionally revised in the Salt Shack Dweller's mind.

It called for three-foot-thick base walls. The outer dimensions of the pueblo were to be 50 x 30 with at least two stories and perhaps three. The walls had tapering thickness as they rose, but even at the highest point they needed to be at least 12 inches thick.

One problem would be where to find the heavy beams to support the roof, but that was a long way off. The first wall was still less than four feet high. Progress was slow. The Salt Shack Dweller had only a few hand tools; shovel, wheelbarrow etc.

The pueblo would take tremendous quantities of mud and sand, all moved one wheelbarrow full at a time. Once in a great while Octavio or Raymond would lend a hand, but usually it was the Salt Shack Dweller alone. All great edifices took a long time—unlike the 10-week box houses slapped together that infested and multiplied throughout the Salt River Valley. The Salt Shack Dweller had the rest of his life to build the pueblo, or at least until the great flood came to render any further efforts meaningless.

Water to the pueblo, as well as to the shack and garden, was plentiful. The Salt Shack Dweller had spent the first two weeks of his residence in the Salt Riverbed digging a trench and laying pipe (arguably stolen but also arguably considered forced reparations from co-conspirators of the enemy).

From the shack, the main water line ran through the park and joined Mill Avenue to deliver water to Monti's Steakhouse, Casa Loma, Perry's bar, Restaurant Mexico, and Chris Smith's bookstore. The park was small by park standards, but it had tall, well-watered trees, a huge swimming pool and a baseball field that lit up the night with massive liquid lights.

The Salt Shack Dweller ran his waterline to the edge of the park and then, under cover one dark night, ran his line to the main, connected it, and backfilled his trench. No one was the wiser, and this was not theft. This was public domain water that had been forcibly removed from the Salt River and the Salt Shack Dweller had done nothing more than return it to its proper place, granting himself running water to the shack, the garden, and to the pueblo along the way.

The Salt Shack Dweller's first shack was washed away by a mediocre flood and promptly rebuilt with newly deposited materials. He was rewarded for his loss by the river delivering to him a three-legged dog that he saved by pulling the poor creature from the flood. This dog was the only domestic canine the Salt Shack Dweller did not detest.

It was independent and resourceful, fending for itself, going off alone for days at a time. This dog did not crave human attention. The dog confirmed the Salt Shack Dweller's belief that infirmity-built character and, besides, he had saved the dog's life.

The three-legged dog had been gone for several days, since the night of the hawk blood ceremony, but now returned, as always, hobbling on the grapefruit sized rocks of the Salt Riverbed. 50 paces behind the dog, also stumbling, was a man approaching, walking alone. The Salt Shack Dweller saw the visitor long before the visitor saw him. Soon he was recognized. The visitor was Harold, a friend of the Salt Shack Dweller from student days, now a lawyer of all things, mi padre.

The Salt Shack Dweller was alone. Raymond had gone to his grandfather's hut on the reservation, for further sorcery instructions. Cecilia was at work, at the hospital and Octavio had gone to the citrus fields northwest of Phoenix to accumulate dollars for the benefit of his sick mother. The Salt Shack Dweller met Harold at the entrance to the shack, inviting him in, out of the direct heat of the midday sun.

"My God, it's stifling in here," Harold began as always. "Why don't you at least have some window openings for ventilation? It stinks too. This place should be condemned and demolished, it's not fit for human habitation. On the other hand, I'm not sure you're still human. I should tell the authorities for your own good. You are obviously incompetent to manage your own affairs."

Harold scoured the shack's interior with critical eyes, immediately focusing on the cache of insects. "Look at those. Be they alive or dead? My

God, they are alive. Don't you know that those things are poisonous? They shouldn't be kept inside. They could easily escape. Jesus, there must be 50 black widows and scorpions, and what are these, a colony of praying mantis? Don't leave your books and papers piled up that way in such a God damn awful mess, it's a damn fire hazard."

The Salt Shack Dweller allowed Harold to go on as long as he had breath. It was Harold's way. At least, Harold had come with some respect, without his three-piece suit.

But when there was a pause in Harold's diatribe the Salt Shack Dweller spoke up softly. "May I offer you some food, Harold?"

"Yes, please, it is my lunch hour, the only time I could get down here."

"You haven't been here to visit me in a long time."

"I'm busy," claimed Harold. "Besides, a normal person gets damn tired of coming here. It was cute at first, but no one thought you'd stay this long. At a minimum, you should make some effort to reciprocate by coming to visit us."

"I can't," said the Salt Shack Dweller flatly.

He gave Harold some cooked meat, corn bread and an orange. Harold opened a small, nice bottle of wine that he had brought. The Salt Shack Dweller drank from a gourd while Harold drank from the bottle, worried there might be a black widow lurking in any vessel in the shack.

"And why exactly can't you come out to visit us?"

"You're all working or going to school during the day, and at night the killing rays are out."

Harold mocked the Salt Shack Dweller, "Oh yes, the deadly, invisible rays. You know, they're going to fire up those rays before long and then there will be countless rays at all times that you won't be able to escape. Then what will you do? Tear the whole damn thing down. And if you somehow fail to tear it down?"

"Stay in the River bottom where the rays can't reach me."

"Until another flood flushes you and this pigsty out?"

The Salt Shack Dweller smiled, "Yes, until then and beyond."

The smile on the Salt Shack Dweller reminded Harold of carefree days of the past that he was so fond of recalling. He wanted to say something nice.

"Hey, this meat is good, did you BBQ it this morning?"

"No, I got it last night."

"Where?"

"At Monti's."

Harold looked up from his food with a question already forming on his face. "Monti's? Monti's a first-class restaurant. You ate there?"

"Of course not."

"Then how did you get the meat from there."

"From the back, after they're closed, of course."

Harold screamed, "This meat came from the garbage at Monti's?"

"Yes," answered the Salt Shack Dweller quietly and calmly, ignoring his friend's agitation.

"It's close and convenient. The food is plentiful and good."

Harold spent 81 seconds spiting, shaking his head, staring at the dirt floor of the shack. Then he spoke again. "Less than a year ago you were one of the top graduate students in the microbiology department. Now you're nothing more than a scavenging derelict."

"The cost of freedom is high, Harold."

Harold tossed the rest of his meat to dog. The dog ignored it. Harold sweated, drinking the wine that he had brought. He looked very hot and very uncomfortable in his casual lawyer clothes even if it wasn't his three-piece suit.

Finally, he complained. "Jesus Christ it is hot…the humidity must be in excess of ninety percent in here."

"That's because white eyes brought all of his foreign plants and trees to this valley."

"No, it's because it's August," answered Harold.

"You need to learn to dress right for the climate."

"Like you? Do I need to buy my clothes at Goodwill? I need to wear old, beat-up wingtips without socks like you, and I need to walk down first avenue in a loincloth or whatever the hell that is you've got on? Do I need to shave my head as well?"

"It might help."

"Not on your life."

"Harold, I need your assistance," said the Salt Shack Dweller. This piqued Harold's interest though he tried not to show it.

"Yeah, what is it?"

"I want you to represent me in court."

"I knew something would happen if you continued to live like this. What have you gotten yourself into?"

"Nothing. I want to sue the airport. And Salt River Project after we're through with the airport."

"Oh God…and what do you want to sue them for?"

"Listen," said the Salt Shack Dweller, pointing up. They didn't have to wait long. A jet on approach thundered overhead, shaking the shack, and rendering conversation impossible.

"Sometimes they takeoff in this direction, and then it's even worse," said the Salt Shack Dweller after the roar calmed a bit.

"So what? They have to land and takeoff somewhere. They can't levitate."

"A matter of opinion, but even if so, not here."

"Why not here? It's the best place. There's nothing of significance to disturb along this flight pattern."

"There is my peace and tranquility. My home is here."

"You are out of your mind. What would you sue them for, anyhow?"

"An injunction to stop them from flying over my home."

"And you want me to represent you on this—you want my good name to go on your fantasy lawsuit?"

"Yes, that's right."

Harold laughed then, as if it had been foolish of him to take one word from the Salt Shack Dweller seriously. But then he thought…two could play this game.

"Well, let's see now. From your surroundings, I would not say that you are a wealthy man. So, excuse me for being crass, but what arrangements do you anticipate for paying my fee?"

"I would trade you for your services. I have runners who can acquire all kinds of fruits from the lush fields of the far end of this valley. Here on the floodplain, I grow some of the sweetest corn, and richest beans, and the most beautiful squash anyone has tasted."

"I have plenty of jojoba plants from which you can acquire fantastic oils that smooth and heal the skin. My mesquite flour has the best texture and taste in the hemisphere. I have secret connections through which I can receive thick slabs of meat, some with the bone and some without."

"Insufficient," replied Harold.

The Salt Shack Dweller thought. From the expression on Harold's face, it appeared to the Salt Shack Dweller that he was anxious, if not desperate, to strike a bargain.

After a minute's contemplation, the Salt Shack Dweller stood and led Harold just outside the shack where they could see the black train bridge that spanned the once mighty Salt River 20 yards to the west. The Salt Shack Dweller pointed to a cluster of pigeons that nested in the super structure of the bridge.

"Harold, do you see those hawks in that massive stand of dead trees just downriver a bit? They are great birds, Harold. They hunt along the river here in the morning and in the evening."

"They take fish from the river and small game from around the river. These are the mightiest birds of prey on any portion of this great River. I've watched them work and hunt and play."

"I know their every move. I can catch one of these birds for you, Harold, to be your constant companion and protector. I will catch one for you in return for your legal server services."

Harold only stared at the pigeons that the Salt Shack Dweller was pointing at and talking about.

"This is a pointless conversation. I've got to go back downtown to work. I'll give you two pieces of advice, however. The first is that you cannot bring your lawsuit because you do not own the land, and the second is that you get your ass out of this dried up, useless river bottom."

"I can't leave this land, Harold. I do own it. It is mine. This is the land of my ancestors. My father lived here and his father before him and his father before him and so on for countless generations."

"I am just a link in a long chain, but I must stop these airplanes, or this land will be no good for my sons and daughters. And even more important I must save the Salt River from the relentless onslaught facing it by the developers and their corporate co-conspirators."

"We are running out of water, Harold. We use all of the river's water and puncture the underground water table for more, going deeper every year. The Earth is sinking, Harold."

Against his better judgment, because curiosity got the best of him, Harold said, "Don't give me that crap. I knew you when you were a kid. You water skied in the canals being pulled by a car on the service road along the canal."

"You surfed down the moss-covered section of the canal where it dropped 50 feet at the Mesa Country Club and you ran away when the security guards showed up."

"You swam naked with the girls in the huge water tanks filled with Salt River Project domestic water after midnight. Your youth revolved around everything that Salt River Project provided even though they didn't provide it for the uses we conjured up."

The Salt Shack Dweller smiled and after a full minute of silence he said, "When I was a child, I talked like a child. I thought like a child, I reasoned like a child. When I became a man, I put childhood behind me." 1 Corinthians 13:11

Harold took a very deep breath. "I can't believe I'm standing here in the heat, with you, of all people, quoting scriptures to me. I am leaving. I hope you recover soon."

The Salt Shack Dweller considered responding in kind but decided not to. "Harold, water is life. That's why the Gods just let it flow free on top of the Earth, all over the Earth. That's why we look for water on other planets. It's the sign of life. It's a resource that cannot be replicated. We can't continue to abuse it, Harold." The Salt Shack Dweller paused, and then said, "Goodbye, my friend. I hope we meet again soon."

3

The Salt Shack Dweller was not dissuaded by Harold's lack of enthusiastic assistance in bringing his lawsuit against the airport. He simply cleared a space at his desk, blew the dust from a typewriter (picked a scorpion from the typewriter's carriage) and began drafting out his own writs and briefs and complaints.

As he progressed, he concluded that he was happy that Harold had declined to assist him—he didn't need some first avenue lawyer to fight his fights for him. He didn't need a substitute mouthpiece. Any decent warrior fought his own battles, regardless of where the battlefield was.

When he filed his papers with the court (the worker bees in the courthouse clerk's office gathered to gawk at him, in his sockless wingtips and loincloth and madras shirt), a woman clerk kindly told him that he had to send a copy of the papers to the airport authorities or to their authorized legal representative.

She told him the date that the Judge would hear the case and told him to bring his witnesses, if he had any (which made the worker bees laugh). The Salt Shack Dweller thanked the woman for her help. It was more than Harold had done for him.

The Salt Shack Dweller was quite encouraged by the response he had received at the courthouse. They had accepted his papers and even given him a court date. This must have meant that they recognized the gravity of the lawsuit and wanted to give it priority because the Salt Shack Dweller had read that most cases took two years or more to process.

Probably he would win, he thought. Sufficient money had been borrowed from Octavio's sick mother fund to make copies and pay postage to send the airport authorities copies of the Salt Shack Dweller's brilliant legal pleadings.

Prospects for victory looked good on Wednesday night, the night before the court hearing. Not only did Octavio showed up from the fields but three of his compañeros had arrived from Mexico and had come to the shack where they knew, from word of-mouth and legend, that they could get a night of shelter.

The three were called Anastacio, Carlos and Miguelito. Anastacio and Carlos were veteran illegal aliens; Miguelito was a boy of 16, a virgin in every sense, a soft, gentle looking young man who spoke not a word, but watched everything in this foreign land with cautious but excited eyes.

All three were headed for the fields. As if by fate or telepathy or sorcery, Raymond also arrived on Wednesday night. With him were his two brothers and a sister who were on their way to the Jefferson Street bars for a drink or two. Raymond's sister, with thick, beautiful black hair was called Donella and she took an immediate fancy to mystified Miguelito.

Raymond's brothers were large and very silent. The Salt Shack Dweller asked the brothers what their names were and when they answered in their native dialect Raymond laughed long and hard, so the Salt Shack Dweller named them Brahma and Stallion.

Anastacio and Carlos smiled proudly when Donella offered to share her bit of whiskey with Miguelito. They could sense that they were carrying out their duty of caring for Miguelito in the finest tradition. If only his Mama could see him now.

Not only did Raymond's brothers and sister have whiskey as well as peyote but Cecilia arrived with two generous jugs of wine. The Salt Shack Dweller saw the necessity of disposing of the business at hand before it became impossible to do so. He called an executive meeting consisting of himself, Octavio, Raymond, and Cecilia. He excluded the others, lit a candle, and started to speak but was immediately interrupted by Octavio.

"I must speak to my good friend, Raymond, before this business begins."

"What is this matter that you must speak to me about, Octavio?" asked Raymond.

But Octavio hesitated to speak and then he looked nervously in the direction of Cecilia.

The Salt Shack Dweller, recognizing awkwardness, intervened. "You may speak in front of Cecilia. She's not a normal woman, she is a doctor."

Cecilia smiled at sweet Octavio and said, "It's sort of true."

Octavio looked up to Cecilia, nodding and acknowledging his understanding of her unique status.

Then he spoke to Raymond. "What you said to me is correct, I think. It appears to me that it is possible that Miguelito may attempt to seduce your sister this very night without the benefit of matrimony or even a proper period of courting."

"Or she him," said Cecilia, unsolicited.

"It appears the same to me," said Raymond.

"In Mexico, a man can find a knife in his back after he has seduced an unmarried woman. And the knife usually belongs to the woman's brother. I would not like to see that happen to Miguelito."

"What a barbaric custom," said Cecilia, unsolicited.

"The same thing can happen on the reservation, Octavio."

"What I need to know," said Octavio, "is whether that will happen here. Miguelito is not in my family, but he is from my village and probably of my blood. He is young and passion rises quickly in the young. There are things he does not know or will ignore. I want to protect him from that fate."

"There is no need, Octavio. My sister is of my family and blood, and she is also very young and cannot be completely controlled. I do not try. She is not stupid and if she would be happy to have Miguelito take her to his bed perhaps to produce many children, my knife would remain sheathed."

"Then it's settled," said Cecilia, unsolicited. "But not many children, not more than two."

"If what you worry about occurs," said Octavio to Raymond, "I will assure you that the children will be raised properly as Catholics."

"If they are raised as ravens or sorcerers, I will be satisfied," said Raymond.

"Catholics, ravens, sorcerers, it's all the same," said Cecilia unsolicited.

The Salt Shack Dweller said, "The important thing is that the seed and the egg of the different races get mixed and remixed until there is only one race. Mexican and Indian is fine but what we need more of is Mexicans and Anglos and Indians and Africans and Asians and all others. We need to bring some young females to this place to kickstart this necessary human leap forward."

"Yes, females and many young males," contributed Cecilia, unsolicited.

"Now, then," said the Salt Shack Dweller, "let's review the testimony for tomorrow's court battle. Octavio, you are first."

"I am not a citizen of this country. Are you sure the authorities will permit me to speak."

"Of course, they will, Octavio. This is a free country. What did we decide that you would say."

Octavio sighed, uncertain of this business, but certain that there was danger in it. "I will tell how the airplanes make me very afraid when I am coming up the river bottom because I am always sure that the airplanes are radar equipped and used by La Migra to catch me and send me back to Mexico without any money. Then my poor mother would have no money for doctors and medicine."

"And if the planes no longer flew above the river bottom," asked the Salt Shack Dweller?

Octavio shrugged at the obvious. "Then I would no longer be afraid."

"Good…Cecilia, what will you say?"

"I will say that the county hospital was built on cheap land and that the existing flight pattern is too close to the hospital and that the noise disturbs the patients."

"Is it true?" asked Octavio, gravely concerned.

"A little bit," answered Cecilia.

"Say it with gusto, it might be true" instructed the Salt Shack Dweller.

He then turned to Raymond and said, "And you?"

"I would say that when I am walking up the river bottom after a week downtown that the jets hurt my head and make it very difficult to walk—"

"And?"

"And how when I hear the jets, I have flashbacks to when I was a soldier in Vietnam and I sometimes fling my body onto the rocks for cover, hurting myself, and that I fear that one day I'll have a serious flashback and destroy the nearest neighborhood, mistaking it for a Vietcong village."

"Good…all very good. And I will testify that the noise and vibration interferes with my peace and tranquility, rattles my home, and gives me migraine headaches for which I have employed the services of a chiropractor."

"Quacks," said Cecilia, unsolicited.

"Everybody got their parts straight?" asked the Salt Shack Dweller. Raymond, Octavio, and Cecilia nodded. The Salt Shack Dweller then passed Cecilia's jugs of wine. "Alright then, we depart at sunrise. It's a long walk."

The Salt Shack Dweller and his entourage began their long walk with the sun at their backs, casting long shadows toward the steel, glass, and concrete towers of their destination. A jet broke the peace of dawn. Even though it had been difficult to get the group started after the previous night's whiskey and wine, they were all anxious to be on their way; Raymond's brothers to see their friends again and share a drink; Anastacio and Carlos to earn many U.S. dollars for their sick mothers back in Mexico.

And Donella because any morning after a night such as she had experienced was something to look forward to anytime, anywhere. It had been an evening of silence for the Salt Shack Dweller. He had been content to sit outside his shack with the others, sharing the wine and the whiskey when it came his way, listening to Anastacio and Carlos relate their adventures in international travel—their bus rides from the Mexican state of Oaxaca to the U.S. border and their border crossing out in the middle of the desert, their dark walk through the desert to the highway where the Papago Indian woman picked them up in a truck with a camper and transported them for a fee of $100 each to the edge of Phoenix, where they were on their own again.

They were seasoned, experienced men who told their story with obvious pride in the fact that they were able to support their families, despite the obstacles and hardships. They were professional illegal aliens but of course the border was illegal in itself—how can something stolen become legal? And they were proud to be passing on their knowledge and skills to Miguelito—baptized by Donella just this previous night.

And to listen to Raymond's brothers, who only began speaking when the wine and the whiskey was half gone. They spoke of the proposed Orme dam on the very river that would flood so many of their homes and much of their land. They spoke with great bitterness and anger and were significantly inspiring to the Salt Shack Dweller.

They spoke not of passive resistance or reasoned responses. They spoke of war, of sand in the fuel tanks of heavy equipment, tearing down every brick that was placed and most of all of employing the services of every sorcerer they could lay their hands on.

And to listen to the desperate but fresh love cries of Donella and Miguelito, somewhere out in the dark, in the hot sand of the fertile river environment; so great and perfect in pitch were their combined cries that the coyotes moved in to eye-glowing range to join in the love song.

"Listen to Miguelito," said Cecilia with a smile that showed her happiness for the young lovers.

"And to Donella," said Raymond with the same smile.

"And to the coyotes," said the Salt Shack Dweller.

The Salt Shack Dweller carried a rucksack with sufficient water, dried meat, fruits, and nuts, for everyone. As they made their way the walking was made easier by the music from a reed flute that Octavio carried with him always. When they began their journey, the sun lay on the horizon and the temperature was 93 degrees.

Now that they had been walking an hour the sun had gained altitude and the temperature had easily surpassed the 100-degree mark. Yet neither of them expected anything different and they hiked along without complaint about the heat.

The first stop came when the band of warriors reached the Hohokam ruins of Pueblo Grande in East Washington. This was a sacred place; this place was treated with reverence. A place of shade along the north bank of the river (that was no more) was used for resting.

The Salt Shack Dweller removed his load and climbed up to the level of the floodplain above the river bottom to see the still standing adobe walls of his inspiration. Once again, he surveyed the site and found it appeared to be in order. What remained were the half-wall outlines of various rooms, each one connected to the next until there was an entire unified village.

There were no people but there were the spirits of those who once inhabited the village many centuries before. The Salt Shack Dweller could hear their whisperings in the dry desert wind. They told him why they had abandoned their village after century upon century of residence: drought and discord, they whispered to him.

Without water there was no life, they continued to whisper. Without water there was only the ruins of interconnected adobe walls for man in the future to speculate about. Take care of the water, they whispered, take care of it as if it was all the children of your village.

Suddenly the Salt Shack Dweller could hear Octavio's melodious flute rising up from the river bottom, taking him back in time to when the ruin was modern, or perhaps forward in time to when the ruin would be much more extensive and yet there would still be a reed flute player accompanied by the hot desert wind.

The Salt Shack Dweller cupped a hand full of dust from the floor of one of the ruins and washed himself with it, asking the Gods for success in his present battle as he did so. However, just then the man from the visitor center came out to yell at the Salt Shack Dweller, as he always did, for entering the ruin area from the river side (unauthorized) and for touching the sacred dust (not allowed).

The Salt Shack Dweller could not hear the government man's voice, it was from another time, and he could not understand the words, they were from another tongue, so he ignored the man as he walked slowly away from the ruins, like a spirit himself.

But this did not stop the man from following the Salt Shack Dweller or hurling threats at him and promising to call police until the government man came to the cut of the river bank and looked down to the band of warriors the Salt Shack Dweller had rejoined, which caused the man of law and order to cease his rude and disrespectful speech and to return quickly to the place he had come from, an air-conditioned office.

The band of warriors continued on. At the eastern edge of the airport, the river curved to the south and then continued west, bordering the airport on the south. At the curve, the major runway ended. In the river, bottom of the curve were massive chunks of runway which had been chewed off and spit out by the river in previous floods.

The warriors cheered these signs of weakness on the part of the enemy. And even though the warriors continued to make wild war cries and jeering sounds at the airport as they passed by, all were silently impressed by the size and strength of the enemy. There were hundreds of airplanes and square miles of asphalt and countless new buildings and jammed parking lots.

There was a landing or take off once each minute and the noise completely drowned out the war cries and the cheers of the warriors—so much so that one warrior could not hear a sound from the warrior right next to him or her. Even the flute was useless.

So, the Salt Shack Dweller, and his band of warriors, were happy to leave the airport behind them and return to the open river bottom. They thought nothing of the noise and confusion of the automobile traffic on the freeway bridge that crossed above them, but it did take a minute before they heard the priest that was standing on the bridge above, yelling down at them. The priest was leaning over the bridge in his black shirt and white collar.

"Where are you going my brothers?"

"To the soul of the beast," called back the Salt Shack Dweller. "To battle the devil of oppression and to return peace and tranquility and water to this river valley."

"Are there any Catholics among you?"

After a few seconds of hesitation, Octavio removed his little straw hat, looked up to the Priest, indicating himself and his compañeros and said, "Si padre, somos cuatro…Y posiblementy un alma no nacida."

"And there are four heathens and pagans among us as well," added the Salt Shack Dweller.

"All the better," responded the Priest. "Wait just a minute. I will park my car and join you on your long walk."

The Salt Shack Dweller leaned over to Cecilia's ear. "Should we permit long-gown to join us?"

Cecilia shrugged. "Who's another sorcerer among us?"

So, the priest climbed down the riverbank with a broad smile. He introduced himself all around (the Mexicans all bowing reverently and submissively). The priest fell into line with the band of warriors…In the tradition of Father Keno.

Now they were eleven. They ate lunch in the shade under the Central Avenue Bridge. The heat of midday was upon them; the humidity was on the rise and any movement of the air had come to a halt. The dangerous part of the journey was before them. It was necessary to leave the river bottom and travel north, along South Central, straight into enemy territory.

They split into two groups, each taking a different side of the busy street. It was difficult to make good progress now. On both sides of the street were shopkeepers, merchants, vendors, and traders of every kind.

4

The warriors among the clan, Octavio and his compañeros and Raymond and his brothers and sister, were enthralled with the sights and sounds of this patchwork of peoples. Too often they were persuaded to stop bartering for one thing or another or to try exotic food or drink. The people they met along the street were shrewd and obviously accustomed to dealing with strangers and foreigners—they enticed the warriors in with laughter and music, pretty women and sweet-smelling food and tobacco and they even spoke to them in their native tongue.

Octavio, who should've known better, almost lost his reed flute and Miguelito, who could not believe his senses, would have lost his machete and leather sandals had not Anastacio and the Salt Shack Dweller intervened on his behalf. Raymond's brothers both traded some silver coins for cold drinks from a brown bottle.

Eventually, however, the band of warriors arrived at the heart of the enemy civilization. There was no more wild war cries and no more jeering. They were struck silent by the obvious wealth and power of this civilization. All around them were monumental towers, one after the next, to what power or God no one knew. There were wide boulevards and sculptures and people so busy that they did not seem to notice, except for a short smile of amusement, when they passed the band of warriors.

The Salt Shack Dweller realized the importance of regrouping and of relieving his warrior's attention to the signs of enemy power that were all around. Directly in the center of the enemy's civilization was a square of grass and trees. This place was called Patriot's Park. It was as if the park was civilization's way of showing just how rich they were; they could squander an entire block of land to satisfy their citizen's childish but harmless desire to stand in the open under the sun.

The Salt Shack Dweller led his band to the park and suggested they sit in the grass under a tree. Donella said it was not a good place to sit. She said the authorities did not want people to actually sit or lay in the grass and in order to prevent that from happening they had planted burrs in the grass and had set the sprinkler system on a random schedule so that it was always popping on and off. No one could believe what Donella had said but Carlos reached into the grass and pulled up a handful of burrs in proof, so they sat on a vacant park bench instead just as the sprinklers jumped up from a secret hiding place underground.

The time of battle was near, so Salt Shack Dweller reviewed everyone's part with them. As he did so he noticed the Priest wore a suspicious little smile.

When he finished with Cecilia and Octavio and Raymond, he turned to the Priest. "Do you have anything you can add to this battle, Padre?"

The priest still smiled. "I could say that if God had intended for man to fly, he would have given them wings."

The Salt Shack Dweller returned priest's smile. "Never mind, Padre, but come along anyhow. Maybe you can work some black magic on the Judge."

It took time to find a courtroom in the court edifice, but the Salt Shack Dweller and his warriors were still the first combatants to arrive. There was a table for them, a table for the enemy and an elevated place for the Judge to sit. The Judge's name was on a nameplate, Judge John Michael O'Sullivan.

Salt Shack Dweller moved the priest to the front row of the spectator's benches and pointed out the nameplate, winking at the priest.

"He must be an Irishman and most likely a Catholic," whispered Salt Shack Dweller. "This is good news indeed. Make sure the Judge is aware of your presence and your righteous nature."

A minute later the airport lawyer arrived along with his young assistant. Both wore three-piece suits, and both stared incredulously at the warriors, not believing what they were seeing. Not a word was exchanged before the Judge and his entourage entered the courtroom from the private back door; the Judge wearing flowing black robes.

The high priest of this world, thought the Salt Shack Dweller. A wooden hammer was crashed down with serious vigor by a female assistant, ordering everyone to stand. Octavio's compañeros did not understand the English command and failed to rise, as did one of Raymond's brothers, who was asleep and snoring lightly. The Judge surveyed the litigants before him.

He took a very long, though silent, examination of the one with the loincloth and sockless wingtips, and madras shirt and shaved head. He read off the name of the case and the number and was ready to begin when he noticed the priest.

His expression changed and he said, "Father, are you here in regard to this case or some other business, that, I may help you with?"

The Salt Shack Dweller turned to the Priest, his back to the Judge and mouthed to him, "Work your magic, holy magic, Padre."

The priest stood when he addressed the Judge, "I have come with these men and women (pointing to the band of warriors) Your Honor. I have no business other than theirs. I come only to bear witness."

"Very well. Shall we begin then?" The Judge indicated for the Salt Shack Dweller to stand.

Before he could speak, however, the airport lawyer was on his feet and was speaking to the Judge. "Your Honor, there are one or two preliminary matters that I would like to take up before we get to the substance of this thing."

The Judge nodded his assent to the lawyer, "Alright, Mr. Jones, what are these preliminary matters?"

"Not to be petty, Your Honor, but I must register my objection to plaintiff's attire. I would like the record to reflect that the plaintiff is wearing no more than what appears to be a loincloth, no socks and a multicolored shirt without a coat or tie. I feel that this is not only disrespectful but also demeaning to this court."

The Judge looked at the Salt Shack Dweller. "Do you wish to respond to what Mr. Jones said?"

"Unnecessary," answered the Salt Shack Dweller with the confidence of Perry Mason.

"Your objection is noted for the record of Mr. Jones. Let's move on."

"Second, Your Honor, there is a woman in the courtroom sitting in the front row who is feeding a baby from her breast. This is certainly not acceptable court decorum. Please instruct the woman to wait outside of the court room."

Miguelito seemed to have understood what the lawyer was saying. He jumped up quite agitated speaking rapid Spanish, waving his arms in distress. The Judge waved his hands in a *everybody relax* manner, and spoke, "The baby is not bothering anybody, counsel. Let's just proceed in normal fashion."

The Priest, sitting next to Donella, stood up to everyone's surprise. "Your Honor, the baby is not a baby. The baby is a doll."

"Even better," said the Judge. "Now everyone can be satisfied that a baby hasn't tarnished this courtroom. The doll is welcome. Thank you for enlightening us, Father."

But the airport lawyer was not satisfied. "Besides all these illegal aliens filling our courtrooms as if the courts were for their benefit, now we have an absolutely new born alien doll being breast fed in our court rooms. There must be an end to this somewhere."

Donella had heard enough. "I'm just practicing, you imbecile. I want to be a good mother when the time comes."

The Judge took a very deep breath and turned to the Salt Shack Dweller. "Do you have anything to add to this baby doll objection?"

The Salt Shack Dweller smiled broadly, thinking quickly, *What the hell is going on? Where did this doll baby come from?* Regardless, he was certainly ready to take advantage of this very weird development.

"Yes, Your Honor. The baby is not an alien, it's a baby doll. The baby doll is an American doll citizen. He or she was born along the Salt Riverbed in the United States of America. He or she was born on the U.S. soil. He or she is a U.S. doll citizen of sorts. This is a public U.S. court."

The Judge could not restrain a minor smile. "Well, thank goodness for that. I don't need to be throwing an American baby doll out of my court room. Welcome to America baby doll child. I wish you well."

Now the airport lawyer was completely exasperated. He spoke with a voice that revealed that he had lost his patience, what little he had for the Salt Clan. "Third your honor, on all of this paperwork, there's no address or telephone number for the plaintiff. There is no way to communicate with him."

"Yes," said the Judge. "I noticed that also."

Turning to the Salt Shack Dweller, he said, "Sir, the court and opposing counsel must have an address and a telephone number through which to communicate with you. Otherwise, this litigation cannot proceed in an orderly fashion. What is your mailing address?"

"I have none. The post man will not come to my residence."

"Where's your residence?"

"In the Salt Riverbed in Tempe."

The Judge stared quietly for a minute and then realized that the Salt Shack Dweller was serious and smiled, more to himself than to the others. "Do you have a telephone, or won't the telephone people come to your residence either?"

"I won't let them come to my residence."

"I see. Well, what are we going to do? There must be a system of communication between us."

"I will send my runner each day to receive any communication," said the Salt Shack Dweller.

"Your runner? Your runner has a car, I presume?"

"Not even a thought of one."

The Judge shook his head. "Well let's get on with it. We will cross that bridge when we come to it. Call your first witness sir."

Cecilia came forward first. She told about the noise and vibrations the jets made over at the county hospital and how it disturbed and upset the patients, inhibiting their speedy recovery and thereby costing the county a great amount of money. She was a very calm witness.

The airport lawyer asked her questions about whether she was really a doctor; apparently not believing her testimony. He asked her if she lived with the Salt Shack Dweller. She answered no. He asked her if welfare medical patients really had a right to complain that their free of charge hospital care was too close to the airport. Cecilia answered that they were not complainers; that she was simply relating the effect that the proximity of the airport had on the hospital.

He asked her, "Which was in existence first, the airport or the hospital?" and she guessed that the airport was.

Next it was Raymond's turn. After he told of the burden, the jets imposed on him when returning to the reservation after a week on Jefferson Street and of his fear that the jets would trigger a Vietnam flashback, the airport lawyer asked him a couple of questions in obvious distaste.

"You just don't like the sound of jets when you're drunk or hungover do you?"

"No sir, I do not when I'm sober and not when I'm hung over. And not when I'm trying to assist one of my tribal brothers to get back to the reservation."

"Have you ever had a Vietnam flashback?"

"Oh yes. They are terrifying. It terrifies me the most because I don't know what I'm going to do during a flashback. In fact, I think one might be coming before the end of this week."

"I see," said the lawyer sarcastically.

Raymond kept talking. "And I am a trained sorcerer too, so I must tell you if the law does not stop these jets, I might just turn them into pigeons."

"I see," said the lawyer again. "Now you are threatening us?"

"Oh no sir," answered Raymond even though the airport lawyer did not expect an answer to his sarcasm.

"My father, who is a great sorcerer taught me to never threaten a person and so I don't. Never, sir."

Octavio took the stand after Raymond. He was extremely nervous, like a man who knew there would be immediate and negative consequences from his actions. Nonetheless he bravely spoke of the problems the Mexican workers had in making their way along the Salt Riverbed when all the time they had to worry about whether or not planes were actually being used to try to spot them. Now the airport lawyer was completely disgusted.

He only had two questions for Octavio. "You and your friends here (indicating Anastacio, Carlos, and Miguelito) are illegal aliens, are you not?"

"Oh, Si Señor."

"You think you are very brave to come here and talk like this, don't you?"

"No, senor. I am very afraid."

"Tell me something else," said the airport lawyer to Octavio, "how did you learn English so well? How long have you been coming illegally to the United States? That's how you learned English, isn't it? From all the years you've been breaking the laws of the United States, right?"

"Si Señor, and from speaking with American children, and watching cartoons, and now by reading Hemingway. Simple words, simple sentences."

Finally, the Salt Shack Dweller told his story. He explained the location of his dwelling and how low the planes flew overhead and how often. He explained the noise and the vibrations. He explained the nervousness and headaches he always felt as a result of the jets. He explained about the glass jars that had scorpions in them that vibrated off of his desk and broke on the floor due to low flying jets.

He explained that the native peace and tranquility of the river bottom had been destroyed by the jets and finally he explained how the jets were a general nuisance, trespassing on the solitude of his life and that of the river bottom itself. The airport lawyer was beside himself with disdain.

"You don't own the land where your dwelling is, do you?" he said quite loudly.

"The land has been occupied for generation upon generation for the people," said the Salt Shack Dweller.

"And you don't rent it legally, do you?" asked the lawyer.

"Before me was my father and before him was his father, as far back as time."

"You are nothing more than a squatter, aren't you?"

"For generation upon generation, unbroken, the land and the river has been occupied and worked and cared for. I am now the one who cares for it. There exists a continuum."

"There exists a nut," said the airport lawyer, even more disgusted.

The Judge spoke to the Salt Shack Dweller. "Are you a Native American?"

"I am of the people," answered the Salt Shack Dweller.

The Judge heard the airport lawyer's speech about what a ridiculous, frivolous proceeding it was that the Salt Shack Dweller had brought and how it was obvious to him that the Salt Shack Dweller was trying to make a fool out of the law. His outrage was palpable and was spilling over onto the table before him. When he had finished stomping and fuming, the Judge said that he was going to take a 15 minutes break in the proceedings to think the matter over and then he left by the back door.

The airport lawyer and his shadow, the assistant, hurried out of the courtroom as soon as the Judge departed, and they were most unfriendly. The priest left a minute later, not indicating where he was going, but the rest of the warriors remained in the courtroom, hardly able to suppress their joy until they were alone. It was clear to them that a great victory had been won.

The Salt Shack Dweller spun around with a mystified look on his face, staring only at Raymond, "How did that baby get in here? Did you have something to do with that?"

Before Raymond could answer, Donella spoke loudly. "It sure freaked me out. All of a sudden there was a baby doll in my arms. It sure looked real. It made sucking noises too!"

Raymond had a soft, fulfilled smile. "Sometimes everything works out. Yes, I facilitated that. I thought the Judge would look more favorably upon us. Catholics love babies. I'm sure that Judge is a Catholic."

"But how did you do that," asked the Salt Shack Dweller who was obviously in total awe.

"I just slipped the doll into Donella's arms when no one was watching. She behaved like a natural mother."

"Wow! Impressive," said the befuddled Salt Shack Dweller.

"When do we get our real baby?" asked Donella.

"In about nine months if I'm following what happened recently along the Salt Riverbed," said Cecilia.

The Salt Shack Dweller, who was still staring in disbelief at Raymond, said, "I need you, Raymond. We are going to make a lot of changes around here, you and me, and the rest of us."

All of the testimony had come off without a hitch. If nothing else, said Raymond's brother, the Judge would rule in their favor out of fear that all of the jets would be turned into pigeons. Donella asked what would happen to the people on the planes if the planes were turned into pigeons. She was not answered, a minor detail, but Cecilia was shaking her head, she did not agree.

The Judge would rule in their favor, but only because he had sympathy for the poor and the sick of the county hospital—she could see it in his eyes. Octavio joined the fun. No, he said, the Judge saw the plight of the workers through his testimony and, besides, Octavio could tell that the Judge liked grapefruit for breakfast, and this was the reason he would decide the case in their favor.

After laughter subsided, Octavio admitted that he was so nervous and excited that he had almost pissed in his pants. After more laughter, he was given directions to the bathroom. Miguelito followed.

But two minutes later the doors to the court room opened and two men in green uniforms entered. La Migra.

They walked immediately to Anastacio and Carlos and asked them in stupid classroom Spanish, "Que es su national?"

Both men, of course, responded that they were Mexican, and they were, of course, immediately handcuffed.

The immigration officer looked around and said, "Our informant said there were four. Who else is not an American citizen?"

They watched the eyes of the rest of the warriors. That was one of their favorite tricks. But they got no response, so they focused on Raymond's brothers, "What about you?" they said to the first brother. "Are you a citizen?"

"Yes," answered Raymond's first brother.

"Who won the World Series in 1957?" asked the immigration officer.

"Milwaukee Braves," answered Raymond's first brother.

"Alright, you're okay." And then to the second brother, "You, who was Ira Hayes?"

"He was Iwo Jima."

"You're alright too, I guess," said the disappointed immigration officer.

When La Migra departed, the airport lawyer and his wide-eyed assistant were waiting at the door.

"I can't find the other two," said the lawyer to the immigration officer, "I really wanted to nail that one smartass son-of-a-bitch."

"Did you look in the restroom? They always run to the restroom when we come. They usually hide in the stalls."

"I looked."

"Well, we'll take these two guys. Call us back if the other two show up again."

When the Judge returned, the Salt Shack Dweller could see that something had changed with him. The priest entered with the Judge and came around to resume his seat. Even though the priest's face revealed nothing, the Salt Shack Dweller could sense victory the way a coyote can sense blood. As soon as everyone was seated the airport lawyer began to speak in a shrill agitated voice. "Your Honor, during the recess—"

But he was quickly interrupted by an angry Judge. "Mr. Jones, I'm well aware of what happened at the recess."

The airport lawyer appeared somewhat stunned but there was more to come.

The Judge continued, "I am going to grant the preliminary injunction. The airport is temporarily enjoined from using the Salt Riverbed as a flight pattern until there can be a full hearing on this matter."

"What!" The airport lawyer seemed to have been shot from his seat. "This is an outrage. This is the worst miscarriage of justice I have ever heard of or seen. This is outlandish judicial activism. The city needs that airport, you cannot live and thrive without it, we must have continual trade and commerce if we are to keep growing—"

"Save it for another judge in another time, Mr. Jones. I have made my ruling."

"I fully intend to," said the airport lawyer, who was out the door before the Judge had even departed, *A sign of disrespect to black-robes,* thought the Salt Shack Dweller.

He had a strange feeling that this victory had very little to do with anything that he had done, though he did not voice that feeling to the remaining warriors since they were already dancing in the isles, exhibiting their pride in their victory. *No,* the Salt Shack Dweller thought, *the victory was unquestionably a result of a spell put on the Judge by some magic or sorcery.* And while the victory was terribly sweet, the Salt Shack Dweller knew at the same time that magic and sorcery were often not permanent and that spells frequently wore off.

So, the band of warriors left the court room and started for the stairwell. Their leader felt that the elevator was a trap or an ambush—who can say what trick the electricity will play? There was no wisdom in relying on the quintessence of the enemy.

But before they reached the door to the stairwell they were summoned discreetly, "PSST! PSST!"

"Octavio! Miguelito!" said an overjoyed Cecilia.

"Is it safe?" asked the breathless migrants.

"It is safe," called Cecilia in a hushed tone. "Hurry, into the stairwell."

Once in the tomb-like safety of the concrete stairwell Octavio related how he and Miguelito (shaking now like a leaf, not understanding what happened) had escaped the immigration authorities.

"We were leaving the bathroom of the man when we saw the door of the elevator open, and we saw La Migra. I pulled Miguelito through the next-door. This was the bathroom of the woman. With goodness, we discovered the room was empty. I instructed Miguelito to roll his pants up above the knee since he has less fur on his legs than I do and for him to sit on the stool. Then I stood on the seat behind him all bent down. We waited a very long time until it might be safe."

Cecilia hugged both Octavio and Miguelito.

"You acted wisely and bravely. I am happy to inform you that our victory in the courtroom was complete, but I am sad to give you the news that Anastacio and Carlos were captured by La Migra."

Octavio beamed. "The news of the victory, it is truly magnificent. It is a victory for the workers. The news of Anastacio and Carlos is not unexpected, and it is not so sad. You see, the Papago woman who charges them $100 has much competition. She will give a free ride to anyone who can show deportation papers within 30 days of when she transported them. They will return in three or four days. It is good for business."

"Octavio," said Cecilia proudly, "you and yours are shrewd like foxes." The rest of the warriors agreed, and Octavio grinned slyly, "Like a coyote, señorita, like a coyote."

They reached the bottom of the stairs and pushed the outside door open. The hot, dry air felt refreshing to the Salt Shack Dweller after the cold artificial air of the court building. It was late afternoon. Soon would be darkness and the rays. The urgency now was to find shelter from the endless gene-splitting rays.

5

Raymond and his brothers knew where to go to begin the victory celebration. The warriors pooled their money and even the Priest pitched in. They purchased two big jugs of red wine and then walked over to Library Park. Library Park, unlike Patriots Park, had not been planted with burrs or psychologically intimidating sprinkler systems. Using the hostage water as a weapon against its liberator in this way displayed a grotesque form of arrogance to the Salt Shack Dweller. Library Park had, in fact, the appearance of having been abandoned to the homeless wanderers of the Valley of the Sun.

The sun was leaving the valley and as darkness came so would the rays, floating like arrows of death shot from a trillion bows from the mythical desert west of Phoenix. But the Salt Shack Dweller followed his victorious band of warriors.

The residents of Library Park, called transients, despite the fact that many had been in residence for years, were a motley crew, not few in number, whose piles of physical possessions looked like dung heaps. Many of these people knew Cecilia, "Hello Mrs. Doctor, my arm is all better," or "doctor, come here please, my leg still has pain." Or "Look Doctor I removed the stitches where Maria cut me by myself, but Maria's husband knocked out one of my teeth."

And many of them also knew the priest. To him they spoke thus, "Good afternoon, Father, would you care to hear my confessions? I have much to tell you since I last confessed (laughter)." Or from a small man who seemed to be in control of very little of his mind, "Father, Father, you must perform an exorcism on me, I sleep with devils."

"Don't we all," chimed in the Library Park chorus. A man with no shoes spoke up next. "Father, do you have any shoes to give away?"

"Or shirts or pants or jackets?" sang the Library Park chorus.

And all of them knew Raymond and his brothers and to them there were only two things said, "Come share your wine," or "come here, I have some whiskey to share with you."

The Salt Shack Dweller did not know the residents of Library Park and now was not the time to get to know them. The rays were surely coming. And it was not the time to consume whiskey or wine since alcohol made the flesh soft and spongy, easy for the rays to penetrate. Yet this band of warriors were mingling with the people of the park, already engaged in the exchange of ideas and consumable goods. They ignored his warning of incoming rays and encouraged him to depart without them with the promise of meeting up with him soon or maybe in a day or so.

When the Salt Shack Dweller snuck off, into the deserted darkness of the city night, he took note that his warriors appeared content. Miguelito and Donella, still under the spell of each other from the previous night, searched for a place among the wanderers and the derelicts and dung heaps to content themselves. To them the park might have been a Mediterranean isle peopled by proud warriors and statesmen after a glorious battle—campfires aglow all around. They would find a tropical bush to curl up under, they would find solitude among the ruins, they would find the magnificence of the previous night. Their youth would provide.

Raymond was discussing a sorcerer's methodology with anyone who would listen. He was conducting an experiment to see if he could turn a cockroach on the table before him into a giant tortoise. If so, he said excitedly, he would flood the city with them.

Octavio went among the citrus workers of the park. They were many. He was explaining the significance of the great courtroom victory and, incidentally, explaining his crew's crucial role in the battle as well as his near capture by the enemy which surely would've led to torture and incarceration.

Cecilia moved like an angel of mercy among the men and women and children of the park. When she found a soul who had no feeling on his left side, she hailed a taxi, paid the fair and directed the driver to her hospital's ER entrance.

The Salt Shack Dweller could see, to his amazement, that the jets did not approach and did not depart over the Salt Riverbed. How he wished he was in his dwelling to enjoy the tranquility that the absence of the jets would bring and to be where he was safe from the rays. The dwelling was too far, the night too dark, the rays too many. The Salt Shack Dweller would have to spend the night out, exposed to the risk and danger and all he could do was try to minimize his exposure.

When the Salt Shack Dweller snuck off into the deserted darkness of the city night, in search of safety from the hard, dry, and silent rain of rays, he was followed by a figure dressed in black, perhaps a spirit. The bombardment of the rays compelled the Salt Shack Dweller on harder and faster, along the empty concrete walkways through the narrow man-made canyons. He hurried, his shirt collar turned up now against the onslaught, but his bare legs were exposed and burning. The man in black stayed with him, like his shadow, but there were no other lost souls wondering about, they had sense enough to get out of this hard rain.

The Salt Shack Dweller did not slow the pace but increased it until, by the time he reached the east side of the Hyatt-Kiva, which would afford him the maximum possible protection in the immediate area, he was running, as was the dark shadow behind him. When he reached the east side of the Hyatt-Kiva, he sat on the concrete, his back against the monolithic block wall.

This kiva was a block wide by a block long by a block deep with numerable interior walls. To the west of the Kiva, from where the rays came, was building after building that could potentially ensure more protection. Some of the rays would penetrate it all, of course, and some would fall from above or swirl upon him from the corners of the building, but for the most part, the rays would bypass him, blocked out by the countless buildings to his back. This was where the Salt Shack Dweller would pass the night until it was safe for him to make the journey back to his dwelling in the river's bottom.

The spirit figure in black made his approach and sat against the wall next to the Salt Shack Dweller. It was the priest. "Why do you run tonight, my son?"

"I am not your son, black-robes."

"But why do you run when there is no danger?"

"Do not be naïve, black-robes. Look into the night sky and you will see the rays of death. They rush through the sky at an ungodly speed from the west to east."

The priest squinted at the dark sky. "Are they there now? I cannot see them."

"Yes, they are present in the multitudes upon multitudes."

"Does this building protect you from them?"

"Somewhat, at least in conjunction with all the other buildings to the west."

"Where do these rays of death come from?"

The Salt Shack Dweller looked at the priest as if the priest was from another century. "From the Palo Verde Nuclear Generating Station of course."

"Oh yes, now I understand," said the Priest.

"You say you understand but do you see?"

"Do I see what?"

"Do you see the rays?"

"Well, no, but—"

"As I thought."

"But that does not mean that, I do not understand. There is much we do not see that we understand just the same. Indeed, my life is dedicated to understanding that which I cannot see."

"Well, let me make sure that you really do understand if you don't mind," said the Salt Shack Dweller.

"Of course," said the Priest, "please do."

The Salt Shack Dweller took a deep breath. "Padre, do you remember General Jack Ripper?"

The Priest chuckled. "Of course. Dr. Strangelove. How could anyone forget him? Fighting to the death to protect our precious bodily fluids from the evil communists."

"Yes, Padre that's him but it's not our precious bodily fluids that are at risk and it's not the communists who are our greatest threat."

"Who or what is then," asked the Priest.

"It's only about 15 miles away. It's the nuclear power plant firing rays at us non-stop night after night, ripping our cells and DNA apart ostensibly to provide us with electricity, which we don't really need for life, at least not as much as we need our cells and DNA."

"Well, that sounds very serious. I will have to research it and educate myself on this issue."

" Yes, you must, especially given the position of influence you have with your congregation…but I'm curious about something else too. Why do you roam these degraded streets at night? Is your spirit lost or are you trying to catch a glimpse of that which you cannot see?"

The priest chuckled. To the Salt Shack Dweller's surprise and delight the priest revealed a small flask of Irish whiskey, offering to share it with him, which he could now accept because he was no longer directly exposed to the rays.

"No, my spirit is not lost. I come down here because this is where the disenchanted are. This is where my work is."

"Where is your parish?"

Again. the Priest chuckled. but this time in a sad way. It seemed that perhaps he had been pulling on the bottle before he joined the Salt Shack Dweller against the Hyatt-Kiva wall. "As of a year ago my parish is in Scottsdale, the town of my birth and of my youth."

"Where were you before that?"

"I was in Papua New Guinea. However, according to the church authorities I was too active in the region's politics. Their solution was to transfer me to Scottsdale. I think their goal was to retrain me."

"They wanted to rehabilitate you in the land of wealth where there was no need for politics   "

"This is true."

"So, you sneak down here in the evenings to replenish your spirit?"

"I guess this is also true."

"May I have another taste of your whiskey, black-robes? Thank you. Tell me, what kind of magic did you play on the Judge?"

Before the Priest could answer, a policeman approached the two in order to inquire about their purpose in loitering the night away. The priest calmed the policeman quickly, however.

"It's alright, officer, I am hearing this troubled man's confession."

"The fact is," said the Salt Shack Dweller to the policeman, "that I am hearing his confession."

The policeman ignored the Salt Shack Dweller and turned to the priest. "I will leave the matter in your hands, Father. Call if you need assistance."

The Priest nodded his appreciation. When the policeman had departed, he said, "Where were we?"

"You were going to tell me about the magic you used on the Judge."

"None. The fact is that you got a renegade Judge, and he seems to be in search of more renegade than less. He seems to have reached the 'I don't give a shit' mindset. It was the airport lawyer who cast a negative spell that influenced the Judge. When the Judge was in his office, I went to introduce myself. Priests and judges are not so different, you understand. We both wear costumes to create an illusion and a mystique, we both have our rituals and ceremonies. Anyhow, the airport lawyer came in to the Judge's chambers where I was sitting with the Judge."

At one point of the conversation, he made the mistake of saying to the Judge, "The God damn Indians think they have a right to be drunk and the God damn Mexicans think they have a right to come to America and the God damn spoiled young people think they have the right to be world-class smartasses."

"Those comments genuinely pissed the Judge off. You could see his mind boiling over at that moment. What the airport lawyer failed to recognize was that the Judge was a believer in more than commerce and growth. He was also a believer in people."

"Black-robes, I'll tell you this. You may believe what you wish. You may even believe that I am a believer, it doesn't matter to me. But in reality, all you say is much too complicated to explain the Judge's ruling. No doubt what really happened was that Raymond got to him with an act of sorcery or that you got to him with an act of Christian black magic by, for example, flashing a communion wafer at him. Or perhaps it was the combined efforts of you and Raymond that took control of the Judge's mind."

The priest smiled, just smiled, and offered the Salt Shack Dweller the last of the Irish whiskey.

"You too may believe what you wish. It is time for me to return to the park. These are the hours when too much drink and despair may have taken over. The police will arrive. and I can do my best work. I have enjoyed our conversation." The Priest stood up and started to depart.

"Father Keno," called the Salt Shack Dweller, "beware of the rays, go swiftly and remember, your assistance in today's battle is greatly appreciated. If you come to my dwelling sometime, I'll see to it that you are rewarded."

"Rewarded?"

"Yes, with an understanding woman, for example."

The Priest looked hard at the smiling Salt Shack Dweller and then he swallowed slowly. Finally, he turned his collar up and stepped out into the open, under the cloudless sky, into the onslaught of the rays, and then he was gone.

6

It was a long night for the Salt Shack Dweller against the wall of the Hyatt-Kiva, yet he maintained a high degree of stoic endurance by remaining cross-legged and motionless, staring into the black eastern sky and by detaching his mind from his body to the extent possible. Never before had he seen so many rays. They filled the sky like the spears of warriors of the ancient Greek states. They blocked out the stars and the moon. Things were obviously getting worse and seemed to be reaching an unbearable level. Something would have to be done.

When light finally began to creep into the eastern sky, the Salt Shack Dweller started to feel better. The morning was warm and beautiful, there had been a great victory the day before and with the increasing light the rays were retreating. He could see across the road to the plaza. At first, the Salt Shack Dweller could see nothing but the small trees that dotted the small plaza.

With more light, he could see a giant dandelion water sculpture. Then the still and silent human figures of the plaza started to take shape. The Salt Shack Dweller stared at the human figures for a long time, wondering what their silence could mean. When he realized, he wept.

The Salt Shack Dweller stood and walked across the road to the plaza, tears of eternal sadness in his eyes, where the human figures were. There were a dozen of them, all but one female, and all but one young adults the other a female child. They were frozen in time and place, and in different positions of elegant, youthful dance.

Some had their arms and faces pulled back to greet the sun. Others reached forward or straight up. One stood parallel to the Earth, balanced on a single leg while another pointed both arms forward. One dancer had not been dancing but had been playing the flute, perhaps for the rest to dance by. A male dancer was holding a female above him, for the stars.

But their skin was badly rutted, it was turquoise and gold in color. Their eyes were hollow pits and might have been pecked empty by the ravens, and in some of those sightless cavities the Salt Shack Dweller thought he could see and hear a sense of universal anguish that their dances would never be completed. The dancers' clothes had long since been burned away or disintegrated. Each of them was preserved in the most beautiful but sad way; their bodies had solidified, as hard as bronze.

There was only one explanation and the Salt Shack Dweller understood immediately. These were carefree, youthful dancers who came to the open-air tiled plaza night after night, in the warm desert air, to dance together. A man and a child must have joined the predominately female troupe. Night after night they danced for themselves or for any passersby who might want to stop and watch beautiful youth express their joy in dance.

But night after night they were exposed to the rays. Their love for dance, their immunity from death because of their youth, led them to ignore the danger and led them to brush aside the discoloration of their skin and its slow but certain decomposition. Eventually the exposure was too great and before the light of day could find them, they had all unwittingly sacrificed themselves, once carefree but now permanently frozen in the summer nights of the desert.

The Salt Shack Dweller wept silently as he went from one dancer to the other, as he stared into the blank eyes and examined the expression on each face, even in death dedicated to concentrating on the dance that would never be completed. He loved each and every one of them, even in their foolish choice to dance in the open, in the night under the stars over fear of the rays and death.

Now he understood the giant dandelion water sculpture. Certainly, toward the end the dancers could see and could feel the effect of the rays on their bodies. It was burning. So, they had built the water sculpture near to their place of dance and this they could go to, now and then, for some temporary relief to enable them to continue the dance for one more night.

Didn't they know that the burning came invisibly and without a conscience or didn't they care about anything but continuing the dance? Under the circumstances the water dandelion could not have been considered anything but the most utilitarian of devices a number of buckets or horse trough would've worked as well but the dancers even had to make that spectacularly beautiful. Was it ignorance? Was it a protest? Why, oh why hadn't he known of their existence so he could have tried to save them?

If there was a way to restore life to the dancers, it was through their eyes by filling the empty sockets with life-giving water so that they could see and therefore think (and yes, dance) once again. Yet the Salt Shack Dweller could not find a way to pour water into the eye sockets.

If, however, the water was available in its solid form, as it was once in a great while in the winter along the river, then he could simply place a chunk of water in each eye socket of each dancer. The Hyatt-Kiva had a machine to make summer water solid and though use of an electrically generated product repulsed him, the Salt Shack Dweller realized that this was an exceptional circumstance.

He went to the Hyatt-Kiva and appropriated a plastic bucket of solid water and was chased off by a uniformed guard like a mangey stray cat. Each dancer's eyes were packed with chunks of solid water. Momentarily, they sparkled in the morning sun, hinting at renewed life, but soon the solid water returned to its fluid, liquid form and ran like tears from the empty eyes of the dancers.

Having failed to breathe fresh life into the souls of the dancers, the Salt Shack Dweller desperately wanted them to know they were not forgotten and that they were not unappreciated. He wanted them to know that they stood as a monument to the choice of a full and joyful life over hiding from death.

So, the Salt Shack Dweller removed his wingtips and started a solo dance on the tiles of the plaza. The tiles were already warm, the sun was on the horizon casting the Salt Shack Dweller's skinny shadow all the way across the street to the Hyatt-Kiva. He danced within view of the now motionless dancers, and he danced hard, until he was hot and sweating.

He went to the fountain of the water dandelion and stepped inside, as the plaza dancers before him must have done too cool and refresh their bodies. Then he danced again. His sorrow now was that one of the young women dancers could not join him, showing him how to really dance. The Salt Shack Dweller danced alone, with intermittent rest under the water dandelion, until the police came and arrested him for trespassing and loitering. The police took him away and did not collect his wingtips.

In jail, the Salt Shack Dweller saw Raymond and one of his brothers, but they did not speak, primarily because Raymond and his brothers could not be awakened. At 10:00 a.m., he was brought before the Judge. It was Judge O'Sullivan again. The Judge looked at Salt Shack Dweller with a thousand questions in his eyes. But he only asked a few.

"Why are you here?"

The Salt Shack Dweller's sadness about the dancers had gone to sleep deep inside of him and in its place was a quiet happiness generated by his renewed faith and the courage of humans as demonstrated by the dancers.

"It's a complex story long-robe. Come to my dwelling someday and I will tell you everything."

"Is that where you will go if I release you on your own recognizance?"

"Of course. It is my home."

"Alright, one more thing before you go. You should know that the airport was successful in getting a higher Judge to reverse my order. It was all done by 9:00 a.m. this morning. No one could find you to give you notice."

"I was dancing with the immortals. By the way, the county is going to owe me for a pair of shoes if some thief has made off with them from the plaza."

And one had. So, the Salt Shack Dweller started his journey up the Salt Riverbed without shoes. Walking without shade on burning rocks and burning sand on what would turn out to be the hottest day of the summer, with jet after jet screaming down on him as he walked, felt as serene as an Olive tree.

7

Because he was thrown in jail and had lost his shoes, it was late when the Salt Shack Dweller spied on the abandoned bridge underneath which his dwelling was built. The return journey was long and hot and came with burning feet. There was a distinct absence of shade in the Salt Riverbed.

Along the way he stopped again at the Pueblo Grande, this time to give thanks by giving up water from his body to the dust of the ruins. The proprietor screamed at him as if he was in the act of giving up water, but the proprietor did not give chase for fear that a wild band of mongrel warriors waited just beyond the cut bank.

When the Salt Shack Dweller finally arrived his home spot where the shack had stood, there was instead, a surprisingly small pile of ashes. The three-legged dog was there, waiting. Except for the metal components of the dwelling structure and the metal spring frame of the bed, everything else had been burned, including the not-for-sale sign the Salt Shack Dweller had made and planted next to the shack.

The fire must have been a hot one, perhaps started by fuel, even the glass containers holding the reptiles and spiders and scorpions partially melted and all of the creatures had been cremated. The Salt Shack Dweller's desk had not fallen down though it was burned through and through; his books and papers had burned but remained in place in the breathless hours since the fire. The books and papers were reduced to leafy ash. The typewriter was a complete loss. In the sand next to the burned-out shack, there was a message scrolled with the words, 'Die, Bum'.

The Salt Shack Dweller was saddened by the death of the creatures that he had kept in the glass containers. He was saddened by the loss of his books and papers but otherwise the loss was not a great one nor was it a first occurrence. The Salt Shack Dweller had been through floods and fires and the machines of man. The shack was merely a temporary dwelling until his pueblo was

57

completed and its destruction could be viewed as nothing more than a minor inconvenience.

It could be rebuilt in a day; a thousand salt shacks could be built with all of the debris that was thoughtlessly discarded into the river or was washed down from the east to collect against the bridge pilings by the sometimes, annual flood. The message scrolled in the sand, could likewise, not be viewed as a matter for concern since it was obviously directed toward someone other than himself; no one would threaten him by calling him a bum. He was the Salt Shack Dweller, leader of the small but increasingly powerful Salt Clan.

The Salt Shack Dweller knew it would take him no time at all, no longer than a day or two, to rebuild his dwelling. Twice before, he had done so. The first time was when the salt shack mysteriously burned shortly after he had originally built it (explainable only as an expression of displeasure by the Gods of fire, perhaps because that time he had failed to make a fire offering to those very Gods before he began construction, which was all that was necessary to ensure protection from the Gods, a fact that insurance companies astutely kept out of the domain of public information).

The second time that the dwelling had to be rebuilt was when the operator of a bulldozer came through and with one swipe tore down the dwelling and pushed the remains into the landfill pit a distance downriver. When the machine operator was confronted by the Salt Shack Dweller with the fact that he had just pushed someone's home into a pit, the operator argued that he thought the shack was just another stack of debris against a bridge piling—but the Salt Shack Dweller could see the mean sparkle of laughter in the man's eyes, as if he'd known what he'd been doing all along.

It was simply that mean little sparkle, which inspired the Salt Shack Dweller to spend the night chanting and praying to the Gods for advice on the proper way, the warrior's way, to answer the acute outrage that had been committed against him. About four in the morning, when the Salt Shack Dweller's medicinal wine was gone, that the Gods told him to answer the destruction by stuffing pages from Edward Abbey's insurrection book into the gas tank of the bulldozer. The Salt Shack Dweller always obeyed the Gods.

But the dwelling could not be built before darkness and the rays would come again so the Salt Shack Dweller decided to spend the night in the little pit that he had dug to catch the hawk. There he would be safe from the rays of the night. Until darkness came the Salt Shack Dweller sat in the bleachers of the little city ballpark that adjoined the south bank of the river.

He watched the contest with keen interest and noted the strengths and weakness of each team. Soon, however, he realized that he was the object of interest of the teenage boys and girls who hung around the ballparks on hot summer nights, unattended. The not-yet-men-boys eyed him with ill-defined contempt and scorn, like a painted bird.

The almost-women-girls, however, eyed him with precocious maturity and interest. In their eyes, he could see a willingness to explore their curiosity and a belief that he might accommodate them without revealing them to their own society. The way the protector boys looked at him made him feel like a threat. The way the awakening girls looked at him made him feel like an invitation. He turned his gaze from both, enough for now, and watched closely the remainder of the game. To his hawk pit, he took with him two ideas to ponder through the night.

The first idea to occupy the Salt Shack Dweller's mind through the night in the pit (like a convict at Yuma territorial prison he realized) was the idea of challenging one of the surrounding tribes to a day of games and athletics. Perhaps softball or court ball.

The second idea was inspired by the look in the eyes of the young girls from the surrounding tribes, that he had seen earlier that evening. It appeared that their own tribe denied them status as either adult or child, leaving them in an impulsive and reckless form of maturation limbo. It seemed to the Salt Shack Dweller that the girls were looking for temporary relief sanctuary where they could leave prolonged childhood behind for a time and test the adult world without fear of crimination.

The Salt Shack Dweller was willing to give sanctuary—who could say what might come of it? Perhaps the co-mingling of the races would begin. Perhaps one of the girls would turn out to be the daughter of an important leader of the surrounding tribes. Each idea had a single purpose beyond itself, however. It was time for the small but powerful Salt Clan, led by one known as the Salt Shack Dweller, to begin to exert its ideas and values, its customs and ways, beyond itself, to the surrounding tribes and races, out of the ashes of the burned-out shack would rise a new and powerful culture, to be led, of course, by the Salt Clan.

Therefore, it was important that the Salt Clan achieve victory in the games they would propose because domination in every sphere was essential if one culture was to engulf and incorporate all others around it. Likewise, it was important that the Salt Clan control the mind and desires of the young girls of the alien but proximate tribes because they, in turn, controlled the birthrights to their respective tribal groupings.

Before the sun had climbed over the Superstition Mountains, the Salt Shack Dweller had started rebuilding his temporary dwelling under the bridge. As he worked, he considered the importance of the games, he would propose. Only the successful cultures had sufficient leisure time to engage in sport and athletic contests. And those cultures only achieved the freedom of leisure by being ambitious and witty. The less time that had to be devoted to providing shelter and food and warding off the enemy, the more time available to develop such endeavors as art and athletic prowess.

The Salt Shack Dweller saw his disadvantage. Much of his time was spent building shelters, constructing irrigation systems, planting, and tending to his garden, hunting, and battling with his enemies. Without question the Salt Clan had burdens and obstacles to overcome if they were to dominate their adversaries. Such was the test of fire, put to all great cultures, destined to lead the blind to a superior life.

By sunset, the shack had been rebuilt. It seemed, to the Salt Shack Dweller, that this dwelling was nicer than the previous one. He furnished the interior with a broken-down chair and table he salvaged from the landfill after the new bulldozer had stopped working for the day. He cleaned the ash from the steel bed frame and set it back up. Before darkness, he journeyed to the market and commercial quarter of the village called Tempe, only a short distance by foot. He acquired a pair of tennis shoes, a blanket to hang over the shack's entrance, some paper and pencil, candles, and a jug of red wine. The bill was charged to his friend, the lawyer, Harold.

On his return journey, he passed through the park. He stopped at the ball field. One team was practicing before the beginning of the game. He identified the leader of the team and boldly entered the playing area.

First, he offered the leader a taste of the wine, out of courtesy, which was impolitely refused as the leader stared coldly at him.

So, he got to the point. "My players would like to challenge your players to a contest."

The leader continued to stare but finally spoke, "Are you in this league?" The Salt Shack Dweller answered, "No, we are in a league of our own."

The leader seemed perplexed for a minute, which the Salt Shack Dweller, translated as a lack of leadership or competitive experience.

Then the leader shrugged his shoulders and said, "There is an open night a week from tonight. We will be here to practice. If your team wants to play a game that night, we will be here."

"Then it's settled," said the Salt Shack Dweller, again holding up the wine jug to consummate the arrangement.

But again, the leader refused the offer and returned to his players.

8

When the Salt Shack Dweller left the field of play, he found that there was a group of girls watching him the way a female a bit older might look, if he had just disrobed, but he was wearing his loincloth and his tennis shoes.

The group of five, giggled sporadically as they came closer and then the bravest of the group stuck her head out a few inches and said, "I'll try some of your wine."

"Follow me then," the Salt Shack Dweller answered.

He continued walking and did not look back. He walked out of the white light of the ballpark and out of the park itself. Many paces behind him the group of girls were following, loudly but slowly, though not so slow as to lose track of the Salt Shack Dweller who was slipping into the darkness of the river bottom ahead of them.

He was sitting in his new chair facing east in his new shack, burning a new candle when the girls arrived at the entrance to the shack. It took them several minutes to actually enter the shack, and they did so only as a group. The Salt Shack Dweller remained silent. He let the girls take their time, to get the feeling and the smell of the place. He understood that it was all very new and foreign to them, and they first had to decide if there was danger in this place that they had ventured into.

Speaking with his hand he indicated the jug of wine on the broken-down table and with the same gesture offered it to any of them.

When they spoke, they spoke the words of their parents. "Why do you live here? Do you have a job? Why do you dress like that? Do you have a family?" The Salt Shack Dweller let them speak without answering their questions. He was not offended by the questions; they came from the mouths of young people, who should've been taught proper respect by their tribe, but were not.

Again, he offered wine. One by one, they took a taste. All participated. As they relaxed, they said the things that could be expected from them.

They said, "You look funny in those clothes. This place is a dump. You don't sleep on that rusty bed frame, do you? I bet you are wanted by the police."

They all laughed each time one of their number dared an insult to the Salt Shack Dweller but none of them left, none of them bypassed the wine. They were fascinated by the shack and its occupant, if for no other reason, then that, it was quite different from anything they had ever seen before. Though each had been restrained in mental growth by their tribe, each was a healthy young woman.

The Salt Shack Dweller knew this, and he knew, they knew it themselves. This was the important thing, and it was something he had to cultivate. So, he was patient, allowing the girls to say and do as they wish. In this way, they would become calm and relaxed. They would grow to feel at ease around him and his shack. They would come and go on their own. They would choose to return to where they were free. Then they would become part of the ever-growing Salt Clan.

The girls had, indeed, become quite relaxed that first night, drinking wine and making childish jokes when Anastacio and Carlos rushed into the shack without warning, frightening the girls very badly. The Mexicans were possessed by a great agitation.

"Señor, Señor—" They both began, speaking in Spanish very rapidly, both speaking at once.

The Salt Shack Dweller did not understand the language, but he could see, in the eyes of the two men, their great fear. He tried to get them to stop, to calm down and to work through their message in the few words of Spanish that he knew and a few words of English, they would know. But then one of the girls, somewhat quietly agitated, interrupted.

She said, "These men are saying that there is a great tragedy in the desert, and they don't know what to do."

The Salt Shack Dweller looked at the girl but did not have time to congratulate her, on her competence.

"Ask them what the problem is," said the Salt Shack Dweller to the girl.

She turned to Anastacio and Carlos and beautiful Spanish flowed through her lips. Both of the Mexican men tried to answer her at once, until the Salt Shack Dweller muzzled Carlos.

"He says they were coming across the desert today and they came upon six workers who had been abandoned by their coyote…I don't know what they mean by the word coyote."

"I do, go ahead."

"They're saying that the six workers were all dying from the lack of water. The coyote took their water. None of them could travel any longer."

"Quick, what more?" asked the Salt Shack Dweller.

His words were immediately translated by the intent young girl-woman.

Anastacio replied for what seemed like much too long. "He says they gave these workers he doesn't think they are from Mexico, he thinks they're from El Salvador. He gave them the little bit of water that they had but it wasn't enough, so these two men went out to the highway for help."

"A Papago woman picked them up, but no one knew where to go for help. They were afraid of the immigration police. This was the only place they knew, to come to."

"Where did they leave the workers?" asked the Salt Shack Dweller.

"In the desert," answered Anastacio through the girl.

"Where in the desert?"

Anastacio's eyes grew helpless. He pointed south and his only answer was that it was north of the American border, somewhere in the desert.

"Where did the Papago woman pick you up?"

"On the highway somewhere" said Anastacio.

The Salt Shack Dweller could feel the situation deteriorating into hopelessness, until the concept of sacrifice occurred to him. He had the girl ask them if they could find the place in the desert where the workers were left.

Anastacio and Carlos answered immediately and without doubt. "Oh yes, we have been there many times."

The Salt Shack Dweller took the girl by the hand, saying, "We need you to come with us."

He pushed Anastacio and Carlos out of the shack and they were off, the four of them on a mission of mercy, two of them to be possible sacrifices. They sped through the night along the river bottom. The moon was full, illuminating their way and keeping the rays to a minimum. They continued running, up the cut bank, across the park to the pay telephone on the far side of the road. The Salt Shack Dweller clawed through the phone book, to find what he was looking for, and then realized he had no money for the phone. But the girl did. The Salt Shack Dweller dialed the number.

On the phone he spoke with a desperate voice. "Hello black-robes? Yes, it's me, the Salt Shack Dweller. Now listen very carefully—"

And the Salt Shack Dweller proceeded to tell the Judge about the immigrant workers who were dying in the desert. He told the Judge to send officers to the phone booth so that Anastacio and Carlos could show them where the workers were. He suggested helicopters and airplanes and fast cars.

In his firmest voice, at the end of the conversation, taking no chances with the Judge's competence or sense of fairness, he said, "Be sure to send someone who can speak Spanish and one more thing…these men who will guide the officers are heroes. I expect immunity for them."

In no more than five minutes, a screaming police car rushed up to the phone booth. Two officers stepped out and one began speaking, in Spanish, with Anastacio and Carlos. In a minute, the two Mexicans stepped into the patrol car. Anastacio rolled his eyes, as if to say that his life had become a motor vehicle ride between the border of Mexico and Central Arizona.

When the car with the flashing lights had departed with Anastacio and Carlos, the Salt Shack Dweller turned to the girl-woman and said, "Do you live near here?"

"Yes."

"Do you walk home or do your parents come to get you?"

"I walk."

"Alone?"

"Yes, alone. Usually with my friends."

"I, will walk you home. The streets are not always safe. Will you be punished for being late?"

"No, nobody will know or even care."

They walked for a while without speaking until the Salt Shack Dweller asked the girl, "Where did you learn to speak Spanish so well?"

"In school."

"You are in high school?"

"Yes, language is fun. It makes your brain work fast and gives it something to do. I don't like it when my brain doesn't have anything to do."

"Yes, I understand"

Again, they did not speak but in a few minutes the girl was weeping. She tried to stop but could not do so and finally just let herself go. She turned and wrapped her arms around the skinny Salt Shack Dweller and wept against his bare skin.

"What seems to be the problem child?" he asked her.

When she could control her throat enough to speak, she said, "I'm sad and scared and happy."

"Oh." said the Salt Shack Dweller. "That's a lot."

"I'm afraid those people might die."

"They could. It's possible. It has happened many times."

"I'd feel responsible."

"No, that would be very wrong."

"And I feel happy because if they do get saved then this will be the most important thing, I've ever done in my life—"

"You did a good job. We couldn't have done it without you being able to speak Spanish. You should be proud."

"But I don't have anyone to tell. If I told my parents, they would have more than a fit, that I was even involved. They would punish me."

"Yes, parents do that sometimes."

They walked to the girl's house. She had ceased crying. She turned again to him before going in.

"Everyone thinks you're crazy, but I know they're wrong. What is your name?"

"I am called the Salt Shack Dweller."

"That's too long," said the girl. "I'm going to call you Bones. Can I come to visit your shack again sometimes?"

"Yes, of course. What do they call you?"

"Patricia."

"You did a good thing tonight, Patricia. You can be proud."

The girl stepped up on her toes and kissed the Salt Shack Dweller on his unshaven face.

"I like you," she said quickly, before running off to her house, leaving the Salt Shack Dweller standing in the street, feeling quite strange.

How could these feelings be happening to him? After all, he was a great clan leader with a great mission and she was so…young, but not that young.

The moon was going down and the night was dark. The rays were on the rise, and it was time for the Salt Shack Dweller to scurry back to his shack. He ran flat-footed and unencumbered the full distance.

Now that the Salt Shack Dweller had arranged for an athletic contest to be played between the Salt Clan and one of the foreign tribes, it was necessary for him to organize his team. Practice might be in order as well. The game of softball required numerous players.

There was himself and Cecilia and Raymond and Octavio; Octavio would bring Miguelito and Raymond would bring Donella. If necessary, more players could be recruited through Cecilia and Raymond, perhaps through Raymond would be the best, as Cecilia's recruits would likely be invalids from the recovery ward of the hospital.

While the Salt Shack Dweller was working his garden with the dry sun burning down on his already dark brown back like a fire breathing dragon, the Salt Shack Dweller stopped his work and met his visitors with a gourd of cool water. Anastacio and Carlos drank greedily, the Judge hesitated, wondering about hepatitis or worse, then shrugged and drank also. The Salt Shack Dweller waited for the Judge to speak.

"Your friends led the immigration authorities directly to the place in the desert where the workers were. One was dead already; the others should survive."

"Where are they now?"

"County Hospital."

"The survivors were fortunate."

"Yes, they owe their lives to these men." The Judge indicated Anastacio and Carlos.

"It is true," said the Salt Shack Dweller. "And now these men will be left alone by the authorities, will they not." The Salt Shack Dweller's tone was more of an instruction than a question. But the Judge was pensive. A frown crossed his face.

"The immigration authorities will try to apprehend the person or persons who smuggled these workers, and your friends are essential witnesses and therefore they must stay in the jurisdiction to testify—"

"Very well, they will stay then."

The Judge's frown was still present. He was obviously not finished speaking.

"Usually, we do one of two things with material witnesses like your friends. We put them in jail to ensure they will be here when we need them to testify, or we release them into the custody of a responsible party."

The Salt Shack Dweller breathed deep, never taking his eyes from the Judge. "Still there is no problem, is there? They will stay here with me."

The Judge looked about the premises; at the accommodations, at the shack and the barely begun adobe pueblo, at the extensive garden, at the bridges overhead, at the power lines and airplanes and the scorching sun on the bleached sand and rocks, and the three-legged dog laying in the precious shade. He looked back to the weathered face of the loincloth-clad Salt Shack Dweller. "I was afraid you'd say that, so, I made up my mind to trust you with the responsibility of these two men."

"There is no need for you to fear. You have the words of the leader of the Salt Clan. What more could you want?"

"Usually we like a cash bond," replied the Judge.

"Which you know is unnecessary in this case."

"And unattainable," answered the Judge.

"Quite true. And now, that this business is behind us, tell me, how are you at the game of softball?"

The Judge's face registered surprise. Before answering, he admitted to himself that he enjoyed trying to keep up with the unpredictable mind of the Salt Shack Dweller.

"Actually, I'm quite good. Why do you ask?"

"Because you have the opportunity to join the Salt Clan in a game of great importance. The game is only six days away. We begin practice at 05:00 a.m. tomorrow morning."

The Judge smiled. "It sounds like fun. I may come."

"Bring a bat and a bag of softballs with you," instructed the Salt Shack Dweller as the Judge took his leave.

Now the Salt Shack Dweller felt certain they could field a team of nine, perhaps 10, if the Judge showed up. Anastacio and Carlos set about making a camp not far from the shack. They each had blankets, and each had a small bundle of personal belongings, but nothing more. Anastacio, the more industrious of the two, built a small fire pit with a grill on top for cooking tortillas and beans. He began to comb the river bottom for wood, as Carlos departed to investigate the outside world.

Patricia came to the shack in the late afternoon from the south. She carried with her a sack of food, ground meat, bread and beans. The Salt Shack Dweller was working on the pueblo, making mud blocks when he saw her fresh and youthful approach.

She called out to him, "Hello Bones, what are you building?"

"A pueblo."

"It's going to be huge."

"Yes, the Salt Clan is growing."

The Salt Shack Dweller was surprised, again, at the youth of the girl. She was, after all, vulnerable and uncertain, and his duty was to be wise in his decisions regarding her.

"What do you have in the sack?"

"Food. I was going to cook for you. Is it all right?"

The Salt Shack Dweller smiled. "It is all right."

Patricia saw Anastacio. She turned away from the Salt Shack Dweller and walked slowly to where he was. They spoke for a short time in Spanish and then the Salt Shack Dweller saw Patricia turn away from Anastacio and enter the shack. He could tell that she was in tears for the unknown worker who did not survive the desert.

An hour before the sun went down the priest approached from the north. He brought candles for the shack. The Salt Shack Dweller first made a formal introduction between the priest and Patricia (who was trying to bring some order to the interior of the shack and who could give the Latin name, to the delight of the priest, for most of the new insects and reptiles the Salt Shack Dweller had collected since the old shack had burned).

The priest, as it turned out, was an accomplished horticulturist. This had been his primary work, besides the local politics, with the citizens of his first priestly assignment. Until the red sun had been gone from the sky for half an hour, the priest and the Salt Shack Dweller worked the garden, trading agricultural ideas and experiences.

When they were forced to quit work because of darkness (because the rays that the Priest still could not see but did not disbelieve) and because a meal was ready, the Salt Shack Dweller said to the priest, "By the way, have you come for your reward?"

"My reward?" asked the Priest.

"I promised you a reward for the assistance you gave us in the battle against the airport. Have you come to collect that?"

The priest did not answer but swallowed hard and looked to the lightest, most colorful part of the sky. From the west, Cecilia came, her hair so black and her steps so self-assured that she seemed like the approaching night itself. She brought a big jug of dark red wine, almost the color of her skin. Cecilia could always be counted on. In turn, she embraced them all and greeted Patricia as warmly as the others. The Salt Shack Dweller watched the priest and could sense the dryness of his mouth, as he stole quiet glances at Cecilia. The wine jug was opened.

Together they ate the food brought by Patricia along with the chicken that Carlos had brought back from somewhere for Anastacio to cook. After the meal, the Salt Shack Dweller, seeing the sadness filled Patricia, asked her to relay the source of her sadness to the others.

Patricia, already comfortable with the clan, spoke deeply of the workers who had been abandoned in the desert and her sorrow over the one who had died. She explained that her vision of their suffering haunted her and left her with great sadness. When she finished, she was crying silently, as was Carlos.

There was a momentary silence broken by Cecilia, speaking softly and directly to Patricia, "Would you like to meet and visit with the ones that survived?"

Patricia lit up. "Oh yes, could I? That would be wonderful. I could speak Spanish with them. And I could skip school."

"I will take you tomorrow. They are my patients."

The silent priest then spoke. "Perhaps they would like to see a priest as well."

His suggestion lacked conviction and almost asked to be refuted. But Cecilia turned to the Priest and smiled. "Yes, I think after what they've been through, they might like to see a priest. Please join us."

The priest's happiness was evident. The Salt Shack Dweller interrupted the proceedings. "Tell me Padre, tell me Patricia, how are you at softball?"

Patricia said, "Not good, my father doesn't think girls should play, so I have never learned."

"We will teach you."

The Priest found his confidence tongue. "Humility is a Christian virtue but so is honesty—I am quite good at softball. What else is there to do in the villages, when the fields are planted, and politics is of interest to no one?"

"Good," said the Salt Shack Dweller. "We hold our first practice at 05:00 a.m. tomorrow. We practice for a game of honor."

Now, they had enough, if the Judge showed up and if Octavio and Miguelito showed up and if Raymond and Donella showed up.

9

A summer morning before the sun rises in the mythical desert is like nothing on Earth. There is light in the sky and the air is warm, perhaps 90 degrees but not yet fired up all the way by the sun. On this day, the myth feigned reality with the mountains surrounding the river valley brilliantly visible, the Estrellas to the west, the McDowells to the north, South Mountain to the south, and the enchanting Superstitions to the east.

The cars and airplanes hadn't yet come out. There was a slight breeze out of the east. The inhabitants had no need of clothing for warmth but like all cultures they did wear sufficient woven cloth to cover the private areas of their bodies. Everything was very quiet except for the electric buzzing of the high-tension lines and the wind passing through the junked cars down along the riverbed.

In attendance at the first practice was Anastacio and Carlos, Cecilia and the priest, the Judge (late) and Patricia (who had made up a story for her unsuspecting parents in order to be released so early in the morning). The Salt Shack Dweller put Anastacio and Carlos in the outfield because they could run like the wind and for just as long. He put the Priest on first base because of his height and because he was not a young man; at first base the Priest would not need to cover a great deal of territory.

He assigned Cecilia to second base because she was fast and scrappy and would never let anything get by her. He placed the Judge at third base with responsibility to cover the vulnerable underbelly of the defense, the left side, because the Judge was determined, seriously determined. He told Patricia that she would be the catcher because it would be the easiest position to teach a novice. He took up his own position on the pitcher's mound.

He would be the pitcher because he felt assured that he could acquire the knack of the Zen-like arch necessary for successful slow pitch softball. And because he was the leader of the Salt Clan, though the ball belonged to the Judge.

The team was not in uniform. Anastacio and Carlos wore their same peasant clothes though they had removed their sandals and were thoroughly enjoying the feel of the dewy grass of the field under their feet, running back and forth even when the ball was in the infield.

The Judge had full equipment, rubber spikes, knee length socks, gray baseball pants and a blue and white jersey. He also had a cap that read 'the Bench'. Cecilia wore shorts, that revealed her naturally beautiful legs and a white T-shirt upon which her black hair splashed. The priest wore his coolest black, a short sleeve black shirt, and his long black pants. Patricia was in a dress and the Salt Shack Dweller had put on his tennis shoes as well as his loincloth.

The first practice session went well. Anastacio and Carlos could glide swiftly under a fly ball and catch it, without a glove, in their shirt tails, and then laugh promptly. The Judge was aggressive, Cecilia sly, and the priest could handle what was thrown his way by the infield. A few balls got by Patricia, and she threw like a girl, but the Salt Shack Dweller knew that the team would bring her along. Already, he had a feel for the ball and for the distance between the pitcher's mound and home plate. When the ball left his hand, he could see purple trails behind its arch like a slow comet. Consistently perfect pitching, he could see, was a function of perfect physical and mental discipline; beware slow stick swingers.

By the end of four days of practice, the team was complete. On the second day out, Octavio and Miguelito came from the fields. Octavio asked what news there was and was told of the workers in the desert. He personally and warmly congratulated Anastacio and Carlos and, the next morning, Patricia. Miguelito, the fine-looking boy, who was a favorite of them all, asked only for Donella.

And indeed, Donella came in with Raymond on the third day. The Salt Shack Dweller assigned Octavio to the outfield along with Miguelito as the rover. The Judge stayed at third base and Raymond took up the position at shortstop. Donella and Patricia shared duties at the catcher position and this was the only problem area. Though Donella could not catch much better than Patricia, she was a larger target and fewer balls got by her.

Because of her size she had a stronger throw and, also, Donella seemed to believe that it was the catcher's job to keep the team's emotional spirit up, so she chattered, constantly, from behind the plate, "Hey batter—batter—batter…swing!" This, even though, there was no batter at 05:00 a.m. in the mythical desert light.

After the practice session, the team would disburse to the four winds. Cecilia, the Judge, and Raymond would be off to the west; Raymond getting a ride with them since they were all going into the downtown area. The priest would travel north to say his first mass of the day. Donella and Miguelito would go off together, usually to the east, no one being quite sure to where.

Patricia would go south to her school and Carlos, after the sun was hot in the sky, would be off to roam the streets of the surrounding villages. This would leave Octavio, Anastacio and the Salt Shack Dweller to spend the day at work in the garden and on the pueblo; gathering black widows and scorpions, praying mantis's and wasps; looking for rattlesnakes, Gila monsters, tarantulas, and roadrunners. The Mexicans were highly resourceful and in no time, the Salt Shack Dweller's collection of native species, which he planned to help preserve by establishing breeding colonies, grew to healthy proportions.

When Carlos would return from his day of roaming, he would always bring with him some prize he had acquired in one way or another, always with a proud smile. At first, the prizes were small, a couple of squawking chickens, a few petrified rabbits, but then, for two nights running, he out did himself. One night he brought in a goat that gave milk and the next night he returned with a small pig.

Both of these animals were fed and watered and kept alive tied up in the shade under the bridge. The produce from the Salt Shack Dweller's Garden was plentiful and along with the meat Carlos provided, the growing clan could usually be fed. But the staples were diminishing quickly so one evening after the sun had left sky but before darkness the Salt Shack Dweller paid a visit to his flour supplier, through the river bottom, beyond the park, across the boulevard, to the Hayden Flour Mill.

After hours, the Hayden Flour Mill had a security guard to protect against the likes of the Salt Shack Dweller. This man wore a gun and smelled of brandy and was therefore called Brandy-breath with a gun. The first time the Salt Shack Dweller came to the flour towers, he was captured by Brandy-breath, who had snuck up behind him with his gun and had chuckled at his captive. "Here's what I'm going to do with you. I'm going to ask you a question. If you answer correctly, you may take the flour you've come to steal, and no one will be the wiser. If you answer incorrectly, I will shoot you because I've always wondered what bright red blood would look like on these white flour sacks."

The Salt Shack Dweller was helpless. All he could do was wait for the question.

After a period of tense silence, Brandy-breath spoke, "Name the man who first ran the Colorado River through the Grand Canyon?"

The Salt Shack Dweller answered irreverently. "Get serious," he said. "It was the Union soldier who lost an arm at the battle of Shiloh, John Wesley Powell."

Brady breath was true to his word. He chuckled to himself, clicked his tongue, and holstered his gun. He removed his bottle of brandy, offering some to the Salt Shack Dweller, which was accepted.

"Ignorance of history is a greater thief than you," said the guard. "Take your flour and be gone before my supervisor comes by. But expect the same if you ever return."

"OK," said the Salt Shack Dweller. "But I've got a question for you, too. Is that a real gun with real bullets? Because I think it would be worse than reckless for whoever is your employer to give an old drunk like you an actual working gun."

Brandy-breath laughed, "Hell yes, it's real. A real squirt gun with H_2O ammunition."

Always, it was the same. The next time the Salt Shack Dweller went to the flour tower to obtain flour the guard was quite drunk, reclining on a sack of flour.

He did not bother to draw his gun, "Oh, it's you. Alright then, tell me this. Who damned the Salt River?"

The Salt Shack Dweller felt bad for the old drunk historian. "Teddy Roosevelt did grandfather. Herbert Hoover did it at Boulder Canyon in the Colorado and then Eisenhower did it at Glen Canyon. It's always the great white father who does it."

"Don't be disrespectful to our President, or I'll have to shoot you, for what you are, a flour thief. I can tolerate thievery but not seditious behavior or statements. And the Sierra Club gave up Glen Canyon, without even knowing what it was."

"Yes, grandfather, as you say. Do you like the patriotic game of softball, grandfather?"

"Of course, I do. It's the national pastime."

So, the Salt Shack Dweller invited Brandy-breath and his squirt gun to be spectators at the game. Then he took his leave quickly since the sky was growing dark. With a large sack of flour over his shoulder, he skipped across the brightly lit and busy Mill Avenue like a coyote, through the liquid lights of the park, and finally into the safety of the dark river bottom. The rays made an insidious and deadly noise as they passed through the night.

On the day of the game, the team met at the shack for a discussion of strategy. On instructions from the Salt Shack Dweller, they took no food but did drink a bit of wine. Carlos wanted a mascot at the game but could not decide between the pig and the goat and the Salt Shack Dweller tossed in the possibility of the three-legged dog.

Patricia spoke up then and said that she had arranged to have three of her friends present as cheerleaders so they could take all three animals. It was agreed. On instruction from Raymond, each player rubbed their bare feet in the dirt to give them speed and then, he had each soak their arms in a bucket mushy mesquite to give them strength and durability.

Donella had already started chattering like some wild Indian creating obvious sexual agitation in Miguelito. Together in silence, except for their temporary spokesperson Donella, the team marched through the dry air followed by a goat and a pig and a three-legged dog to the field of play.

The Salt Clan's opponents were present at the field and stood immobile and speechless at the clan's arrival, no doubt controlled by a sense of defeat that the Salt Shack Dweller had requested Raymond and the Priest to place them under. The flour guard was present, and he cheered their arrival loudly, as did the friends of Patricia.

The mascots were turned over to Patricia's friends, as the Salt Clan immediately took the field to allow their opponents to bat first (as the home team should). Patricia started the game at catcher. Donella disturbed the opponent's concentration with her native chattering from the bench. The Salt Shack Dweller threw three warm-up pitches, and the game was on.

But there was no umpire to call the close pitches and the plays between the two teams. After looking around and finding no other choice, there was agreement on the old flour guard who claimed extensive experience as an umpire at old Phoenix Muni stadium in the minor league days, big Willy

McCovey. True or not, the old guard walked proudly from the bleachers to the field, biting on a cigar, a flask bulging in his pocket.

The opponents had no difficulty hitting the Salt Shack Dweller's pitches, perfect arches though they were. But they were not able to score many runs or get many men to base because of the Salt Clan's finely tuned defensive ability. The infield was quick and aggressive, allowing nothing to pass, pulling a tight net around the infield. The all-Mexican outfield was impenetrable. They were like hawks onto prey, when a ball was hit in the air to them—sure and deadly for the out. The only way the opponents were able to score, it seemed, was by hitting a home run. Donella gave them no peace.

The Salt Clan, on the other hand, could not buy a hit-off of the opponent's pitcher. Early in the game, the Salt Shack Dweller realized that the opponents had used a little magic of their own, making the ball unwilling to come into contact with the Salt Clan's bats. Instructions were given to Raymond to do what he could, to circumvent the power the opponents had managed to work on them. Between innings, Raymond could be found behind the Salt Clan's bench in a semi-trance, chanting, searching for the formula.

By the end of the fifth inning, the opponents had had hit only one home run, but the Salt Clan had failed to move any man or woman to any base. In the sixth inning, the opponents' first batter hit a fly ball which would've been a routine out for Miguelito, had he been in place, but Miguelito was not at his position. He was discovered at the far side of the dugout in an embrace with Donella, who was still chattering an irresistible call to Miguelito's youthful passions.

The Salt Shack Dweller remedied the situation by putting them both in the game, Donella at the catcher's position, her chattering louder than ever. But the damage was done. With a man on base, the next batter smashed the first pitch well over the fence. It did not matter that Donella made a diving tackle on the batter as he started off to make his rounds or that he couldn't run the bases until Brandy-breath and the Salt Shack Dweller persuaded her to release her captive. The score was still 3-0 when the dust of the sixth inning settled.

And 3-0 was where the score remained through the seventh and eighth until the Salt Clan was faced with its last opportunity. Since Raymond had batted last in the eighth, he was sent to work on full-time sorcery, and he was joined (in prayer however) by the priest. The Judge started the inning with a determined look on his face, and managed to get a hit, reaching first base safely. The Salt Clan and their supporters went wild.

The next batter was Octavio. He made good contact with the ball, sending it to the left field. He was out but the Judge moved to second base, and they called it a sacrifice. Raymond's efforts seemed to be paying off. Carlos batted next and got a good clean hit putting men on first and second base. The Priest came out and swung hard at the first pitch. He hit the ball to dead center, and it looked at first as though it would clear the fence, but it did not and was caught within a few feet of the fence.

The Judge advanced to third and Carlos to second; now there were two outs. The Salt Shack Dweller took the bat. On the first good pitch, he swung for the stars but caught only the tip of the ball, which rolled forward a few feet like a bunt. For a few seconds, none of the opponents could find the ball, allowing the Judge to score and the Salt Shack Dweller to reach first. The score was now 3-1.

Cecilia was up to bat and there was uncivilized excitement in the Salt Clans dugout. Cecilia exhibited excellent concentration and waited for the pitch that suited her. She smashed a line drive to the outfield wall. All base runners took-off. The pandemonium on the sidelines panicked the goat and the pig and they bolted onto the field of play with the three-legged dog chasing and barking. The base runners kept running. The goat went toward second base, while the pig was in the vicinity of home plate.

The opponents started yelling at the animals and the umpire tried to chase the pig, but he fell down. Carlos came across the plate, 3-2 now. Running made the Salt Shack Dweller's loincloth loose, so he was not as fast he should have been, with one hand occupied holding up his garment, but he was saved when the relay man turned to throw the ball but was unfortunately tripped by the goat. The Salt Shack Dweller scored. Score: 3-3. Cecilia was still running, digging for home, herself not far behind the Salt Shack Dweller, the three-legged dog running with her and barking.

The relay man had regained his feet and made a good throw to the catcher who was straddling the obstinate pig at home plate. The dog and Cecilia arrived at the same time as the ball. Brandy-breath had his head in the action, but the dust and the confusion made it difficult to see the play as clearly as he might have preferred. But he did see enough.

After the dog and the pig and Cecilia and the catcher crashed into each other at home plate, it was the dog that came up with the ball in its mouth and gimped away proudly, so Brandy-breath was compelled to yell at the top of his lungs, "She's safe!"

Score: Salt Clan 4, Opponents 3.

The Salt Clan danced away from the ballpark in jubilation, calling out wild cries of victory, accompanied by the squealing pig and the bleating goat and the handicapped dog, who did not bark, who had been awarded the game ball for keeps. They skipped and danced out of the light of the park, into the darkness of the river bottom, their voices fading from the ballpark and a cloud of dust slowly settling back down to the ground behind them.

The opponents stood at the end as they had in the beginning, stunned and silent. Brandy-breath was among them. He smiled sheepishly, quietly laid down his umpire mask and trotted off after the Salt Clan, slowly at first but gaining speed as he chased after the team, which disappeared into the night.

Joy and pride was the name of the stars above them and was as rampant as wine. All the players congratulated each other on the victory several times over, they even congratulated the umpire when he arrived, and they toasted him with wine from a new jug. Cecilia especially was the center of admiration though; she accepted her celebrity status with grace and composure.

The priest hovered near Cecilia, alternately like a proud relative and then perhaps like a nervous suitor, desperate for something to say, always repeating himself clumsily. The girls who had come to cheer were in the thick of the celebration, consuming substantial quantities of wine. Donella and my little one (as she sometimes called Miguelito) were someplace or other, not far away, a familiar sound that the clan was used to hearing.

The Mexican contingent was reliving the game in Spanish while at the same time trying to find enough English to speak with the three young girls. Brandy-breath found the judge, who sat a bit apart watching the celebration unfold, and cornered him, subjecting him to constant chatter concerning local history.

Patricia was quiet, sipping the wine, apparently content when she was near to Cecilia or the Salt Shack Dweller, though she was constantly being employed by the Mexicans or the other girls as a translator. Raymond gave formal thanks to the spirits of athletic contests. Certainly, they had taken an active role by inhabiting the bodies of the goat and the pig and the three-legged dog at the end of the game. Certainly, they had saved the hero goat and pig from the barbecue pit.

10

At midnight, under a tremendous mythical desert moon, the Salt Shack Dweller spoke, "I know a place on this river, not far upstream, where the water has carved out a deep pool with smooth sides and a smooth bottom. The water is clear and fresh, some flowing in while the same amount flows out. Around the pool is a clean smooth sheet of hard stone…let us move this celebration to that place, to refresh ourselves."

The priest and the judge and the flour mill guard all stared in question of the Salt Shack Dweller. Could there really be such a place left on the dried up, washed up, blown away depression known as the Salt River bottom? The foreigners and the youth however did not question him. Neither did Octavio. Cecilia simply smiled (and so the Priest did also, although perhaps involuntarily) since she knew the Salt Shack Dweller far better than any of them. Her approach with him was, don't doubt, just wait, and see. There was great enthusiasm from the celebrants in favor of the suggestion.

Under the moon, the clan stumbled out of the river bottom and passed through the dark park to the opposite corner of the park from the softball field. Soon, after working their way through several buildings, they came to the pool that was mostly as the Salt Shack Dweller had described, except for being built by man rather than by nature. A high fence surrounded the pool and the gate in the fence had a lock. The Salt Shack Dweller called for Carlos, snatcher of chickens and pigs and goats, to snatch the lock from the gate, which he did in less than a minute.

The Salt Shack Dweller passed through the gate first, deposited the jug of wine he carried into a corner along with his loincloth and dove into the pool, smashing the moon's reflection on the water into 1948 pieces. Raymond, Octavio, and Cecilia disrobed and followed the Salt Shack Dweller into the cool water.

When Cecilia stepped out of her clothes, even the moonlight grew brighter. The girls and the Mexicans found themselves giggling. Patricia separated herself from all of them and joined those in the water unencumbered by clothing. The priest and the judge hesitated at the gate, no doubt they both thought that through the gate might lay the path to sin and code violations. But after a moment they walked bravely across the threshold, together arm in arm, while Miguelito and Donella continued their own celebration elsewhere.

Brandy-breath, with a rather aged and ill-treated body, was next into the water with a loud call of, "Geronimo," which inspired Raymond to respond, "Right on, brother."

The pile of temporarily discarded clothing, from peasant's cloth to debutante permanent press, grew but it did not include any that was black. Soon the pile of clothes was topped with a baseball uniform, when the judge tossed caution to the wind, where there was no wind, just a warm, seasonally dry air on another late summer night in the desert. The priest's flaming desire to be in the pool with Cecilia and inability to remove the black enclosure he wore, lead to a compromise.

He removed his shoes and entered the water otherwise fully dressed. The virgins in the pool, except for Patricia and the priest, could be identified by their giggling, by their constant motion and by noting who was being followed from spot to spot with the same keen interest as a hawk displays with potential prey. The priest was huddled in a corner, trying to act as if he wasn't out of place, with his clothes on, praying that Cecilia would not find him odd. The judge swam laps.

Cecilia, Patricia, and the Salt Shack Dweller were in a corner of the salt pool at the deep end. The moon was skipping off their wet skin into the water, warming it even by night. Cecilia noticed how Patricia stayed somewhat apart from the Salt Shack Dweller as if she was deferring to Cecilia's proximity to him.

Cecilia said to Patricia, loud enough for the Salt Shack Dweller to hear, "Have you ever seen such a body as he has? Sometimes you have to look twice to make sure that he really exists."

Before Patricia answered, Salt Shack Dweller spoke.

He was looking at the star lit sky, not at the woman to his right, as if the comment should not be dignified by direct recognition, "A leader's true power is in the power of his mind."

Patricia answered Cecilia with complete seriousness, "I've never seen a man's body at all. I think it's beautiful."

Cecilia laughed, "It is true but keep your eyes open, there are many displays of beauty."

"Well, your beauty is great," said Patricia to Cecilia.

"Everyone has at least one eye on you all the time"

Cecilia turned to the Salt Shack Dweller with a sly grin. "Not all the time, thank God."

She splashed water in her own face. "Take Bones, here. He tries not to let you see where his eyes take him, but I have caught him often, when his eyes were following you."

There was a very short silence until the Salt Shack Dweller, in the same tone as before, said, "Another cup of wine is what my eyes are searching for."

"I'll get it," said Patricia, a drop, too enthusiastic.

But Cecilia put an arm on Patricia and held her into the water, "No, stay here with Bones. I'll get it."

The only light brighter than the moon, reflecting from Cecilia's body, as she walked calmly to the wine jug, was the burning light from the Priest's eyes.

Cecilia returned with a cup of wine for the Salt Shack Dweller. She dove into the water and swam away, toward the shallow end. The Mexicans pursued the virgins endlessly. Repeatedly, Brandy-breath jumped into the pool with the same, Geronimo cry, just before hitting the water. The judge finished his laps and surfaced in the shallow end to meet Cecilia and the priest.

In the shallow water, Cecilia's breasts floated to the surface; one nipple pointed to the judge and one nipple pointed to the priest, who was submerged to his neck, not to hide his body but to hide the fact that he was hiding his body. Cecilia had brought the wine jug with her and the three of them shared the bottle and spoke of religion and morals, ethics and law, medicine, and magic.

When the Judge spoke his mind on a subject, he walked in the water, arms folded, head down, as though giving the matter great thought. But he would stroll to the shallowest part of the pool, ever so slightly, revealing glimpses of his private body to the priest and Cecilia, though the priest concluded that, it was for Cecilia's benefit, that it was done—if it was done consciously, which the priest felt it might be.

Yet he could be wrong, he told himself. He liked the judge and had great respect for him and he wondered if this strange but overpowering feeling he felt for Cecilia could be tainting his other thoughts and beliefs, making them strange as well. He wondered, if he was having feelings of the normal man; feelings denied to him in his daily realm.

At the deep end of the pool, Patricia spoke, "Cecilia is your lover, isn't she?"

This was said as both a statement and a question. She had turned her face to the rim of the pool avoiding the Salt Shack Dweller's eyes, which was unnecessary since his eyes were in the moon.

But he answered gently, "Do not concern yourself, with these matters."

"Oh Bones," she said, mildly disgusted.

For a moment, he thought that he had heard another voice of similar age protesting to him, but the other voice was gone, and Patricia's voice was back.

"I already know because she told me." But the Salt Shack Dweller knew it wasn't true. The Salt Shack Dweller knew Cecilia would not talk about such matters.

"What time must you return to your elders?" asked the Salt Shack Dweller.

Patricia didn't answer but she turned to look directly at him as though she resented him changing the subject. She defied him by pushing off the side of the pool with her feet and gliding through the water on her back, exhibiting her unchildish body to him in full bloom under the nurturing light of the moon as she floated by slowly. She was testing his stoic eyes.

From the other side of the pool, she pushed off again and came by even slower and, of course, he failed the test miserably. Satisfied, Patricia, now answered his question, "I don't want to go home, Bones. I want to run away. I'm like a foreigner there, we don't even speak the same language."

But then the Salt Shack Dweller noticed that several of the clan were out of the water and were casually taking their time in returning.

He called out to them, "It's not good to be out of the water. Tonight is bright and there are still many rays. Too many. It is dangerous. In the water, you are safe. Stay away from the rays."

Only the priest acknowledged that he had heard. The others went on as before.

"Bones, did you hear me? I don't want to go home anymore. I hate it when I'm there." She was almost crying, "I'm only happy when I'm here. Here I am a person…no one knows me or understands me at home."

"Sometimes my father slaps me, really hard. They don't want me to be really alive."

Now she was crying. The Salt Shack Dweller reached out and put his hand on her shoulder, "What is it that you want me to do?"

"I want to come live with you and Cecilia and Anastacio and everyone else. I don't care if Cecilia is your lover."

The Salt Shack Dweller did not bother to tell Patricia that they did not live together and he did not bother to tell her that he and Cecilia had a very long history. He could only be aware of the beauty of youth that he felt with his hand on her shoulder and all at once he was enthusiastic, once again, about the future. Nonetheless he remained outwardly dispassionate as all great leaders must.

"This is something that will require discussion and consideration," is all he said.

"You mean there's a chance you might say yes?" asked Patricia, suddenly excited.

"We shall see," is all the Salt Shack Dweller would answer.

This was enough for Patricia, however. She leaped through the water that separated them and clung to the Salt Shack Dweller, hugging him, and saying, "Oh, please say yes, please hurry up the discussion and the consideration and say yes. I can't stand too many more weeks."

The Salt Shack Dweller could feel the girl's breasts against his skin and her legs against him; even her breath was as fresh as dawn. He could feel the influence of her in his loins and he was worried that in a minute she too would be able to feel her influence upon him. This worried him greatly, it would change everything, but he was powerless to extricate himself from her embrace.

He was looking away from the girl so that she wouldn't see in his face what was rapidly rising in his body: he was desperate. If the girl-woman realized what power she had over his body, how she could make him sing and dance without great effort, everything would be most different. But just then, looking away from the pool, the Salt Shack Dweller saw, in the liquid shadows of big trees, in the moon splashed park surrounding the pool, enemy warriors in blue, sneaking up on the clan from the south.

The Salt Shack Dweller knew all too well the consequences to a tribe caught in a vulnerable position by a raiding party from an enemy. There would be no mercy, only slaughter. He cursed himself for failing to post a look out. He cursed himself for putting celebration ahead of safety. A leader could not be excused for such carelessness.

He could see the pool turned red with the spilled blood of the clan's males and he could see the females, taken captive by the enemy warriors, to be used as domestic slaves by the women of the enemy tribe, to be used as sex slaves by the men of the enemy tribes, and to be pissed on by the children of the enemy tribe.

The Salt Shack Dweller had heard of such things. At once, he cried out, at the top of his voice, a war cry, a cry of warning, a cry that rose up from the power of his lungs, "ENEMY, WARRIORS!...A RAIDING PARTY!...RUN FOR YOUR LIVES!"

The Salt Shack Dweller came out of the pool with great speed and agility, pulling Patricia from the water behind him. They ran along the wet stone, disobeying a sign forbidding them from running, and without losing more than a breath, grabbed up the loincloth and Patricia's shorts, leaving Patricia's shirt behind.

There was no time to dress, slaughter was imminent for the slow or the modest. The Salt Shack Dweller and Patricia were the first to reach the open gate. The blue enemy (two of them) were closing fast. A deft fake to the left as they exited the gate was just enough to give the Salt Shack Dweller and Patricia a several step lead over the enemy.

At the same time, various clan members were desperately trying to escape, and everyone was on their own. They had scattered upon the warning cry of the Salt Shack Dweller. Some were climbing the fence, some were trying to dress above all else, some were screaming their terror into the face of the invasion. Brandy-breath had not even left the water.

Survival was the first order. Hand in hand the Salt Shack Dweller and Patricia raced through the night, keeping to the liquid shadows of the trees, avoiding the moon's tell-tale light. In the dark, streaking across the flat park, they were attacked by the rays, but immediate survival was foremost and required that they endure penetration of some of the insidious rays.

The rush of the warm night air against unclothed bodies quickly dried their skin and their hair in a matter of minutes. They ran so hard and fast that the only sound they could hear was the sound of their excited breathing that was being left behind them. At the edge of the park, they dropped into the Salt River bottom and then danced and skipped their way along smooth rock to the safety of the shack.

The Salt Shack Dweller wrapped and secured his loincloth around him, left Patricia and started back to the site of the enemy attack, catching his breath as he went. In the shadows, 30 yards from the pool, he could make out the events.

The enemy numbered only two, but they had captured all but Raymond, and all of them were lined up inside the fence, dressed now, except for Brandy-breath who remained in the water. The enemy had made a great raid counting many coups. When they returned to their own land, they would be heroes…unless the geology could turn the battle to his favor. There were many rocks all around him.

The Salt Shack Dweller threw a rock into the enclosure from the shadows. The rock landed on the flat stone and cracked loudly when it hit, making the enemy warriors jump and peer into the darkness. He moved into the shadows to throw another rock from another angle. The enemy's attention focused on the new direction of the darkness.

The Salt Shack Dweller kept moving, always with the shadows, always throwing a bigger stone, each time harder. Then he heard another stone coming from the opposite direction. *It could only be Raymond,* thought the Salt Shack Dweller. He hadn't seen Raymond make his escape when the blue enemy attacked but that meant nothing. Raymond might have simply turned himself into a raven and flown away unnoticed at the time.

Now, it seemed that Raymond had joined the Salt Shack Dweller in throwing stones and together they were able to keep the enemy confused and off guard. But it wasn't until a third stone thrower, a very accurate thrower, joined the counterattack that the three throwers were able to bring down a rain of chaos and stones on the enemy warriors.

Danger to their own captured warriors from the stones was minimal since they were lined up against the fence and the stones had to clear the fence to land within the area of the pool. The only real danger was that one would be hit by a ricocheting stone, but this danger was nothing compared to the possibility of slaughter or enslavement, so the reign of terror upon the enemy continued.

Finally, the enemy was looking in all directions and jumping nervously at the slightest sound. Then one of the two enemies left the enclosure to search for the stone throwers. From all directions, the stone throwers threw the rocks at their pursuer and lured him further into the darkness. Now the enemy had made a mistake. There was only one guard for all of the captive clan.

Only one of them, to guard the gate by keeping it to his back and by keeping his captives lined up facing him, on the other side of the pool. With the second enemy neutralized by wandering around in the now silent darkness, the Salt Shack Dweller was permitted to sneak up behind the lone enemy guard, enter the gate silently, and push the enemy from the back into the pool.

At that instant, the captive clan members made their escape, one by one flying through the gate. But the Salt Shack Dweller could not persuade Brandy-breath to make his escape. Brandy-breath remained in the water, willing to submit to any indignities or punishment the enemy warriors decided to bestow upon him, perhaps more a victim of a failure to oppose authority throughout his life than anything else. All of the others were free.

Back at the shack there was great happiness. A bold and brutal enemy attack had been successfully repulsed with only one casualty, an older man who could not pull himself from the salt pool. The second stone thrower had been Raymond, who had indeed made his escape by turning himself into a raven but what the Salt Shack Dweller hadn't known was that he'd maintained the raven form during the battle and had dropped his stones on the enemy from overhead, like a bomber, instead of throwing them from the ground.

The Salt Shack Dweller praised Raymond's value as a warrior and the others called out their agreement and gratitude, which Raymond accepted in the ordinary course of the evening. The other stone thrower was Patricia, who had indeed snuck back to assist the clan. She also was lavishly praised.

There had been a minor problem with Miguelito, Donella, and Patricia. On her way back to the scene of the battle, Patricia had inadvertently approached Miguelito and Donella in the dark to tell them of the enemy attack, but she was still shirtless. Miguelito saw only beauty and Donella saw only rage, believing that Patricia's purpose was to entice beautiful and virile Miguelito away from her. By insult and many words, Donella had threatened to pull Patricia's hair from her head.

Patricia had made a rapid explanation of things both in English and Spanish and the matter was put aside during the counterattack, but now, at the shack, Donella spoke up.

She said to the Salt Shack Dweller, "You tell that girl to stay away from my Miguelito, dressed or undressed."

The Salt Shack Dweller smiled secretly and looked at Patricia, in her eyes he saw soft, silent pride and a full willingness not to argue. He, therefore, repeated Donella's demand to Patricia who politely nodded her assent.

Yet the rescued needed to express their gratitude. The Mexicans were grateful because capture would have meant another round trip between Central Arizona and the Mexican border with a long hot walk back through the desert. The virgins were grateful because capture would have meant facing their fathers with the facts of their lives—it would have meant an end to the illusion of childhood carried only by one party to the father-daughter relationship.

The judge was grateful (an unusual emotion for him, he admitted) because it taught him that he could still be grateful (an unusual reasoning thought the Salt Shack Dweller) and because, as he admitted, it might have been awkward for him, a judge, to appear in court on charges of trespassing and indecent exposure. The priest, with his black robe dry but wrinkled, was humble and direct in his gratefulness.

"I do not think that the people of Scottsdale could have accepted this," he said, "at least, not from one of their priests."

Cecilia was not grateful (though she was not ungrateful), rather she was happy, because everyone else was, which was how she liked it.

11

In the morning, the mythical desert was hot and quiet with no true recollection of the details of the previous night's celebration. The morning light washed the night away, it would have been just the same if the clan had become captives of the enemy instead of successful in repelling the attack. The morning light was silent and indifferent and could not be any other way. The universe did not care.

In the previous night's lateness, the Salt Shack Dweller had instructed the priest to see the virgins safely to their homes. The Salt Shack Dweller once again walked Patricia home himself, taking in more rays than he had in many months, but willing to do so. There was no more talk of running away from home and joining the clan but when she left him to crawl through the window of her bedroom, she kissed him in a woman's way, not, as before, in a child's way.

In the morning, everyone was gone except for the Mexicans but even they were not within sight. An hour before noon, when the sun had fired itself up and sweat ran like a river from the Salt Shack Dweller's body, he worked on the pueblo. Progress was as slow as the growth of a saguaro cactus, which was pleasing to the Salt Shack Dweller.

He expected the project to take maybe 20 years. To do it right, it would take roughly the same amount of time for him to build the pueblo as it would take the rain and wind to wear it down. He heard a salutation called out by a figure in black, wearing a wide brimmed white hat, approaching from the north. It was the priest and the Salt Shack Dweller wondered what brought him back so soon.

The two men met at the shack and shook hands before the Salt Shack Dweller offered priest fresh water from a gourd and an orange. The priest accepted and drank deeply. He asked if they could enter the shack to speak and the Salt Shack Dweller answered by pulling the blanket that covered the entrance to the side and indicating for the priest to enter first. The priest sat on an upturned wood crate, giving the big chair next to the insects and reptiles to the Salt Shack Dweller who stoked up a bowl of tobacco, which he shared with the priest.

"Tell me, Padre, did you have a chance to say mass this morning" asked the Salt Shack Dweller.

The Priest smiled gently. "Yes. I was just in time to say the 6:00 a.m. mass. I felt very good. I had not had time to prepare a formal sermon, but I gave one, nonetheless. On situational ethics."

"A fine subject for Christian contemplation," agreed the Salt Shack Dweller.

"Let me tell you what I've come to speak with you about."

The priest was clearly nervous but determined to speak. "I must speak with someone, and you seem to be the one I should speak to. I hope we can keep this between us, however?"

"You may believe it," answered the Salt Shack Dweller.

"It concerns the woman, Cecilia."

"She is worthy of concern," affirmed the Salt Shack Dweller.

"My belief precisely," smiled the Priest, who was then silent for a minute, apparently contemplating his belief with that schoolboy smile he wore.

"However," he began again, pulling himself up from thought, "I believe, I may be in love with her."

The Priest blurted out this last belief much as countless confessors blurted out their worst sins to him in the confessional over the years.

The Salt Shack Dweller was not surprised. Many men believed that they were in love with Cecilia. It had been happening to her since she was 10 years old. She was the kind of a woman that a man of good judgment would jump off mountains for. Yet, as with all women of this type, this power came to her honestly and naturally, it wasn't something she consciously cultivated, it was something she was born with, just as she had been born with those dark eyes and black hair. In response to priest's confession, the Salt Shack Dweller relit his pipe and said, "Yes, I can believe that."

"I've never felt this way before," said the Priest.

The Salt Shack Dweller sighed. "Love can make a man superior to other men or it can destroy him, Padre."

"In the church, we teach that love can save a man's soul not that it can destroy him."

"It's a nice belief. But in church you are talking about a different kind of love than you are talking about on the street."

"Yes…is Cecilia your woman?"

The Salt Shack Dweller took a deep breath, "No, she is not. She is not any man's woman."

The Priest nodded, "I wondered about that."

The Salt Shack Dweller smiled, "I once told you that you could be rewarded with a woman in return for your assistance in the battle of the airport. Are you looking for a woman?"

There was genuine shock on the Priest's face. "Oh, good Lord, no. How could you think such a thing? A woman's name should never even be associated with such a thought, no woman should—"

"Just wondering, Padre, because quite honestly, I could not have fulfilled such a request if you were, you understand, things are different and…you see at the time, I made the offer I had in mind, some virgin or perhaps a captive, someone who would be honored to be given to man like you—"

The priest was still slightly outraged, "No woman," he repeated, "should ever be spoken of in this way."

"It's certainly not the modern way, is it?"

"No and thank God (the Priest made the sign of the cross upon reference to the Almighty) that it is not."

"Please forgive me, Padre, if I offended you. I asked to be sure, I understood the meaning of our conversation and to avoid confusion."

"Forgiven," said the Priest as routinely as a judge would say, innocent. "Back to Cecilia. I need your advice. You seem to know her as well as anyone—"

"It is true, I do."

"And I need to know what to do. I've never loved a woman before. I feel like, I'm acting like a fool when I'm around her."

"Excuse me, Padre, do you mean to say that you have never loved a woman in the physical sense as well as the emotional sense?"

"Of course," answered the Priest, surprised that the Salt Shack Dweller should be surprised. "I am a man of the cloth. I am married to the church. I do have my differences with the church, but so far, those differences are limited to political and social justice questions."

"Not even a desperate parishioner?"

"Not even any woman," the Priest said with emphasis.

"I see," said the Salt Shack Dweller, thinking ahead.

"So perhaps, you can see. I have no experience in these matters. All I know is that she is always on my mind and when I am near her. I lose all control…did you see how ridiculous my position was in the pool, last night?"

The Salt Shack Dweller smiled. "Well, yes."

"You did? Did Cecilia speak of it?"

"No, Padre, she did not."

"You, see? I am always worrying about what she thinks and what she says and how she feels. Is this love? It's not all good, if it is. I feel like a fool sometimes, but I can't seem to stop myself."

"Maybe someone put a spell on you."

"Do you think that's funny? That's how it feels, and I don't even believe in spells, well not in most spells. I do believe in love though, only this one aches."

"Excuse me, Padre, but I must ask. Does it ache in your loins?"

The priest looked at the Salt Shack Dweller, wondering, whether he should answer the question, but then he abandoned wondering to resignation. "Truly and really, it does."

"You've got it," answered Salt Shack Dweller definitively.

"I know, I do. I cannot deny it. This is why I need your advice. I think, I could die, if I could not be near her."

The Salt Shack Dweller spoke confidently. "You might die anyway. My advice is for you to go to Cecilia. Speak with her as you have with me. Say to her, 'I am a man who has never loved a woman. I have an ache for you in my soul and in my loins. I want you and I need you'."

The Priest blanched, "I could never say such a thing to that angel of a woman. Besides, my interest in Cecilia begins on a higher plane. The ache in my loins is secondary…it is something I cannot deny but I will not be controlled by it."

The Salt Shack Dweller raised his eyebrows but not to argue with the priest. These were subjects upon which some (very few) men differed, and argument was pointless. Instead, he paused and looked deep into the priest's confused eyes.

"Tell me, Padre, are you prepared to be defrocked? As I recall, the church takes these matters rather seriously."

"Of course. I have considered that. and I hope it does not come to that. It is something, I know, I must pray about and seek guidance from the Lord."

The Salt Shack Dweller nodded his head. "Padre, do you know the poet, José Marti?"

"Yes, of course," the Priest answered, wondering what on Earth José Marti had to do with his love for Cecilia. Then the Salt Shack Dweller began to recite a verse and quite quickly the Priest joined him:

Yo soy un Hombre sincero
de donde crece la palma
Y antes de morirme, Quiero
echar mis versos del alma
I am a sincere man
from where the palm grows
and before I die, I want
my soul's verses to bestow…

"Beautiful and sincere, is it not?" asked the Salt Shack Dweller of the Priest.

"Very."

"This is the way you must approach Cecilia, if you want my advice on the matter."

"But if I did," complained the Priest, "and even if, God helped me (another sign of the cross), and she accepted me, I have no experience with women. I wouldn't know what to do."

"Don't worry about that, Padre. It would all come naturally at that point. I assure you."

The priest sighed heavily; no burden had been lifted from his shoulders. His face was troubled, "Well, thank you for the suggestions. I will consider them. I admit, I am a desperate man and perhaps I can and will do things that seem impossible to me. I will take my leave now."

"Goodbye Padre…and the best of luck to you."

93

The priest and Cecilia, an interesting idea, mused the Salt Shack Dweller as he left the shade of the shack and returned to the white-hot heat of midday. As he walked to the pueblo construction site, he checked the valves that he had installed (after splicing into Tempe's water line) to control his water system to make sure none was leaking.

This was a daily ritual with him because he knew that the Gods would, sooner or later, (they were busy) deny water to those who wasted it, negligently or otherwise. In this regard, however, he was safer than most since any spillage or leakage would occur in the Salt Riverbed, where it came from and where it belonged.

He checked the valve on the line going to the garden, and the one to the outdoor shower, and the one heading in the direction of the pueblo which was presently sealed off, all dry and in perfect working order. He wondered, how Cecilia would receive the priest's confession of love.

The Salt Shack Dweller had been back to work on the pueblo for less than an hour, when he heard greetings called out to him from the west. He turned and saw the judge in running shorts and a sweatband around his head, jogging up the riverbed toward him. He met up with the judge at the shack and offered him fresh water from the gourd. The Judge was sweating profusely from running in the midday heat and he drank deeply and gratefully from the gourd.

The athletic judge spoke first. "Thank you for the water. I usually swim laps in my lunch hour but I wanted to speak with you, so I decided to run up here."

"Where did you start from?"

"I left my car at the 24th St. crossing."

"Tread carefully," said the Salt Shack Dweller. "Heat exhaustion can kill you."

"It's true…listen, I wonder if you have a minute to speak with me about something."

"Certainly. Would you care to go inside where we can be out of this heat?" The Salt Shack Dweller held back the blanket over the entrance to the shack and the judge entered first, selecting the big chair by the insects and reptiles for himself. The pipe was filled with a fresh bowl of tobacco and lit, two men smoked, despite the added heat.

"I am a lover of life," began the Judge as the Salt Shack Dweller sat back to listen.

"I love everything I see and everything I do. I love this heat and I love this place (he obviously did not specifically mean the salt shack, rather he was speaking more expansively, like the mythical desert, for example)."

"I do everything with full dedication and full intensity. It has always been this way with me. When I was a very young man searching for a career, I was devoted to order and logic, so, I chose law. You can see that I've been successful—I'm quite young to be a judge in case you haven't notice."

The Salt Shack Dweller nodded that he had noticed. The Judge continued speaking, "My only goal has been to be able to honestly say that I have lived a full life, and have no man be able to say that I was small or unfair. or that I did not recognize the beauty of this life."

"A worthy goal," affirmed the Salt Shack Dweller, wondering what such a man could possibly need to speak with him about. Just then he found out. The judge ceased speaking of himself.

Now he asked a simple, direct question of the Salt Shack Dweller, "This woman Cecilia, is she your woman?"

The Salt Shack Dweller did not betray a thought. He had years of practice. "No, she is not. Cecilia belongs to no man. Why do you ask?"

The Judge actually looked relieved, "Well, that takes care of one problem."

"What problem remains?" asked the Salt Shack Dweller.

"You see, in Cecilia, I believe that I have seen my perfect female counterpart. In her own way, she may be as intensely dedicated to life as I am. I have to admit that I am obsessed with her, to tell you the truth. I cannot think of anything but her, I cannot get my work done, I cannot do anything. Besides all of that she is beautiful beyond words."

"Perhaps someone put a spell on you," suggested the Salt Shack Dweller.

The judge nodded in agreement, "Yes, that is what it feels like, and I sure hope, no one removes it. I have never considered myself in search for a perfect counterpart. Actually, I believed that concept was better left to country song writers. I have a good wife and two fine children. But I did not believe a woman existed who could make me feel like how Cecilia does."

"Then it is not for a wife and mother to your children that you look for in Cecilia," said the Salt Shack Dweller.

"No, never. I don't believe she was born for such life."

The Salt Shack Dweller thought it odd that the judge would opine on what Cecilia was (or was not) born for.

"I see. What is it that I can do for you then?"

"I think, I need advice. I've never hesitated before, but this is different. This is like waking up to discover gold dust in your hands and feeling it will blow away before you can save it or like finding yourself thirsty in the desert with cupped hands full of water and worrying that it will leak away before you can consume it."

"Actually, it's worse than those things. I've awakened to something very precious and something that will be gone, like a wonderful dream, if I make one mistake or one wrong move. I need your advice how to approach this woman."

The Salt Shack Dweller sat pensively for quite some time. The silence was great. Sweat dropped to the floor from both men but neither paid any attention, they were used to it. They were veterans of many years living in a desert.

The Salt Shack Dweller finally spoke, "My advice to you, long robes, is that you go to Cecilia and speak with her as you have with me. Say to her, 'I am a sincere and hungry man with a great ache in my loins for you. I need you and I want you'."

The judge's face registered disbelief and almost shock.

"Can you be serious? Could such an approach impress a woman like Cecilia? Relief for the ache in my loins is not the primary interest I have in Cecilia. I am no mere schoolboy, and she is a woman with a great deal more to offer than her body."

The Salt Shack Dweller was nodding slowly as if to say, *trust me, I know of what I speak.*

But instead, he said, "Trust me, I know of what I speak. What better way to get to know someone? All relationships must start in some way, this is a good way. Cecilia is a doctor for all the world. The one thing she understands and appreciates above all else is sincerity. Do you know the poet, José Marti, long robes?"

The judge did know the poet, Jose Marti. Together they recited a verse in Spanish:

> *Yo Soy un hombre sincero*
> *de donde crece la palma*
> *Y antes de morirme, Quiero*
> *echar mis versos del alma*

"Beautiful and sincere, is it not?" asked the Salt Shack Dweller.

"Very"

"This is the way you must approach Cecilia, if you want my advice on the matter."

Still in confusion about the advice he had received, the judge, without further discussion, stood and shook hands with the Salt Shack Dweller.

"Thank you for your time and your advice. I will give it serious consideration. I trust that this conversation may remain between us."

"You may believe it."

The judge nodded once more slowly and then he smiled. He took another drink of water and stood up to leave.

The Salt Shack Dweller spoke again. "Please remain seated for I have a question for you."

The Judge sat back down and crossed his legs.

"Is it because of Cecilia that you have joined our Salt Clan?"

The Judge smiled as if he had known that he would one day need to answer this question.

"No. And I have not joined your clan, although I must admit, I am strongly attracted to it—there is a sense of raw purity here that I realized was fully missing from my life."

"Then why do you try to help us and risk your position of prestige in the world of our adversaries—why do you favor us when we come to you about the airport? Why do you help us when our Mexican friends are lost and dying in the desert?"

"Why did you join our athletic team in the contest against the rival tribe? Why did you swim naked in the night pool? Were you rendered helpless by a spell, or a trance imposed on you by Cecilia or Octavio?"

The Judge smiled deeply before answering, "I'm sure, either Cecilia or Octavio has the power to impose such a spell but that is not the answer. The answer is that I am a weak man, despite what I said earlier. As a young man, I sought power. I was ambitious."

"What is better than being a judge? But I have learned, painfully, that a judge is a mere puppet of those with real power, who make the laws that favor them and oppress others and I am then obligated to enforce those laws."

"Why would I send a young man or woman to prison for smoking a bit of weed and laughing for a few hours? I might as well shoot them because prison will destroy their life. Why would I send a homeless man to prison for stealing food?"

"Why would I evict a single mother with three young children who cannot pay the rent? The answer is that so far, I have not had the courage to defy them. I need time, training and courage. I guess, I hope that this world I've stumbled into, will be my training ground. I do need a new world view; I need the balls to live with a new world view."

After a long silence, Salt Shack Dweller took a deep breath and said, "No one chooses to become a member of this tribe. They either are or they are not. Nature and the spirits make sure of that. You are a member. You are a welcome member."

There was a pause before the Salt Shack Dweller continued, "One more thing about Cecilia. You have a wife and children, do you not?"

The Judge spoke quietly. "I do."

"Are you prepared to lose them? That is a possibility, is it not?"

"It is," was the judge's response before he turned away.

The Salt Shack Dweller watched as the judge stood, smiled ironically, sadly, and started running down the river bottom into the white heat, the sweat already glistening on his back like aluminum foil.

12

Ordinarily the Salt Shack Dweller worked until the hottest part of the day was upon him and then he would stop work to seek shade and rest for three hours, after which he would return to work. Much of this day had been consumed in the role of advisor with very little physical labor. He had hardly worked up a sweat.

Nonetheless the day's scorching, silent and still hours were upon him, and he decided not to return to his work on the pueblo. He filled the gourd with freshwater and took some dried meat, fruit, and a tortilla to the shade of a sand bar coming out from one of the piers of the railroad bridge. There he sat and slowly ate his midday meal, watching the ravens and the buzzards hang lazily on the rising thermals.

In the heat, after a morning of mental and physical labor, and after a full meal, the Salt Shack Dweller grew sleepy, his chin falling onto his chest…and he dreamed:

The river was flowing but only a small amount, a narrow channel of water within the great wide banks which were full only on the rarest of occasions, one of which had come in the last time of desert cold water. Now, however, was the time of the sun and he walked along the bank in the morning shadows of the trees, hopeful of seeing the beautiful young maiden who had been catching his eyes frequently the last few months and giving him a sensation of a dry tongue and a dry throat.

If he did not see her this morning, he would not have a chance again until the end of the long day because he had to go a long distance from the village to work. The great flood in recent time of the cold air had ruined large sections of his village's man-made diversion canal and it would not carry water to the fields anymore.

The slow, arduous repair process wore him out every day but every day he marveled at the task his ancestors had undertaken in the first place to divert water from the river to a place of their choosing, to a place where they planted beans and squash and melons and corn and jojoba and agave.

His people were truly superior, just as the songs and prayers said. He was proud of his people above all others and was happy to be assigned to work on the repair of the river-of-the-people, despite how hard the work was, but he wanted a chance just to smile at the girl. After all, there was more to his life than digging ditches each day.

When he looked up, she was there, on the path before him and she was just as startled as he was. They were alone and she smiled, radiantly.

Proudly, he said to her in a most serious tone, "I'm going to work on the repair of the river-of-the-people so that water to our fields can once again be properly directed."

He believed this would impress her and it did. She pressed a pomegranate into his hands, smiling again, and then she hurried down the path. What a life, he thought. He would savor each juicy seed of the fruit that she gave him. He would repair the river-of-the-people so that it could never be washed out again, no matter how great the flood. He would hunt small game and make his garden the most productive of any.

She would see. He would...

The Salt Shack Dweller awoke from his dream to loud harsh words, "They caught me! They caught me!"

It was Brandy-breath the flour guard, standing next to him in the warm sand. After a minute, he pulled his chin from his chest and looked around for the girl who had given him a pomegranate but sadly she had disappeared as quickly as his dream.

With some hesitation, entirely appropriate in the heat, he answered Brandy-breath calmly, "Yes, they did, you did not get out of the pool and escape."

"They had uniforms," said the flour mill guard, who did not smell like brandy just then.

"Yes, they did."

"I spent the night in the jail."

"Was it bad to be caged?"

"Not too bad but they didn't serve brandy."

"No, they don't usually do so."

"They subjected me to psychological torture."

"They're known for that throughout this region. What information did they want from you?" asked the Salt Shack Dweller.

"They wanted the names and addresses of everyone who was at the pool, especially the one who pushed the uniformed officer into the pool."

"Yes," said the Salt Shack Dweller in contemplation, "that would be me. They want to know which tribe to retaliate against. Did you tell them?"

The flour mill guard looked deeply hurt that anyone, especially the Salt Shack Dweller, would think he might have squealed on the clan.

"I did not. They could've tied me to an ant hill and poured honey over me and I still wouldn't have talked. They could've cut my eyelids off and staked me to the ground facing the sun. They could have tied a sack of rattlesnakes over my head. They could've bound me to the middle of an ocotillo tree and left me to die. I wouldn't talk. What is there if there isn't loyalty?"

"There is nothing, old man, there is nothing."

"That's what I say…they may get me yet, though."

"How's that?"

"Well, if they tell my employer of this incident, I will no doubt be fired. However, I have a solution for that as well."

"What's that?"

"I am an old man. If I can no longer contribute anything and if no one wants me around any longer, I'll have to shoot myself. I've always wanted to shoot something like the outlaws used to do—that's why I took the job as a guard."

"I thought, I might get my chance, but I never had the heart to do it. I couldn't even bring myself to shoot you and you were an out-and-out thief if I ever saw one. I caught you red-handed…or, I guess, white-handed."

"I understand—"

"So, I'll shoot myself and I'll do it in the flour mill, so that the blood falls on the white flour. I always thought that would be something to see, like blood on snow, something like Shakespeare would write about, but we don't even get snow here, so, the flour would have to do. Of course, I wouldn't actually get to see it, but you could be there and see it for me."

"It won't be necessary old man. If they fire you from your job, you can join the clan. We will need you. We will still need flour and your knowledge and information, and expertise will be invaluable to our raiding parties. In fact, I think we might have you be in charge of flour for the clan."

"Do you really think that could be?" asked the flour guard.

"Yes, I believe so. And in the meantime, if there's a chance that you will soon be fired, we should consider storing a year's supply of flour."

"Yes, that would be a good idea. Where would we store it?"

"Underground. In a deep pit"

"I will plan the raid," said the flour man.

"Good. The clan relies on you already! Quit your job today, so they can't fire you. Then your resume won't show that you were ever fired."

The flour guard fell silent in thought. He was pleased with his new found meaning in life.

After a minute, he spoke again, "That Cecilia sure is a beauty…I wish, I was a younger man."

The Salt Shack Dweller laughed, "I wish you were too, old man. I could give you some advice about her."

In the late afternoon after the flour, guard had left to report to work and to learn his fate and after the hottest three hours of the day had passed, the Salt Shack Dweller returned to labor on the much-ignored pueblo. To the east, towering over the Superstition Mountains, the sky was building with the great thunder clouds of a late summer storm, ready to roll down into the Valley of the Sun.

Most commonly this daily bragging on the part of the towering thunderheads amounted to nothing, like impotence. Most often the storm clouds would hit the wide (mythical) desert floor and collapse, spread out thin, raise the humidity a few marks, signaling nothing. Then again, those same clouds would sometimes just bring ugliness, gathering up torn apart dirt and dust along the way and blowing ferociously through the valley leaving everything with a layer of dry Earth covering it.

But once in a great while, however, thunderheads would be more than equal to their boasting. They would roar into the valley, slowly and confidently, building as they came, spitting lightning bolts after lightning bolts like a snake tongue, shaking the valley's floor with thunder, growing darker as they came until the sun was gone.

Pressure would mount until there could be no more and then the storm clouds would explode into desperate rain as if the extreme dryness of the Earth forced all the water it could, in as short a time as it could, from the heavy, moisture laden clouds overhead. But the thunderheads would fight back with more lightning bolts aimed at the Earth, trying to tear itself away from the greedy, magnetic grasp of the Earth, all the while crying out in its thunderous rage against the Earth's effort to devour it in one place at one time.

And once in a great while, the thunderheads would not escape; they would not survive the merciless pull of the Earth and when the battle was over, the thunderheads would be dry and dissipated and the Earth would be saturated.

Such storms came only once or twice in the season and once was always at the end of the hot, dry summer season as if to announce that the grip of the furnace—like, heat was about to be broken by the coming of the mild season. This afternoon, as the Salt Shack Dweller watched these thunderheads building in the east, would be that storm.

The Salt Shack Dweller was a storm-watcher with many years of storm watching behind him. So, when a moist breeze began to stir and the eastern sky turned deep blue and gray from horizon to heaven and lightning bolts began to strike the Earth in the first volleys of the coming battle, he stopped his work and turned to the east to face the storm. In a matter of minutes, the storm obliged and was upon him where he stood, in the river bottom with his face turned skyward.

Lightning struck all around him, thunder shook his body and the ground he stood on and the rain came fast and hard, trying to beat him to the ground. He withstood the onslaught and entreated the proximate storm Gods to let the rain, in this fierce way, go on and on and on for day upon day until long after the ground was saturated—let it go on until a terrible violence of water had nowhere to go but to run into the washes and arroyos and dry river bottoms and finally into all the natural drainages leading to the unnatural lakes and reservoirs.

Let the rain come to the lakes and reservoirs spilling over their walls and barrier dams and run down the great, now dry river bottoms, taking out all dams in their way. The Salt Shack Dweller asked for this from the storm Gods even though he was pretty sure it wouldn't happen in this way, not with one summer storm no matter how violent, but he asked anyway, never wanting to let the storm Gods believe he'd abandoned his prayers for a great storm that would cut across the state east to west and north to south, a great storm that would flush away obstructions and choking, a storm that would force rebirth.

But such a storm was not to be this storm though the hard rain persevered for a long time, perhaps more than an hour and the Salt Shack Dweller came out of it, feeling like he had been beaten by several million wonderful pebbles.

After dark, after the storm died leaving the air thick and heavy with moisture, the Salt Shack Dweller remained inside the shack, watching the new tarantulas, black widows, and scorpions that he had been able to gather, following the storm. The old ones, fat and lazy, he fed. The candle flame was dull and short in the moist air, and it was difficult to see by, to see which spider and which scorpion was willing to accept the live feed given out by the Salt Shack Dweller.

"Do some of them fail to eat?" asked Cecilia, who sat on the bed, drinking a cup of wine that she brought when she came to the shack just after dark.

"Yes, some do. They die off and become food for those that remain."

"How long are you going to stay here, Bones?" asked Cecilia.

"Why do you call me Bones now?"

"That's what that pretty little girl, Patricia, who is in love with you, calls you. I like it."

"As long as necessary," said the Salt Shack Dweller, taking more wine for himself.

"But the river may never run again," said Cecilia. "At least not like it used to-not like you pray for it to."

"This is a place of power, a place from where the Gods will hear and listen."

"Do you think you might ever go back to school?"

"Never, that place is full of false Gods."

"I hope you stay here forever," said Cecilia. "I love coming here. I love the people that come here."

Without significance the Salt Shack Dweller added to Cecilia's last comment, "They love you too."

Cecilia knew the ways of the Salt Shack Dweller. She knew how his mind worked, "What do you mean when you say, 'They love you too?'"

"Expect cries of love from the priest and the judge…maybe Brandy-breath as well."

"The priest and the judge?" repeated Cecilia. "Tell me what you know and how."

"I have spoken all that I can speak."

"The priest and the judge?" she said again as if disbelieving. "Life gets funny when you grow up. It is not what I expected."

"No?" questioned the Salt Shack Dweller.

"No? Is it different with you? Is this what you expected?" She indicated his world in the shack.

"I could not have asked for more."

"That's not the question. The question is what did you expect out of adult life?"

As usual Cecilia had him. "No, this is not what I expected." She continued now. "And did you expect that a 17-year-old girl would fall in love with you?"

"Cecilia—"

"Did you?"

"She's a child. She doesn't know how the world really is."

"I wonder sometimes if the judge and the priest know how the world is."

"We are educating them," answered the Salt Shack Dweller.

"And we are most certainly educating the girl as well." Cecilia looked at the Salt Shack Dweller with purpose. "Like it or not, and I expect you to like it a lot, you most of all are educating the girl about the love between a man and a woman, you are being asked to make her a woman."

"A great honor and likely a great pleasure. I'm sure you will teach her properly. I have no doubt about it. I've talked to her Bones. She wants you to love her as a woman."

"She's a child," repeated the Salt Shack Dweller.

"In some ways, yes, but she is becoming a woman and part of the privilege and responsibility of that process has found you."

"I never asked for the responsibility."

"It's true but the question is how do you exercise it now that you do have it…and you do know that you have it."

"The same question faces you with the priest and the judge. Do not doubt my words, they are coming."

"I do not doubt you; you are usually right about such things. I'm looking forward to them. Maybe the Priest most of all," laughed Cecilia.

"You should be."

"There's someone else coming, by the way," said Cecilia quietly.

"Who else is coming?"

"Your wife is coming."

The Salt Shack Dweller said nothing. Cecilia continued, "She called me at the hospital today. She's coming tomorrow to see you."

After less than a minute, the Salt Shack Dweller poked his head out of the shack and called out, "Octavio!"

A voice came from the campfire, "Si Señor?"

"Are you going to the fields for work tomorrow?"

Octavio answered, "Si Señor."

"What time does the train come by?"

"05:30."

"I will be with you."

"Bueno!"

When the Salt Shack Dweller returned to the shack, he paced nervously for a minute, mumbling of his hope that his wife would not come before the train arrive, before he was able to hop a train with his Mexican friends for the fields of labor. Cecilia watched his pace, laughing deeply at his anguish. But finally, Cecilia put down her cup of wine and took the Salt Shack Dwellers hand, pulling him to her.

"Come lay beside me, Bones. I want to make love with you."

The Salt Shack Dweller did not hesitate. He never hesitated with Cecilia. As always, together they were like the late summer storm that had graced and replenished the river bottom that very afternoon—she the Earth and he the sky. There was something about being in the river's bottom, that place of power that made their love better than ever, that left the Salt Shack Dweller drained and released and left Celia fully satisfied. It had always been so; it was just more so in the river bottom.

13

The train was on time. It rolled onto the black bridge and almost stopped, as if it had come specifically to pick up the five passengers: Octavio, Carlos, Anastacio, Miguelito, and the Salt Shack Dweller. The morning was cool after the previous afternoon storm. The aroma of the mythical desert's moistness, led by the perfume of the creosote bushes, was in the air.

The train started up and moved down the tracks a quarter of a mile and then it stopped again. The failure of the train to keep moving did not concern anyone; the distance they had to go was 30 miles and it could take all day.

Soon Anastacio would pull out the cards and try to win the daily wages that would soon be coming to the others. The Salt Shack Dweller was content once the train made the first quarter of a mile; it was a sufficient distance from the shack so that if his wife came early, she would not find him.

Around noon, the train had traveled west not far beyond 24th St. and was once again at rest. The Salt Shack Dweller gathered money from his compañeros, departed the train and ran the back way to the Mexican restaurant El Molino on 22nd St.

The cost of the lunch was twice what he had been able to extract from the workers but he made up the difference with some of the money he had borrowed from Cecilia; soon he would have a fruit picking income and he would be a man of means. The proprietors of El Molino knew him and greeted him warmly.

They gladly accepted the mixture of pesos and dollars and took special care in preparing the order once the Salt Shack Dweller explained that the food was for a group of his friends who he wanted to treat with true Mexican food. With the food, the Salt Shack Dweller bought five Mexican beers and above the din of Mexican American radio, called goodbye to the proprietors, who shook their heads, who were happy they no longer worked the fields.

The train was rolling once again when the Salt Shack Dweller reached the tracks, but slowly, and he simply waited for his box car to roll up to him. When it did, he handed the food and beer to Carlos and jumped aboard. Once the workers overcame their guilt and self-indulgent feelings about eating restaurant food they all enjoyed it and thought it very good with a single complaint that the tortillas were too soft, like white American bread, not so hearty and rugged as they were used to.

Miguelito had been quiet and pensive all morning and everyone thought it was the result of the fact that he would be deprived of Donella's love for way too long. And perhaps in part it was this but while they were eating, with Octavio translating, he spoke to the Salt Shack Dweller.

"Did he (the Salt Shack Dweller) believe that the girl, Patricia, had meant to seduce him (Miguelito) that night when she approached him in the park with her white breasts exposed?"

The Salt Shack Dweller could hear the hopefulness in Miguelito's question. He answered, "He could not say; Miguelito would have to find that answer in Patricia's eyes."

Miguelito said, "He had tried but couldn't tell, he thought it was quite possible; he contributed that he had heard that it was the way of American girls."

To this there was no response to be made, the Salt Shack Dweller could only smile and nod, yes, certainly it was possible. Miguelito's eyes burned with the possibility, he speculated out loud what kind of heaven it would be to have two women to sing to the stars with. When the men laughed deeply of Miguelito's concept of heaven, he looked hurt and embarrassed and returned to silence, refusing to eat any more of the restaurant food which left more for the others.

For a while, in the ruins of downtown Phoenix, the workers thought that their boxcar was going to be left behind. In the rail yard, a string of train cars, including theirs, had been disconnected and left without a locomotive. They sat idly for an hour looking for a train to transfer to, but then their car was reconnected and eventually they were off again. When the train turned the corner and headed northwest along Grand Avenue, they knew they were headed to the citrus fields.

Grand Avenue was not so grand. To the Salt Shack Dweller it looked like a blight, a sore, an abscess on the body of the mythical desert. It was a parasite growth on the city, denied by the city, but existing, nonetheless. It was where the stragglers, the busted, the small-time schemers ended up, never having made it to the land of their dreams, California. They were broken down and abandoned in the outer ring of Phoenix. Truly it was a freak, absolutely rejected by the desert to its far side and unwanted and an embarrassment to the city to its inside—a place in existence but a place ignored.

Further down the track, when the city's ugly tail, known as Grand Avenue, finally began to yield to the country of open fields, the Salt Shack Dweller could see, in the distance, the farmers favorite cash crop; box houses. For every green field, he could see there was another field which had cut the ground for sewer lines, water lines, gas lines, electrical lines, slab foundations, slump block walls, pebble yards, driveways and not a drop of shade.

The return on this crop was excellent even if the yield per acre was poor. Admittedly, it was a once in a lifetime planting. After the housing crop was finished and sold at market, the work of the farmer was over and he would retire from his life of labor, he could even retire on his former farm, if he wished, purchasing for himself one of the fruits of his labors, and that of his father and his grandfathers.

The train had taken the workers into a strange world that the Salt Shack Dweller did not understand at first. It was a separate universe, walled off from the streets and railroad tracks, each house looked exactly the same, as did the pebbled yards, as did the nonexistent trees, as did the streets. Life existed in the city, the sun fell on it, there was an unnatural quietness, a sense of too much order, too much agreement, too much consistency, too much sameness.

There was an unfortunate lack of conflict, divisiveness, or struggle; there was a passive serenity side-by-side with the apparent day-to-day conduct of life and to the Salt Shack Dweller this was incongruous and mutually exclusive and in need of explanation.

The first explanation that came to mind was that the train had skipped the track and exited its familiar world and entered a form not explained by usual homo sapiens standards. This theory was unsatisfying and rejected. But perhaps this place was the place where the physical body resides once the spirit soul has departed.

This theory could explain what the Salt Shack Dweller saw but was also rejected when he noted grocery stores, beauty salons, restaurants, and Chevrolets. There were churches but there were no schools, no children, no faux tough boys, no astonishing girls walking in a group, talking. This started the Salt Shack Dweller to think and mandating further observation. He examined the inhabitants; they rode three wheeled bicycles, drove golf carts, walked, and a few, the boldest, drove cars under 18 mph.

Soon he was able to detect their common trait; no one was under 60 years of age. At once, all of his questions were answered. He understood the situation precisely. He knew that all cultures have their own way of dealing with the old people of their society though he hadn't known, until now, what the cultures surrounding his Salt Clan did.

He knew the old Eskimos who could no longer contribute, who slowed down the progress of the tribe, who could only consume, would voluntarily walk off into a storm never to return. Or, if they weren't willing to go voluntarily, they might be left on an ice floe or so some said. It was the same, with slight variations, with other cultures. Rather than snow storms and ice floes, the place where the old would go might be burning deserts or high mountains but there was always a way to deal with the old and the unproductive.

This was apparently how the culture surrounding him handled the situation; build a city for the old people where the old people could be quarantined to live out their lives in undisturbed and quiet but close enough to visit with relatives and far enough so that the city could go on with its life in its pursuit of youth without the daily reminder of old age.

Interesting, thought the Salt Shack Dweller, pragmatic but hardly in furtherance of the concept of pluralism. He thought of his own clan. He determined that he would bring in the old flour guard who knew so many stories of the past and who would know how to make a successful raid on the flour mill.

And he would go to the other end of the spectrum by bringing Patricia and those of her virgin friends who wished to come along, who were full of youth and enthusiasm, who were ready and willing to learn the culture traits of the clan and who, above all, would be in a position to pass on the clan's wisdom one day.

14

The five workers waved their thanks to the passive conductors and departed the train at the intersection of Grand Avenue and Bell Road. From there, they walked through the desert (and around part of the city of the old citizens) to reach the citrus fields where they would be able to find work.

It was growing dark in the western sky when they came to the fields; Octavio led them into one citrus orchard where they expected they would find a camp of workers. Inside the orchard was dark. They walked down the center of the rows in mud due to a recent irrigation.

For quite some distance, they saw and heard nothing, but then, out of the darkness above them, came a voice in Spanish. Octavio stopped and answered and the next minute a young sentry jumped to the ground from his watching post in a lemon tree. The sentry shook hands all around. He was about the same age as Miguelito.

He led them to the worker's camp in the middle of the orchard. Notice of their approach was relayed ahead by a network of invisible sentries. By the time the five emerged from the darkness into the campfire light, they were expected.

The camp was populated by about 30 men, most of them were young men in peasant clothing and sandals but a few of the men were at least 40 or more. There was a small campfire in the depression between two rows of citrus trees. Several bricks enclosed the fire pit and. a grill rested on top of the bricks.

Scattered around the campfire was a small kitchen of beat-up and blackened pots and pans. Stretched between the trees, several feet above the fire, was a tarp to keep the rain off the fire and perhaps also to keep lemons from falling into the fire. Not far from the fire was a large pile of garbage consisting of cans and bottles and some hard plastic, the paper having been burned.

Dotting the ground in an ever-expanding ring around the campfire were the sleeping spots of the workers. Though the sleeping arrangements appeared to have no order to it, there was in fact, priority. The leader of the camp, a husky man in his 30s, to whom all others deferred and took their instructions from, El Jefe, had a mattress and a sleeping bag on the ground near the fire in the center of the ring.

The next best accommodations were not as close but were still in proximity to the fire and these spots were taken by torn and stained mattresses with most of the stuffing gone, foam rubber pads with a single blanket, broken metal box springs and plywood. All of these bedroom sets, including El Jefe's relatively fine mattress, came from a nearby landfill and one had to wield considerable power to coax another to go with him to the dump to help them carry the useful material possessions back to the camp.

The rest of the workers, the majority, had only blankets, that they spread on the ground wherever they could find a spot beyond the established dominion of the leadership core.

Many of the workers knew the Salt Shack Dweller. Some had passed his shack on their way to the fields and had stayed the night. Others remembered him from the previous spring when he had spent a week picking grapefruit. Still others, though they had never met him before, had heard of him.

He was greeted warmly and sincerely by the leaders of the camp first and then by the other workers. The new arrivals were encouraged to take some food from one of the pots that had been placed on the grill to heat along with tortillas that were being separately heated by one of the workers.

As the Salt Shack Dweller squatted near the fire, helping himself to some of the food, he saw a familiar five gallon can being used as a water container by the workers. He had seen these cans before. The label was still on the can but certainly none of the workers could read the English small print on the label or understand its meaning; he himself understood the words on the label only because of his knowledge of chemistry—and because of the little black-and-white skull and crossbones also printed on the label.

It seemed to him a five-gallon can of chemical pesticides should have a big skull and crossbones, perhaps even a different color, perhaps bright red? The Salt Shack Dweller was surprised that the workers were not all dead. Not wanting to interfere in the world of the workers, the Salt Shack Dweller mentioned the water container to Octavio quietly.

Octavio whispered back, "Oh, it gets rinsed out before we use it."

The Salt Shack Dweller had brought his sleeping bag with him. He unrolled it some distance from the camp. He was happy to be sleeping outside. The night was mild and the stars, between the trees, were bright. He could not sleep outside as often as he wished at his shack because lately the rays had grown so thick that they sometimes dipped down into the riverbed on the worst nights.

But here in the citrus fields he was far north of the source of the rays and the prevailing wind patterns were in another direction. Also, the acres and acres of trees created a strong barrier. He did see an occasional lonely ray glide by in the sky, but one ray was nothing to worry about. He felt safe and immune, and he would sleep soundly once he got used to all of the snoring and farting that surrounded him.

In the morning, the Salt Shack Dweller was issued a heavy canvas bag with shoulder straps and a pair of gloves along with all the other workers. The bag was designed to be worn to the front of the body, like a pouch. The bottom of the pouch was not permanent; rather it consisted of an overlapping flap which could be secured to seal the bag, but which could be undone, allowing the bag's contents to simply drop out as a means of emptying a full bag.

The bag was checked out to the individual worker and did not need to be paid for if returned in good shape. The cost of the gloves was deducted from the worker's first paycheck. The foreman did paperwork on the new workers that were present in the morning and the fact that each of them used the same social security number did not cause the foreman to bat an eye.

Picking lemons was never as easy as it seemed like it would be when the day started. At first, there were plenty of lemons hanging low on the branches, ripe for picking. But with 30 or more men picking in a selected area, the easy lemons faded rapidly. Since the lemon picker was paid by the bag, the lack of accessibility cut severely into his production and therefore his pay.

After the easy pickings were gone, the workers climbed through the trees with great agility. This was not always the safest of work; once in a while, a worker would lose his balance and the weight of his bag would pull him to the ground.

One worker among them had lost his sight in one eye the previous season when he was poked in the eye by a sharp, narrow shot of a limb that he was working on. Not only did the lemons grow scarce as the day went on but the heat of the day, and the humidity of the grove, combined took a toll as the day wore on.

When a worker's bag was full of lemons, he would take it to a huge bin, unclasp the bottom to dump his load and then give the pay foreman (always a Mexican with American citizenship, always a man indebted to the owner) his name so the foreman could give him credit in his little book for another bag.

The foremen had been known to cheat the illiterate workers on occasion by failing to record a bag here and there but the foreman who did so ran the risk of having his blood run through the orchard along with the irrigation water.

There is a belief among the workers (and most foremen) that the strain of grapefruit known as ruby-reds, known for their pinkish red meat, first came into existence in an orchard where the foreman cheated the workers and the workers retaliated co-mingling the foreman's blood with the irrigation water that seeped into the soil and was quickly sucked up by the roots of the grapefruit tree.

It is said that ruby-reds are the forbidden fruit of the foreman and that its existence serves as a reminder to all foremen. If a foreman looks at an exposed cross-section of a ruby-red while a blood-red moon is dipping behind the western mountains, it is said that he will not see the dawn and that the orchard owner can look forward to a lucrative crop of the prized ruby-reds.

The length of a workday depended on how much citrus the grower wanted to ship on any particular day. Frequently, the full shipment order might be picked and packed by 02:00 or 03:00 in the afternoon and then picking would stop.

The workers then had rest of the afternoon to buy their beer and groceries from the company store that was always happy to run a tab with interest for the worker, making proper adjustments to his pay before it is given to him, to mail home to his sick mother or wife or children. It was also the time for the workers to bathe in the irrigation ditches.

To the Salt Shack Dweller's mind, revolution was the only answer. Revolutionaries sneak into the camps at night when the orchards belong to the workers; when the foreman, the owners and their families know that it might be unsafe to roam through the orchards. The Salt Shack Dweller had heard the workers speak of them. They were a ragtag group of ex-workers, political activists, groupies, novice lawyers, knee-jerk liberals, and Catholics.

The were called MOP or MOPS in the plural. While the Salt Shack Dweller believed MOP to be an acronym for Maricopa Organizing Project, Octavio believed the name had a literal meaning, especially after the Salt Shack Dweller defined the English word mop for him: a tool used to clean up a mess. Octavio assured the Salt Shack Dweller that the condition of the peasant workers was a mess and that it was MOP'S goal to clean it up.

MOP sent only their most seasoned organizers into the camps at night; only men who were fluent in the language and who understood the social network of the camps. The MOP people brought boxes of blankets and cans of food to the camp but did not distribute them to the workers, rather they were left for distribution with the camp leader, El Jefe.

In this way, an alliance was formed. MOP offered legal and medical services to the workers. MOP would mail a registered letter with a worker's money order back home to the worker's mother or wife in Mexico. MOP would drive workers to stores with more favorable prices than the company store for groceries. MOP would bring fresh drinking water to the camps.

MOP spoke to the workers on the mild nights around the campfire of organization and worker power in solidarity and of labor strikes. To the Salt Shack Dweller's mind, the idea of a labor strike by workers who were present under (politely stated) legally suspicious circumstances, was ludicrous. The workers greatly feared the idea of a strike.

After all, it had taken a great investment for them to get to the American citrus fields in the first place. Second, while wages were not great, there was little or no work back home and what there was paid very little. And third, everyone knew that the immigration authorities tolerated their presence because the city growers needed them for the harvest of America's citrus but, sweet Lord, immigration officials and the growers certainly would not in a thousand years sit by and do nothing if the workers refused to work.

Was MOP crazy or what?

Many workers even feared the talk of a strike. They feared that the growers had spies in the orchards at night to listen to the workers talk and to listen to MOP and that there would be severe punishment for such talk. As a precaution, camp's sentries were ordered to their stations when MOP came in the night to the camps.

MOP was dangerous. MOP gave much to the workers. Nothing needed to be decided right away. A strike was something not to be taken lightly by any means. MOP seemed in no hurry. They would continue to talk, they would continue to visit the camps, they would continue to provide a range of services for the workers. And one day, the Salt Shack Dweller thought, *They would call in their chips and exert all the power they could muster and then it would be known if the workers would make fools of MOP or whether they would stand with them against rather convincing odds.*

The Salt Shack Dweller greatly admired MOP'S boldness and vision. He hoped to meet these crazy MOP leaders. And that very night his wish came true. Two of the MOP leaders, Lupe and Jesus, both Mexican American citizens arrived to share a meal and a beer with the workers and, of course, to do a little organizing.

After introductions, the Salt Shack Dweller got right to the point.

Speaking directly to the MOP leaders, the Salt Shack Dweller said, "Let me get this straight. These workers are here illegally. They are breaking the law by entering the United States without permission, they are working illegally, and they are breaking the law by using false social security cards, right?"

Lupe and Jesus smiled pleasantly, "Yes, that is all true," they answered proudly.

"And your organization is attempting to convince them to go out on a public strike from their jobs, right?"

"That is also correct. And in addition to that, it is also illegal to strike during the harvest, which by the way, is the only time they are working here."

"Wait, wait," said the Salt Shack Dweller. "How did it become illegal to strike in America? I thought that battle was won many years ago."

Lupe and Jesus smiled and shrugged their shoulders in unison. "Well," said Jesus, "the Arizona Legislature passed a law that makes it illegal to strike during harvest. It is that simple."

Laughing while he spoke, the Salt Shack Dweller said, "So you want these illegal workers to go on an illegal strike in public view?"

"Very much so," answered both leaders simultaneously.

"What will happen if they do? Will they all be deported?"

"Oh, no, that won't happen. The growers need the workers far too much to let that happen."

"Well then, what will happen?"

"A court will order the illegal workers to go back to work in these citrus field."

The Salt Shack Dweller broke into uncontrollable laughter, "And the absurdity of the worker's condition will be revealed to the world, right?"

"Absolutely," smiled the two leaders like the proverbial cat that caught the mouse.

"Brilliant," said the Salt Shack Dweller. "I am impressed beyond words."

One day he would try to integrate all of them into his clan or forge an alliance with them. But for now, he had to be realistic, they were out of his territory, too far away to wield power over or with. Before he could extend the Salt Clan's influence on the western reaches of the valley, he had to solidify his domination over the east and central portions of the valley.

In the east and central areas was where the transportation, communication, commercial, and educational centers existed and these had to be controlled first. It was true that much, though not all, of the agriculture came from the west and it would be mandatory that the Salt Clan control the west one day, but for now, let MOP have it.

But MOP's effectiveness was suspect. That very night after they were gone there was an immigration raid on the camp. The first warning came from a sentry stationed south of the camp; he made the call of the mourning dove. Some workers had already gone to sleep while others were in preparation. When the warning call came, the worker's escape plan went into immediate effect; every man for himself; scatter in every direction into the darkness of the orchard.

Run, run, run, and when you could run no more climb an obscure tree and stay silent. The Salt Shack Dweller stayed where he was, in the shadows of the Orchard, about 15 yards from the fire, as calm as Sunday. Like sound following light the immigration authorities rushed into the camp only a minute behind the scattering workers but for the workers it was a precious minute; a fleet-footed peasant could disappear rapidly on a dark night into the depths of the orchard.

The immigration authorities were not new to the mechanics of the chase. The raiding party consisted of 10 men. All but two ran through the camp, knowing the workers had scattered, and tried to find them in the darkness. They carried powerful flashlights to look up into the trees and they listened for movement and heavy breathing. It was much like a deluxe version of the children's game hide-and-seek; the immigration authorities as in some Greek comedy were perpetually 'it'.

The two members of the raiding party who did not pass through the camp began to vandalize it. They kicked the pots and pans into the night, bent the grill in half and dismantled the bricks enclosing the fire pit. They poured the water containers onto the bedding and then removed their pocket knives to slice the mattresses, sleeping bags, and blankets to shreds. The Salt Shack Dweller stepped from the shadows and into the light of the still burning campfire. When he spoke, he brought the two enemy soldiers out of their skin.

"What is it that you think you're doing here?"

Both soldiers turned, frightened, trying to hide their fear, "Who are you?" one demanded.

"Just a poor worker trying to get some sleep. What are you going to do with those knives?"

The knives slipped back into the pockets they had come from but there was no answer, only another question, "Are you a citizen?"

Now the Salt Shack Dweller recognized the two opposing soldiers. They were the same enemies who came to the courthouse the day of the airport battle. The Salt Shack Dweller felt no fear.

"Of long standing," he answered calmly.

"Where were you born?" they demanded.

"On the banks of the once great Salt River," he answered.

"Name the capitals of North and South Dakota," demanded the other one, desperately wanting in on the interrogation.

"Bismarck and Pierre," he answered. =

"Now, let me ask you something. Do you remember Judge O'Sullivan? I think he had a little talk with you a few months ago. I don't think the Judge was happy with you."

Great uncertainty and insecurity crossed over the fire illuminated faces. They both stared at the Salt Shack Dweller starting to recognize him and recalling the incident in Judge O'Sullivan's court room. As if involuntarily, one answered that yes, they did know him. The Salt Shack Dweller nodded knowingly and then he asked another question.

"What do you think he would say about all of this destruction?" he asked, indicating the vandalized camp.

The vandals could not remain long enough to answer. After the question had been asked and after several seconds of dead silence followed, the vandals suddenly thought they heard a criminal in the trees not far away and the chase was on.

When the raid was over, the workers began to drift back to the camp. Three workers, none from the Salt Clan, had been captured. The destruction of the camp was considered minimal and for this the Salt Shack Dweller was thanked by the workers. The sentries returned to their posts and one worker played songs from the homeland on his guitar until the fire had gone to ash and all of the King's men had gone to sleep.

The Salt Shack Dweller worked for a week in the citrus orchards. He ate very little, not wanting to give any of the money he earned back to the growers through the company store. On Friday afternoon, after they finished work for the day, the men were paid by the foreman.

All the men of the camp tossed $3 of their pay into a hat and a group of workers, headed up by Carlos, went off to purchase beer from the store and a goat from a local villager. Another group of men dug a pit and laid a fire in preparation for the goat. The Salt Shack Dweller planned to leave the next morning but first he wanted to drink beer and eat roasted goat and listen to guitar music with his compañeros.

Carlos and his party returned with much beer and a live goat. The goat was slaughtered a short distance from the camp and its blood ran in a stream of the irrigation channel between the lemon trees. The goat roasting process was a slow cooker process; the goat might not be ready to eat until midnight or later, but the men were in no hurry—they had beer and it had already been announced that no lemons would be picked the next day. And they had money in their pockets.

Later that night, before the goat was done, the irrigation water came without warning. It came swiftly, darkly, and silently. Before the men could dig the goat up, the water spilled into the pit and filled it, causing thick smoke and stink to rise. It was too late to save the goat; the workers were scrambling to save their bedding and other personal belongings.

The Salt Shack Dweller stood in running water now crawling up to his ankles. He knew this was stolen water. He knew the lemons should be called salt lemons, the oranges salt oranges, the grapefruit salt grapefruit, as they were an aberration of nature.

He wept into the irrigation water, he wept for the indignity of it all, the water trapped and accumulated and then released by the turning of a valve on some timetable of regularity, to run in mild little orderly rivulets, one after another as far as the eye could see by the light of the moon.

He ceased his weeping and cursed the water mongers who appropriated the summer downpours and winter snow for their own profit, turning the precious moisture into lemons and lemons into dollars, leaving his river as dried and bleached as an old bone, and turning the desert to myth, desert brown to waxy green and dry to humid.

The workers were standing on higher ground, silenced by the abrupt end to their fiesta. Irrigation had put a sure end to the campfire, leaving them in darkness except for the light of the rising moon.

Suddenly, four powerful lights encircled and trapped the workers. There was nowhere to run as the lights moved in on them. At first, everyone thought the lights were immigration officers but when the lights moved closer it could be seen that each of the four lights carried long barrel guns, rifles, and shotguns: these were thieves from some nearby village.

They knew it was payday, perhaps tipped off by the fact that Carlos and his crew had been spending money freely that afternoon. Only one of the four thieves spoke, and he spoke in Spanish. They stayed behind their lights and could not be seen. They made the workers line up in two rows facing each other still enclosed by the four bright lights.

A burlap sack was handed to the first worker, and he was ordered by the thief to put all of this money into the sack and then pass it on to the next worker. Any worker who did not put all his money into the sack would be shot, they were told. The workers did as they were told.

The last worker to get the sack was Miguelito. When he put his money into the sack, the thief came forward to take it from him. As the thief reached for the sack, Miguelito bolted for darkness. The gun came up and gave off a tremendous blast, immediately closing the distance between the thief and Miguelito.

Miguelito went down like a bird knocked from the flight. The explosion from the gun caused panic among the workers and they broke ranks, scattering in chaos. The air smelled of acrid, thick gunpowder. The thief that brought Miguelito down splashed through the irrigation water to retrieve the burlap sack of money but the blast from his shotgun had disintegrated the sack; the money was blown away, scattered in the darkness; it was being carried away by the still silent flow of irrigation water down the straight and countless rows of the orchard.

The thief swore out his frustration, threw down the useless burlap and then ran from the scene to join the other thieves, now on the run, all of whom knew that the workers would slit their throats, like so many goats before them, if they could catch them.

Octavio and the Salt Shack Dweller were the first to reach Miguelito. Others ran after the thieves. The damage to Miguelito was impossible to determine in the darkness; it was severe, but he was alive. As far as the Salt Shack Dweller could determine the shot had been off to the right, ripping apart the burlap sack along with much of Miguelito's right arm.

No doubt the real damage was that Miguelito would bleed to death in the darkness and the mud and the irrigation. The Salt Shack Dweller, realizing that an ambulance could never get into the orchard, instructed Anastacio and Carlos to make a stretcher from the canvas citrus bags and to carry Miguelito to the closest road.

The Salt Shack Dweller started running down a single row in a straight line, running as hard as he could run out of the orchard to a phone kiosk. He ran faster than the wind with his feet hardly touching the ground. He ran past one of the thieves but did not hesitate. He ran through the insidiously creeping irrigation water. He ran strong, barefooted, his hair streaming behind him, his left side lighted on and off by the bright moon splashing on him between the trees.

His call was to Cecilia who was on duty at the emergency ward. The real damage, she agreed, was that Miguelito would bleed to death. She asked for his location. She would accompany the helicopter ambulance. It was another seven minutes before Octavio, Anastacio, Carlos, and a fourth man emerged from the orchard, carrying Miguelito on the makeshift stretcher.

The Salt Shack Dweller rigged a tourniquet as best as he could. Another seven minutes passed before the air ambulance arrived; Cecilia took immediate charge. By the light of the flying machine, they could see Miguelito clearly for the first time since the shooting. He was caked with mud and blood. His color was bad.

He was only semi-conscious, and his right arm could not support its weight, it hung together by only bloody threads. In a minute, the helicopter was gone and Octavio with it to translate and once again, the night was dark and quiet but far emptier. The Salt Shack Dweller turned away from the orchard. He wanted to walk through the night, through the desert and through the city in cover of darkness.

It was bad water that brought the terrible events of the night, the fouling of the roasted goat, the thieves, the gunning down of Miguelito, and the only way to stop it was to stop the water, to stuff it back through the pipes and ditches and canals that cross stitched the valley like a web matrix. Run it back to the point of beginning and free it, remove its confusion and its desperate state of confinement, release it to run free under the sun once again so it has no more reason to carry darkness with it.

15

The Salt Shack Dweller returned to his residence late next day, after waiting patiently by the train tracks all night for a freight train, which did not come until first light. He walked first to his garden, concerned that his week of neglect would be its ruin but at the garden he found, Brandy-breath. His garden had been well cared for, watered, and carefully attended to, by the proud old man.

He said, "The Priest had come by on two occasions to instruct him on proper horticulture." He said, "His employers had learned of his arrest and terminated him."

The Salt Shack Dweller laid an appreciative hand on the old man's shoulder and said to him, "Sell your belongings and move down here with us. Plan a raid on the flour mill. We will need much flour."

The shack was clean and well cared for; the three-legged dog, the pig and the goat had been fed and watered daily. Patricia was responsible for this, and she sat in his chair in the shack, reading one of his zoology books, watching the spiders and scorpions in their little cages. She was startled when the Salt Shack Dweller pulled back the blanket and entered the shack.

He could see in her eyes that she was happy to see him, but he could see she deliberately cover her happiness from him and retreat.

He said to her, "You have taken good care of the scorpions and spiders." Patricia nodded.

"You have cleaned this place and made it nice." She nodded again.

"You have fed and watered the dog and the goat and the pig." Once more she nodded but tears were welling up in her eyes.

She took a folded piece of paper from the table next to her and handed it to the Salt Shack Dweller.

She spoke with tears flowing down her face now, "And I have met your wife. Your wife told me to give you this note."

Patricia cried hard. She said wife, as if the word was a brick resting on her neck. It seemed clear that she had been anticipating a confrontation with him for days, but she hadn't planned on the river of tears, and they embarrassed her, so she ran from the shack, ran to the river bottom, and ran across the flats toward her native village.

The Salt Shack Dweller opened the many times folded and unfolded note. He recognized the writing. His wife was coming to see him in an hour. This time, he did not run and did not hide; he merely waited with Miguelito on his mind.

She came, she spoke, she listened, and then she left. The Salt Shack Dweller couldn't help but think of the wailing that would go up from Donella when she'll learn of Miguelito's tragedy. His wife spoke to him and as he sat listening to her, watching the western sky soak up Miguelito's blood: he felt like a ghost. He occupied two realms. He was physically present next to his wife, but his spirit and his mental being rose up and floated above both of them, observing without passion.

She spoke of the humiliation he caused her by living like an animal instead of a mature man. She spoke with disgust about his shack, saying it was filthy and infested, calling it a health hazard, not fit to live in. She asked if the derelict she had seen earlier (certainly meaning Brandy-breath) inhabited the shack as well. She spoke of economic security and how they could have it and a family if he would return to the university and teach.

She did not speak of these things in a pleading or passionate way. She didn't say this to hurt him but only to make him realize the urgency of the matter.

The Salt Shack Dweller felt bad for his wife. He knew that she could never understand him (sometimes he could not understand himself) and he knew that he could never return to his past life. He also knew that he owed her an attempt to explain the inexplicable. He moved closer to his wife and looked at her in her beautiful eyes while his eyes demanded moisture.

"I've only known one war, maybe all wars are similar, I don't know. But the war I was in, changed me forever and I will never be the same man you knew or for that matter, the man I knew."

"Speaking just for myself and not ever asking for pity I will tell you that when you see napalm poured on men, women, children who cannot outrun it, you are a changed person. When you smell Agent Orange, you can't get rid of the smell, it's with you for life, even though it was never intended that you would smell it since it was made for others but, you know, accidents happen in war, and you are a changed person."

"When you hear a crack, and turn to your war buddy and see, for a nano second, the expression on his face as an enemy bullet smacks him between the eyes, exits the back of his head and bounces off of your shoulder you are a changed person."

"That will make you wonder what you're doing there; that will make you change your outlook. That will make you swear to rely on your own instinct and your own conscience; that will change every cell in your body."

"I am not the same person. I am not and never will be the man you married. I want the world I now have, along the dry Salt River. I want to make the Salt River a gushing river. This is not temporary. I cannot return to normal society, whatever that is. You would not be happy with me as your husband, I would not be happy living in the world you want to live in."

The Salt Shack Dweller's wife sighed, "These things are usually temporary, especially if you get help. It's pretty clear that you have what they call PTSD, but you can get over that with professional help. I can help you get better, and I will help you get the services you need."

The Salt Shack Dweller smiled at his wife, "I appreciate your words, but I don't have PTSD, and in an odd way that I can't really explain, my war experience has enabled me to reveal myself to me and it has freed me to try to change the world I live in, to make it a better world and I have the energy to take on the biggest projects that threatens us. I'm anxious to do my duty. This is my home. I loved you and I still do in my own way, but this is my chosen home."

Out of nowhere Octavio appeared. He bowed humbly. He whispered the news of Miguelito into the Salt Shack Dweller's ear. He felt defeat and loss. Miguelito was alive but he had lost his arm. The Salt Shack Dweller excused himself from his wife. She said she would see him again. With small, soft tears in her eyes, his wife departed.

Cecilia came to the river bottom that night. Brandy-breath was present as well as Octavio. Cecilia brought wine, over which they discussed the one-armed young man named Miguelito.

"Life will be hard for him," said Cecilia. "The arm had to be removed above the elbow."

"Life has always been hard for the peasants," said Octavio. "But we are not people to cry and complain. It is true that this will bring great difficulty to Miguelito. I don't think he will be able to pick the fruit."

"He must stay in the hospital for at least another week" said Cecilia, "and after that he should stay around for therapy. Where will he stay?"

"Here, of course," said the Salt Shack Dweller.

"It is better that he stay here than return to his village," agreed Octavio, "in his village there is sympathy but no therapy."

"When he comes here," said Cecilia, "it is important for him to know that he is cared about, but he should not be wept over; he should not come to believe that self-pity is acceptable."

"He must learn to do for himself," said Octavio.

"That is correct," answered Cecilia.

The old man, pulling on a small bottle of brandy offered his thoughts. "That Indian woman is the important one. If she will still have him, things will probably be fine."

The truth of this observation from age and experience was universal within the walls of the salt shack, recognized and fully accepted.

They drank to the old man's wisdom and insight before the Salt Shack Dweller spoke, "Here is what we will do then. Miguelito will come here to stay. Before he comes, we will execute a raid on the flour mill for sacks of flour and on Monti's for meat, so that we have a store of provisions for this difficult time."

"We will send a runner to the reservation to tell Donella the news and to prepare her for Miguelito's return. We will plan a fiesta so that he may feel honored as a hero of the clan. We will roast a pig or the goat, whichever he prefers."

"We will bring the workers from the fields and the Indians from the reservations; we will have all of Miguelito's friends here. We will have games and contests between black widows and scorpions; wagers will be accepted. With all of this and with Donella's help, Miguelito will not have time to think about the arm he lost."

The plan was unanimously agreed on. The old man and Octavio departed the shack and built a small fire at their camp a short distance away. Overhead, as always, the big jets bore through the darkness of night leaving huge gaping holes in their wake. The day had been long and demanding, one that left the

Salt Shack Dweller weary. He laid in the bed once the old man and Octavio had left.

Cecilia came to him then, undressing as she came. She made sweet and gentle love to him for a considerable length of time; she brought a level of peace back to his soul. Following their lovemaking, after several minutes of silence except for the cicadas, Cecilia spoke from beside him.

"How is your wife?"

"The same."

"Oh."

The Salt Shack Dweller smiled softly, "Tell me about the priest and the judge. Have they come to you yet?"

"Yes, they have both arrived to speak. I see each of them almost every day. The Priest comes in the morning, the Judge comes in the late afternoon."

"Does one know that the other also comes to you?"

"No, I have not told them. I don't want them to think there is any kind of a conflict or competition because there is not."

"What testimony or confessions do they make to you?"

"None, really. They are both honest, sincere men. The Judge told me straight away that he was married, just as an honorable man should. The Priest told me straight away that he was married to the church all of his adult life, which was his way, I think, of telling me that he is a virgin."

"That's pretty exciting. They both, rather nervously, made reference to an ache in their loins and for a number of days, I wondered, if they were speaking of love or medicine."

Both the Salt Shack Dweller and Cecilia laughed, rolled over and kissed each other deeply until the laughter over powered the kiss.

The Salt Shack Dweller then said, "Which one, if either, will you have? Have you made up your mind, how to approach this?"

"No," answered Cecilia, "it's kind of fun though somewhat different, proceeding slowly with this. They are both uniquely interesting."

"Yes, and each day they become more dedicated to the Salt Clan."

Cecilia nodded, then moved on to Patricia, "But speaking of going slow, I must tell you again that you must do something about Patricia. She came to speak with me again, after she met your wife; your wife treated her like a peasant. She has great desire for you, her only concern was that I might object but I assured her that was not an issue. She is young but she is ready to be a woman."

"A woman so young as she, with as much desire as she has is controlled by the spirits and is not predictable, if left unattended. She needs and deserves a responsible person, a mature man, to lead her through this time and if she doesn't find one then no person can make her account for her actions."

"The spirits of passion are not from an evil camp but once they have a hold on a young woman like her, they do not release her easily."

"It is the same for the Priest. He needs a good woman to guide him."

"I have thought of that," smiled Cecilia.

The Salt Shack Dweller paused, then frowned. "You don't think Patricia would bring her friends, you know, to watch? They're all virgins you know."

Cecilia exploded into her infectious laugh that prevented her from speaking until it finally melted into gasping giggling and allowed her to say, "That's a wonderful idea. Would you like that? I'll tell her to bring any of her virgin friends. It's the duty of leaders of the clan to give direction to the youth in their time of confusion. It solidifies their position within the clan."

"Well, that's true," said the Salt Shack Dweller. "But no bystanders allowed. It might intimidate me."

Cecilia continued laughing so the Salt Shack Dweller added, "Seriously, don't get carried away my beautiful Cecilia. I need you with me, calm and level headed like no one else in the world."

Some minutes of silence followed until the Salt Shack Dweller spoke again, "Was it like cutting off your own arm when you had to cut off Miguelito's arm?"

"I did not want to do it. I was going to have someone else do it, but Miguelito asked me to be the one to do it. Octavio said it was the way it should be…and speaking of that beautiful boy, I must go now to see how he is doing. I told him I would be gone only a few hours." As Cecilia dressed, she said, "Think of what I told you about Patricia tonight."

"I will. Do not forget the judge and the priest."

"I will not. Good night, Mr. Salt Shack Dweller." And then Cecilia was gone, into the night, and the Salt Shack Dweller fell into a deep sleep that lasted until dawn.

16

Within a few days, Carlos and Anastacio arrived at the Salt Seabed via freight train. Both were severely grieved to learn of Miguelito's fate; both renewed vows to find the thieves who had done this thing to Miguelito and to take revenge by flaying the guilty man's skin with their knives. There was no doubt that the two men would carry out their threats, if they, ever found the thief who shot Miguelito. God help any innocent man who got in the way.

The Salt Shack Dweller needed a runner to go to the reservation village to find Donella and Raymond and to give the news to them and to tell them to join the fiesta the coming weekend.

Between Anastacio and Carlos he chose Anastacio; both had permits from immigration (because they were being held in the United States as material witnesses against the smugglers who abandoned the immigrants in the desert) so both could travel about freely but the night of the raid on the flour mill was coming and the Salt Shack Dweller wanted Coyote Carlos to be among the raiding party.

Besides, Carlos might pick up a few stray chickens or another pig or goat in his idle time; there would be a lot of people to feed at the fiesta.

Before the night of the flour raid, the Salt Shack Dweller went to see Patricia. He went late at night and stood outside her window to call to her with the song of the mourning dove. He knew this was a dangerous behavior, especially in enemy territory, but he remained steadfast, repeating his song until her curtains parted.

She looked at him from behind closed windows for a full minute and then motioned for him to wait where he was. When she appeared outside, she was wearing a full-length white dress and she looked beautiful, like a young maiden preparing for initiation. She waited for the Salt Shack Dweller to speak.

He said to her, "Come to the river bottom Saturday. Miguelito lost his arm in a battle. He will be returning to the river bottom this weekend and there will be a major fiesta. You may wear that uniform if it pleases you. It certainly pleases me. You may bring your youthful friends."

Tiny tears appeared in Patricia's soft eyes and two of the tears dropped onto her cheeks. "Miguelito?" she said sadly.

"Yes," answered the Salt Shack Dweller while dual tears filled his eyes.

As Patricia had done once before, she went up on her toes, balanced herself with her hand against his bare chest and kissed him. In her breath, the Salt Shack Dweller could tell that, yes, here was a woman.

Patricia whispered to him, "I will come. Thank you, for coming to me." She turned to go but then turned back and spoke again, "I hope Cecilia will be there. It's different with Cecilia. I wish she was my sister."

"She will," answered the Salt Shack Dweller.

Though there was deep sorrow in his heart for Miguelito the Salt Shack Dweller could not deny his happiness over Patricia. He did not know what would become of the matter. As he crossed the road that effectively separated his Salt Riverbed territory from the territory of the adjacent tribe, he could not help but give expression to his joy.

Since the mild season had begun, he rarely wore anything more than his loincloth; even shoes where unnecessary to protect his feet from the burning ground of summer. His spirit was light, there seemed to be no one around, so the Salt Shack Dweller jumped as high into the night air as he could and clicked his heels.

But there was somebody around. In a parked car, along the road, two enemies in their blue war costumes, were out of their car and after him before he had come back to Earth from his leap of joy. Because of this they had the jump on him and in a minute they had him pinned against the stone wall of the park.

Steel bracelets were locked onto his wrists; both enemies had a secure hold on him and for the moment escape ceased to be possible, so, the Salt Shack Dweller quit active resistance and went limp.

One of the enemies said to the other, "Are you sure this is him?"

The first enemy replied, "How many tall, skinny men with hawk noses frequent the Salt River bottom wearing nothing but a loincloth?"

"Yeah," the other enemy responded, "Hey you, what's your name?"

The enemy was speaking to him, but the Salt Shack Dweller did not say a word. The enemy tossed him into the back of their patrol car which was like a cage and a terrible place to the Salt Shack Dweller. He maintained silence. The two enemies looked at him from outside the cage, as if, he was a wild animal.

The one said to the other with a laugh, "His wife is right. He's crazier than shit."

Both laughed and then one of them took up the radio and spoke, telling their chief that they had captured the lunatic of Tempe wearing, of all things, nothing but a loincloth, on the banks of the Salt River and that they were transporting him to the state mental hospital at 24th St. Van Buren.

So that was it. It had nothing to do with the attempted slaughter at the big pool, an event which now was part of the proud history of the Salt Clan, an event told around the fire many times and would be repeated many times more and thereby, be preserved. Instead, he realized, this was the fulfillment of his wife's threat to have him committed.

This would be interesting; the Salt Shack Dweller was looking forward to it. He only hoped he would return to the Salt Riverbed in time to make a raid on the flour mill before the fiesta. He hoped that the old man, Octavio, and Carlos don't go through with the raid without him. He relaxed in the moving cage of the enemy. Silence was the proper approach.

At the mental hospital, there were administrative details, which the Salt Shack Dweller fully ignored, refusing to answer any of the questions they asked and refusing even to acknowledge that he heard a word that was said.

There were two enemies now, one blue and one in white. They talked and laughed and drank coffee together, so, it was safe to assume that they were allies working together; no doubt their strategy was to join forces in order to dominate the smaller tribes of the region. *Nonetheless,* thought the Salt Shack Dweller, *one day soon the Salt Clan will have grown to a level of power where they did not need to fear the enemy in white or the enemy in blue.*

"Is he dangerous," White asked Blue.

"We don't know," answered Blue.

"Is he violent?"

"All we know is what his wife said, that he's a lunatic living like an animal in the wild."

"I'm wondering if we should give him some drugs to sedate him."

Now panic shot through the Salt Shack Dweller's mind when he heard them speaking of drugs. Drugs altered reality and if the Salt Shack Dweller prided himself on any one thing, it was that he understood and lived fully within the boundaries of reality, while the rest of the population (with some minor exceptions) lived their lives outside of reality; dependent upon the drug of modern society. Drugs would be a torture to the Salt Shack Dweller; he did what he could to look passive and sedate and non-threatening.

"He looks about as passive as a bowl of Jell-O to me," said one male orderly big enough to instill passivity in most any person.

This black giant of a man led the silent Salt Shack Dweller to a chair in the main ward.

"Tomorrow they will decide your fate friend. You will have very little to say about it—but that does not make you much different from the rest of us; we are all committed in one way or another. In your mind is the only place you can be free and from the looks of you I would say, you are a free man. I salute you." Which he did.

The Salt Shack Dweller would have liked to have spoken with this big but gentle man. He would like to recruit him into the Salt Clan. Perhaps later. For now, the approach was silence. He folded his arms across his chest, fixed the expression on his face that he would maintain without change until they ordeal was over. He was prepared to wait out the night.

From his place of silence, the Salt Shack Dweller observed the prisoners of 24th St. By morning's first light, he could classify each prisoner into one of three categories and each category had a specific diagnosis.

First, there were the prisoners deprived of love and Gods with the resulting depression that caused social dysfunction. Second, there were the prisoners who were powerful and talented but were never given the opportunity to express their talent resulting in a destructive frustration that was expressed in chaotic action of an unpredictable nature designed to demand recognition of power and talent but doomed to failure.

Third, was that group of prisoners who had consumed too much electricity or been exposed to excessive amounts of rays from the Palo Verde Nuclear Plant or had devoured too many of modern society's prescription drugs. Sadly, there was no hope for these individuals; they were vegetables and the only good thing that could come of their tragic existence was if they served as an example to the vulnerable youth of the Valley of the Sun.

The Salt Shack Dweller knew that he could cure the maladies of the first two groups in a matter of weeks by incorporating them into the clan. Tribal love would be theirs and the clan had a multitude of Gods to choose from. Each one would be free and encouraged to use his other powers and talents for the good of the clan; it would not be wasted.

For the third group, the Salt Shack Dweller could do nothing but free them and permit them to wander out for the rest of their days in a perpetual state of overdose. The others, he would welcome into the clan. One day, the Salt Clan would liberate this cold institution at 24th St.

The Salt Shack Dweller was scheduled to go to mental health court at 11:00 a.m. essentially to have a determination of his mental competency conducted by a member of the enemy tribe.

At 10:00 a.m., a young lawyer appointed by the court to represent him at the competency hearing showed up at the hospital. But the Salt Shack Dweller did not want a lawyer. He wanted no foreign mouth to speak for him. A leader and a warrior could speak for himself or choose not to speak at all, but a warrior did not have a walking fashion show to do his speaking for him, especially one who was a stranger. What a ridiculous procedure! The problem was how to get the lawyer to go away without letting anyone from the hospital hear him violate his vow of silence.

He waited until he was alone with the lawyer and when the others had moved away. He waited, until he could lean close but whisper harshly and viciously.

He bared his teeth like a mad dog and said, "Go away from here or I will bite your heart out."

The lawyer jumped away as though he'd been given electric shock. Slowly, the Salt Shack Dweller allowed his upper lip to drop back down to cover his teeth. The plan worked. In a minute, the lawyer was gone, explaining to the hospital staff that he had all of the information he needed and that he was going to the courthouse. But the Salt Shack Dweller knew that the lawyer would be conveniently late.

The lawyer did not show up, but the Salt Shack Dweller's wife was present with her spokesman, another walking fashion show with a flash of hair.

Still, the Salt Shack Dweller's silence was maintained with his arms folded defiantly, across his chest. He was accompanied by two male orderlies from the hospital, one of whom was the big gentle black man. He would put the system to the test. Yet it turned out not to be much of a test.

Either, the Gods of chance or selection, or more likely an act of human intervention, saw to it that a judge named O'Sullivan presided over the Salt

Shack Dweller's commitment proceeding. The judge covered his initial surprise at seeing the Salt Shack Dweller before him by quickly calling the court to order.

The spokesman for the Salt Shack Dweller's wife cataloged a list of social atrocities for the judge to hear. In the middle of this discourse, his wife began to audibly cry. To the Salt Shack Dweller, she sounded like a dying rabbit. But the Salt Shack Dweller did not listen to his wife's tears.

His attention was focused on what her mouth piece was saying, though he refused to show that he was listening. He simply stared straight ahead, refusing to even acknowledge the proceedings. All that was being said about him made him proud. He did not have a job and hadn't had one for more than a year.

He lived in a shack made of flotsam and windfall junk in the Salt River bottom. The shack had no plumbing or electricity. (Partly incorrect, there was plumbing of a sort) His companions in the shack were live scorpions, black widows, tarantulas, snakes, mice, and maybe more, they couldn't guess.

He cohabited with illegal aliens and Indians and drunkards and possibly underage girls. He dressed hardly at all (no argument there). He looked like a pagan Indian with a loincloth. He had totally abandoned his responsibilities to his family and society.

Had the Salt Shack Dweller been in a speaking frame of mind, he would have cheered this diatribe. It was eloquent and all true. The judge turned his gaze upon the Salt Shack Dweller, though it was not acknowledged in this formal setting, and asked if he cared to make a response to the court. He did not. Silence was his response. Folded arms was his defense.

With nothing left to do, the judge rolled out swift justice. He turned to the eloquent spokesman for the Salt Shack Dweller's wife.

"It seems to me, that what we have here is a failure of communication; it seems to me that what your client needs is a divorce decree, not a commitment order. The petition for an order of commitment is denied."

And that quickly the judge brought down the gavel and disappeared through a secret door behind the bench. The Salt Shack Dweller's wife wept louder as her spokesman consoled her and as they departed the court.

The big orderly gave a little laugh and slapped the Salt Shack Dweller on the back, saying, "Good show, Chief Silence, I salute you." And then he did just that.

His partner was urging him to hurry, saying, "Let's go so we can beat the rush at El Molino."

They started to the door, but the Salt Shack Dweller called out to the big orderly, "You have treated me well during my time of captivity. You have heard where I live. Come visit us sometime. You will find it like an island of welcoming, in this harsh world."

When the big orderly heard the Salt Shack Dweller speak, he laughed, a deep full laugh that loved life. Before departing, he assured the Salt Shack Dweller that he would come to the Salt bed for a visit before seven days have passed.

The Salt Shack Dweller was alone in the courtroom but only for a minute. The judge stuck his head back in, to see if everyone else was gone and when he confirmed it, he returned to the courtroom without his black robe and sat near the Salt Shack Dweller.

"How did you get yourself into this one?" The Judge asked.

"It wasn't a provoked attack. I assure you. But do not worry. I do not plan any specific retaliation."

"I'm relieved," said the Judge.

"Have you heard of the tragedy that has befallen Miguelito?"

"Yes, Cecilia told me about it."

"There will be a fiesta on Saturday in his honor. Will you be there?"

"I will be there. I would not miss it."

"Good."

The Judge hesitated then, searching for words, an apparently unusual condition for him, "Did you know that the Padre is interested in Cecilia as a woman?"

"I have heard this, yes."

"It is a most unusual situation. I never expected to be in competition with a Priest for the affections of a woman."

"How goes your pursuit of Cecilia? Did you tell her about the ache in your loins?"

"I did but maybe not exactly in those words. It goes well, even though I cannot say for sure that I've made much progress. The more I know of her, the more I want to spend time with her. Do you understand the feeling?"

"I understand it well…and how are things between you and the Priest?"

"Strangely, we have become very good friends. We do not view ourselves as rivals."

The Salt Shack Dweller nodded his approval and wondered to himself, if there was anything Cecilia could not do.

"So, all is well except for Miguelito, and we do what we can for him. Come, give me a ride back to my territory. I have much to do and I am tired of the long walk."

No one had missed him. Upon his return to the Salt bed from the prison on 24th St., the Salt Shack Dweller instructed the old man to finalize his plans for the raid on the flour mill; the raid would be that night after dark. He went to the nearby open-air camp of Octavio, Anastacio, and Carlos.

Anastacio had already departed for the reservation to take the message to Donella and Raymond. Octavio and Carlos were informed that the flour raid would take place that night. For the rest of the afternoon, until dark, the Salt Shack Dweller slept.

The old man's plan contained the element of simplicity; he employed the distraction formula. Under cover of darkness, but not until the midnight hour, the old man, Octavio, Carlos, and the Salt Shack Dweller crossed the Salt Riverbed, crossed the park, crossed Mill Avenue, and made their way around the huge building to a back door that the old man was certain would be open in order to give some ventilation to the old building.

It was. The old man, then left the three and returned all the way around to the front where the office was. The old man's weapons were a bottle of brandy and a knowledge of the new guard. He noisily (to allow the three to follow his movements by sound) made his way into the mill building and engaged his replacement in conversation.

The old man and the new guard, also an old man, knew each other and greeted each other loudly, sitting on sacks of flour and breaking the seal of the brandy bottle to renew their friendship. The Salt Shack Dweller stuck his head in through the door to see if the old man had succeeded into distracting the new guard. He had. The Salt Shack Dweller smiled at Octavio, who in turn, smiled at Carlos.

Carlos always smiled, as though he had something up his sleeve, like a chicken or a goat. The rule was silence and the most silent among them was Carlos. He was instructed to enter the mill and to return with a sack of flour until they had three sacks.

The first time was successful, as was the second. On the third effort, Carlos tripped and fell and had to survive a search by the new guard who was constantly being diverted by the old man and his brandy bottle. When the guard was seated again, Carlos made his way out the back door with the third sack of flour.

Each man hoisted a sack of flour on to his back and made his way to the side of the building to where they could see Mill Avenue. When there was a break in the traffic, so that no car could see them from any direction, one would scurry across the brightly lit street.

The Salt Shack Dweller went first with his skinny stick legs, topped by a shapeless and oversized white torso with no head; some kind of a mutant white rat from the flour mill exposed to excess nuclear generating rays would have been the only exclamation from marijuana induced stoned college students who may have witnessed the weird figure crossing the road.

Once in the safety of the shadows, they took their time moving slowly under their burdens. Walking on the floor of smooth, odd sized rocks in the river bottom, under the weight of a flour sack was slow and difficult but by 3:27 a.m. they had reached the shack. The pit from which the Salt Shack Dweller had called the hawk, was deepened and expanded to a sufficient size so that the three sacks of flour could comfortably rest in the bottom of the pit.

The flour was marketed under the name of Rose Flour. Each sack had a single multi-petaled red rose stamped brightly at its center. In the pit, the bright roses were facing up so that fresh air and light could maintain the freshness of their delicate petals and so that the petals would not be crushed under the weight of the flour. The three red roses on the flour sacks formed a soft triangle that glowed red in the pit and in the night.

By 4:00 a.m., the old man had returned, proud and somewhat drunk. "Declare the flour raid a success," he called out happily as he stared at the three roses of the (mythical) desert.

17

By Saturday, the day of, the night of the fiesta, preparations were almost complete. Anastacio had returned from the reservation; he had succeeded in finding Raymond and Donella and giving them the news of Miguelito and of the coming fiesta in his honor. He reported back that Donella had broken into a river of tears upon hearing the news of Miguelito and that Raymond had set to work on a sorcerer's curse to be inflicted upon the one who had maimed his sister's lover.

He told Anastacio that the guilty one would be recognizable if ever seen again as a man with a progressively shriveling penis. Donella had desperately wanted to return with Anastacio but was told to wait until Saturday when Miguelito would also arrive at the shack and to spend the time on the reservation gathering up available women to bring to the fiesta to ensure its success.

Patricia arrived in the Salt Riverbed in the late afternoon, dressed casually, looking as light and delicate as a butterfly. There was a calmness and happiness to her youth that brought an added measure of joy to the Salt Camp. The Salt Shack Dweller greeted her warmly within the confines of his role as the leader of the clan while everyone else greeted her without reserve, making sure she knew that she belonged on a welcome and equal footing.

She joined Carlos in the plucking and cleaning of some chickens he had found roaming aimlessly about some unidentified place. Carlos had already killed them for which Patricia was thankful. They chatted away in Spanish and the Salt Shack Dweller, gathering wood for the night's campfire, felt his mouth go dry, every time he passed by lovely Patricia.

Raymond, with eyes that could see into the world of magic, followed by Donella and three other women, came to the camp before the sun was gone, bringing corn and squash from the reservation garden along with a little whiskey and wine. Donella sat on a rock and wept in anticipation of

Miguelito's arrival, but Raymond scolded her for this and got her to stop crying. The three girlfriends brought to the Salt Camp by Donella did not weep; they were busy getting to know Octavio, Carlos, and the old man in the best way they could with awkward tongues. Once again Patricia was invaluable, along with Octavio, in providing a common tongue.

The judge and the priest had both desired to arrive at the fiesta with Cecilia, but Cecilia was bringing Miguelito, so the priest and the judge came together, and together they arrived bearing a beautiful dish of paella, just as the sun was being consumed by the edge of the Earth. Neither would say who had cooked it or when.

Everyone, the Salt Shack Dweller expected to attend the fiesta had arrived as well as one he had not expected.

Harold arrived out of nowhere. It was a strange appearance. He explained that he had dinner at Monti's on the other side of the riverbed with some potential employers, county and state lawyers looking to hire young, recent law school graduates.

He said, "He had seen the glow of the fire pit as he was leaving the restaurant and knew he would find his weird friend tending to the fire in a stupid loincloth and wingtips."

He said, "He was surprised to see so many other people who looked sort of normal. He asked the Salt Shack Dweller who they all were."

"Members of the ever-rowing Salt Clan," the Salt Shack Dweller answered.

The Salt Shack Dweller invited Harold to stay and enjoy the evening, even though he knew from their conversation several months ago, just after the Salt Shack Dweller took up residence in the Salt bed, that Harold was severely disparaging of his so-called lifestyle.

Throughout the early part of the evening the Salt Shack Dweller attended to his business, but he noticed that Harold spoke only briefly with the judge, the priest and Cecilia. He did not speak with any other members of the clan. He did not eat any food. He declined the wine and whiskey that was offered him.

The flames of the campfire reached higher into the night sky as darkness came to the Salt Riverbed. There was a vast pile of dry wood gathered from all around, that was more than sufficient to burn through the night. The food had been prepared and was kept warm for anyone to take as they wished; wine and whiskey and the music from Anastacio's guitar surrounded them.

A lanky one-armed boy-man entered the ring of light from the world of darkness to peer silently at all of the people. One by one the people noticed his presence. In silence, they began to drift toward him, until Carlos looked up from his cooking fire, saw the empty shirt sleeve and cried out, "Miguelito!"

Carlos jumped over the campfire to embrace Miguelito. Noticing that they were standing in rich sand, he engaged the bewildered Miguelito in a friendly wrestling match on the spot. Cheers of approval and desperate cries of protest went up at once. Donella could not now hold back her hysterics at the sight of her disadvantaged loved one being rustled to the ground by another.

The old man jumped into position to referee the event. But before anyone could do anything about the outrageous spectacle, Cecilia emerged from the darkness and put a stop to it in the same casual way she did most things. In each hand, she carried a jug of wine. By swinging, the jug in her right hand ever so slightly, she was able to give Carlos, a good-natured crack on the head.

"Knock it off," she said mildly. "Miguelito is not ready for it tonight; next week he will whip your ass."

Carlos did not understand each word spoken by Cecilia and Patricia and Octavio experienced some difficulty making a translation, but Carlos got the point and abandoned the match. Miguelito pulled himself up from the sand wearing a grin and after he had brushed the sand off, he gave Carlos an affectionate one-armed hug.

Cecilia set the wine jugs down and said to the priest and the judge, "There are two more of these in my car, will you guys go get them?"

The judge and the priest responded like schoolboys; they disappeared into the darkness in an instant. Between Miguelito and Donella there was shyness and anxiety. They did not allow their eyes to meet but Miguelito joined the fiesta without difficulty and Anastacio resumed playing his guitar.

Except for the shyness between Miguelito and Donella, the fiesta progressed well. Sufficient wine had been consumed so that the gift of speech seemed to have been given equally to everyone. Foreign tongues spoke with foreign tongues; the judge and the priest had Cecilia sandwiched between them and they both spoke and laughed at once and it was as if she was two people the way she could deftly handle the affections of both men.

In the case of Octavio, the wine brought forth a singing tongue and in the case of the old man dancing feet. The wine went down quickly when there was something to wash it down with; great quantities of chicken with chili and tortillas, paella and spiced corn were consumed. Patricia made no special effort to be in proximity to the Salt Shack Dweller. She helped herself with wine and food and moved comfortably from one conversation to another and even joined Octavio in song, when he sang the one, she knew.

Yet, a fiesta is more than food and wine and song and dance. It is a time for communication between people who do not always see each other.

Therefore, it was no surprise that just when the Salt Shack Dweller had taken a seat next to Patricia and had been the recipient of one of her lovely smiles, that Raymond approached him, saying, "There are matters I wish to speak with you about."

Raymond and the Salt Shack Dweller left the center of the fiesta that was gaining momentum as the guitar played faster and the songs came from deeper, and the old man danced harder around the fire. In the shack, a half empty jug of wine was set on the floor. Before they spoke, they smoked tobacco, blowing smoke in the four directions.

"What is it that's on your mind, Raymond?" asked the Salt Shack Dweller when the necessary preliminaries were over.

There was a sadness hanging over Raymond that contrasted greatly with the gaiety of the fiesta.

"The enemy threatens us once again," he announced.

"The enemy is always a threat. Until we have grown and become powerful, we must be wary. What particular threat are you speaking of?"

"It is the greatest of threats to my people. We were pushed from our land to one place or another for a hundred years until we were pushed to an obscure corner of the desert that the enemy considered a wasteland. They did not want it."

"This is true."

"But we are strong and resourceful people. We have made our homes in this corner of the Earth and we have survived. As small and as dry as our land is, it is now our land. It is all we have."

"This is also true," said the Salt Shack Dweller, drinking wine and passing the jug to Raymond.

"Now they plan to take this as well. Without our land, our people will be scattered by the wind because they will be rootless people and we will cease to exist."

"The threat you speak of is the new dam the enemy has proposed?"

"Yes. This dam will be on the Verde River, just where it meets the Salt River. This dam will be downriver from our land and the lake behind this dam will swallow our land. It will wash away our sacred burial grounds. It will consume our houses. People cannot live under a lake."

"What have you done to stop this dam?"

"Everything but no one hears our voices. My grandfather and I have turned to sorcery as the only hope."

"A wise decision," agreed the Salt Shack Dweller.

"But it is hard. Do you understand? Sorcery is the most personal art. It is necessary to have some specific person or object to concentrate on. With this dam, there is neither."

"The dam does not exist yet except on paper and there is no specific individual to attack. The dam is in the mind of the planners and bureaucrats, and it is difficult to find a place of responsibility, so that the magic can be properly directed. Sorcery needs a place to send its curse."

"I know of no power greater than sorcery. What is it that I can do?"

"I want you to think like the enemy. You were once a part of them. You know, how they think."

The Salt Shack Dweller did not blink. He did not like to have his past life much discussed. He preferred to let it slip silently into the darkness of history.

"It is true that I once lived among the enemy, and it is true that I learned much about how the enemy thinks. I will try to devise a plan of attack to counter the enemies' threat to your people and to your land and to the river itself."

"And my grandfather and I will continue the effort to find the proper place in the enemy bureaucracy to direct the power of our magic."

Just then, from the area of the campfire, a great commotion arose and though it sounded like a thousand voices in mortal verbal battle, Donella's hysterical rage easily lead the way. Raymond and the Salt Shack Dweller rushed from the shack to the camp. There they found Donella being restrained by one of her friends. Blood-red violence was in her eyes. Across the campfire from Donella, was Patricia, standing but bewildered, being shielded from Donella by Cecilia.

All the men remained seated, afraid for their lives to come between the females. As Raymond and the Salt Shack Dweller arrived, Donella began screaming out the source of her anger. It seemed that, while Donella and Miguelito had still not overcome their lover's shyness, that Patricia had strayed too close to Miguelito, perhaps to say something to him, to welcome him back or to express her sorrow for his misfortune. But Donella could not see this. She could only see Patricia's pink flesh and she deeply believed that Patricia was trying to take Miguelito. Therefore, she attacked.

It was Raymond who persuaded Donella to calm down and to resume her seat on the cottonwood log by the fire, next to Miguelito(Miguelito was grinning; he fancied the idea of the two women fighting like cats over him even if they weren't). Cecilia squeezed Patricia's hand and relinquished her to the Salt Shack Dweller who took up a seat next to her.

Quietly and diplomatically Anastacio took up the guitar; the old man jumped back to the fire circle and Octavio gave forth with a deafening cry from the Mexican soul; let the fiesta resume. The judge and the priest leaned across Cecilia and commented to each other on the incident; love was controlled neither by the laws of man or even the laws of the wild universe.

Patricia turned to speak softly to the Salt Shack Dweller. Instead of fear or anger in her eyes he saw happiness.

She said, to his ears only, "I love this place, Bones. I think these people care about me and they treat me like one of them. Even Donella takes me seriously, if incorrectly."

The Salt Shack Dweller could not restrain a smile. He nodded as to the correctness of what Patricia said.

Then he spoke, "Donella did act out of haste, but her actions were understandable. Be bold and magnanimous beyond your years. Go to her and make peace."

Patricia did not hesitate. She called Donella out into the dark and spoke with her alone. They were gone for several minutes and whatever was said between them was not known to the rest but it was successful; both returned having left their differences in the dark under a large rock. The event did accomplish a goal of major importance, however; Donella returned and took a seat next to Miguelito and held on to him tightly.

When Donella had resumed, her seat it appeared that all were present. The Salt Shack Dweller began to speak. He wanted to set the stage for the coming battle between the black widow and the scorpion. A battle without historical background was foolish. But he was interrupted by the sudden appearance in the ring of light of a huge man carrying a small child on his shoulders.

The Salt Shack Dweller recognized the man at once; he was the big orderly from the state hospital, the one the Salt Shack Dweller had seen potential in and had invited to the Salt Camp. The Salt Shack Dweller stood and formally welcomed the visitor to the camp. He introduced the orderly, (named Francis), to the clan.

When the introductions reached the Judge, Francis broke into a sly grin, "Ah, Ha," he laughed. "You get around don't you, Your Honor?"

To which the Judge replied, "I follow the path of justice."

The Salt Shack Dweller handed Francis the jug of wine after Francis greeted the judge and the priest with a warm handshake.

"Drink, eat your fill and feed the child all he can eat and then drink some more and tell us who your little friend is."

Francis, now kneeling in the sand with the big-eyed little boy, still on his shoulders did drink.

Then he brought the boy down and held him in front of himself and said, "The boy's name is Carl. He is older than he looks but he hasn't grown so well. He doesn't talk. Everyone thinks Carl hasn't got much of a brain, but Carl and I know better, don't we, Carl?"

Francis gave Carl a little squeeze, but Carl made no response, he merely stared at the fire and all the new faces surrounding him.

"You see, Carl has spent most of his short life locked in a closet and he hasn't been out very long. Since I adopted him, I just figure that all he needs is a little time to get used to this old world and to see as much wide-open space as possible. That's one reason I brought him with me tonight; show him how life goes outside the closet."

Cecilia reached out and gently persuaded the boy to come to her, so that she could look into his eyes. The judge and the priest gave her room.

Cecilia said, "Bring him to the county hospital and I'll run some tests on him."

Then the Priest spoke up, "Then bring him to my church. The church will care for him when you're working or need a break."

And the Judge said, "Bring him to my court. We will see that justice is done by him. The county can and should be providing services for him."

"All in good time," answered Francis with an appreciative smile. "This land is run by God, by law, and by science now. One day, this fine little guy will need to know all three but for now I think all he needs is a friend…Excuse me, Chief," he said to the Salt Shack Dweller, "I think you were talking when I came up, but I have to ask you, don't you worry about the floods when you're living down here?"

"We pray for them," answered the Salt Shack Dweller.

At the same time, he was answering Francis' question, he looked over Francis' shoulder and saw Harold's face. Harold caught and held the Salt Shack Dweller's eyes. Neither blinked. Looking in Harold's eyes, the Salt Shack Dweller could see that Harold did not approve of Francis or any of the rest of the clan. Without a word spoken Harold stood, turned his back on the fiesta and took his leave. The Salt Shack Dweller wondered if he would ever see Harold again. In a way, he hoped not.

When the new visitors had eaten their fill and had answered all the questions presented to them by the curiosity of the Salt Clan and when the new visitors were comfortably situated in the sand by the fire, the Salt Shack Dweller asked the old man and Carlos to build a spider's battlefield in the sand. After supervising the location and size of the battlefield, the Salt Shack Dweller went to his shack to get the combatants.

According to tradition, the scorpion had been removed from its fellows and placed in a glass jar on one side of the room 24 hours earlier. The black widow had likewise been segregated and placed alone in a glass jar, on the opposite side of the room. They were kept apart so that there would be no danger of them becoming familiar with each other. Neither had been fed for 30 hours.

The black widow was a deep, rich black color, supple and ample in body. The scorpion was almost albino white, small, and deadly looking. Ordinarily, it was against the laws of nature to promote a battle like this for sport. On the other hand, there were (and needed to be) ways in which the Gods spoke to man and through spiders and scorpions was one way. And just that night, it so happened, there was a need to communicate with the Gods.

A dam was a difficult foe to defeat. Surely in opposing the dam the Salt Shack Dweller and Raymond would be on the side of righteousness, but evil was a powerful force, gaining more power each day and if there was to be any hope of success, it would be necessary to obtain advice from the Gods on how to proceed and what tactics to employ.

Should they attempt to defeat the dam with force and a straight forward attack like the ancient scorpion or should they be seductive and subtle, dark and furtive, sleek and fast. Should they woo and trick their opponent like the black widow? The proper procedure would be revealed by the black widow and the scorpion in battle.

Since there was a legitimate purpose to be served by the scorpion versus black widow battle there was no reason not to combine some sport with the event. The Salt Shack Dweller returned to the fire circle with the jars containing the combatants, dangling calmly from each hand. He gave the jars to Francis and asked him to hold them but not to shake or agitate them.

It was important to be respectful and kind to each of them, for they had been transformed from common (mythical) desert creatures to messengers of the Gods. While Francis held the jars (to the boy Carl's intense but silent interest), the Salt Shack Dweller took Raymond into the dark, away from the fire, and explained to him the greater significance of the battle, (which Raymond already knew but politely listened to).

Neither of them would be permitted to bet or wish for the victory of one creature over the other. The two of them must watch and listen very carefully. They must pay extreme attention to the battle because, though revealed in the old way, the battle was a divine message to them on a mission of great importance, the destruction of the river and people in exchange for liquid light and blood-red grapefruit.

Raymond and the Salt Shack Dweller returned to the fire. The Salt Shack Dweller received the jars from Francis and held them as high in the air as he could.

Silently he beseeched the Gods, "Bless these creatures and through them communicate wisdom and tactics to us dumb humans who are bound to this Earth, for this time and who are trying to do your will."

After he made this prayer, he spoke to the people of the clan, "You may bet, and you may wager on this contest. Both creatures have been prepared for this battle according to tradition and neither has a known advantage over the other."

The Salt Shack Dweller, then proceeded to show the combatants to each of the spectators, but he held tight to the jars—it was not yet time for them to be stirred up. Raymond stared into the jars but also past them. The fire reflected in his eyes and already he was putting himself into a trance, so that he could better receive the communication of the Gods. Patricia thought they were both the most beautiful creatures she had ever seen as the Salt Shack Dweller held the jars up for review, with the fire illuminating the jars from the back.

The old man and the Judge both offered to referee the contest, but the Salt Shack Dweller assured them that, death would be the only referee. The priest offered to bless the event, but the Salt Shack Dweller said, that while he meant no offense, greater powers had already been involved in the matter.

"Get on with it then," said Cecilia.

The Salt Shack Dweller set the jars on the ground and removed the lids. Already the perimeter of the battle ring was crowded with curious people, vying with each other for a superior position. After waiting for an airplane to pass overhead, the Salt Shack Dweller came to the edge of the smooth stone ringed field of battle. Swiftly and somewhat violently, he tossed the creatures from the jars to face each other in combat. After a second of orientation, the scorpion straightened itself and started to survey the enclosure with no particular interest in the black widow.

Those with bets on one or the other were screaming encouragement to their chosen creature. The Salt Shack Dweller had to wonder if either the scorpion or the black widow were affected by the chaos. He concluded not. He concluded that they were receiving last-minute instructions from the God of insects.

Suddenly the scorpion lunged at the black widow, but the spider danced quickly away. A dozen times, the scorpion attacked. Each time, its segmented stinger would curl back up to a cocked position above his body. The deadly stinger was poised to strike in a downward fashion, like a silent arrow let loose from the night sky. A dozen times the stinger failed to strike its mark.

Then the black widow started undulating as she might in preparation for seduction, abandoning the hypnotic movement only when the scorpion renewed its attack. Watching dispassionately, the Salt Shack Dweller recognized the universality of the undulating movement employed by the black widow as well as the depth of its black color, as deep as a starless, moonless night sky. The dance remained the same. The black widow faced the scorpion, undulating softly, until the scorpion made its run, at which the black widow would move quickly out of range.

The Salt Shack Dweller looked into the faces of Miguelito and Donella. Though they had originally bet on the scorpion both their eyes were fixed on the seductive black widow; she had them mesmerized and dry mouthed. Donella held Miguelito's one hand so tight that they were both white knuckled.

But then, in an instant, it was over. After countless attacks and retreats and with constant undulation in between, a slight but deadly variation occurred. The scorpion made its move as usual while the black widow was undulating but instead of retreating immediately the black widow hesitated for but an instant.

As she hesitated, she drew her torso back somewhat further than she did for ordinary undulation and then she moved. Instead of moving away, however, she moved forward and met the scorpion as it came—she met the scorpion with an upward slam of her torso, her stinger exposed and dagger like transmitted her poison to the scorpion.

The scorpion's stinger came down in retaliation, but it had been caught off guard and the strike missed its mark and was ineffective. Immediately, the black widow withdrew. In a short time, the scorpion was in the throes of death and soon, thereafter, it was still.

There was a flood of emotion released by the spectators. They all spoke at once, but none, not even the betting winners, boasted of their victory. Patricia had quiet tears in her eyes. The Salt Shack Dweller was approached by Raymond.

"The Gods have given us beautiful and clear advice. The way of the black widow shall be our way. Our approach must be subtle and secretive."

"Which translates to fraud and artifice for us men," said the Salt Shack Dweller to Raymond, as they exchanged significant glances with each other.

From the darkness of the river bottom came, what sounded like the cries of coyotes and rabbits and of mourning doves all put together. The sounds captured the attention of the Salt Clan and they all stopped to listen.

The sounds came faster with increasing intensity and passion. The sounds evolved from animal sounds to the sounds of an unreasoned pleasure; indeed, there came to be so much pleasure in the sounds, that they could only be death-defying; they could only be human. The listeners searched for their numbers. Missing, of course, were Donella and Miguelito.

The clan waited patiently for the conclusion of the concert, just as they had waited for the conclusion of the battle between the black widow and scorpion and then they cheered loudly into the night sky. They cheered the beauty of both performances and throughout the cheering, the fingers of Patricia and the Salt Shack Dweller were laced together.

It could be said that drunkenness prevailed. The Gods had spoken freely to Raymond and the Salt Shack Dweller, in response to prayers and requests for assistance. Miguelito had been quickly brought back into the clan. The tragedy had diminished and there was reason to celebrate. The old man had built the fire up to a blaze and he was dancing about like a wrinkled elf.

The Mexicans, Octavio, Anastacio, and Carlos had become sufficiently acquainted with the Indian women brought to the fiesta by Donella. Always, it seemed, there was a pair in the sand continuing the music of love begun by Miguelito and Donella.

The beautiful music was now accompanied by the guitar and the voice of Anastacio who was strumming the music of love until someone else took up the guitar, Cecilia. Anastacio, though a man of many talents, could not play both forms of music at the same time. Jugs of wine and bottles of whiskey were stationed all around like squat soldiers.

In a world of their own, the judge, the priest, and Cecilia sat together in the sand, leaning up against a cottonwood stump, laughing about lofty matters made earthly, being witty and in the case of the judge and the priest being taught by Cecilia, the meaning of freedom. She was between them, and she had an arm around each.

The friends of Donella were lovely and generous young women. The ancient glow of a mesquite fire reflected beauty in the ancient color of their skin. They could see that they were outnumbered but no one wanted the music of love to be stopped and so…they gave of themselves most generously. The old man could hardly believe his good fortune. When he realized, what waited for him, he beamed yet brighter than the fire and cursed himself for dancing so hard and expending so much energy.

Raymond's mind was tangled with black widows, dams, subversive concepts, poison, fraud, and Edward Abbey. At first, he could not be coaxed into the dark by the young friends of his sister but then the undulations of the insects entered his mind and then he went quietly and willingly. Finally, late into the night, when the mortal Goddess of love came for, he smiled while the beautiful females giggled among themselves over Francis' tremendous physical stature.

They argued playfully over which of them would endure his pleasure. Francis thanked the Salt Shack Dweller for his first-rate hospitality.

The Salt Shack Dweller quietly accepted Francis' gratitude but then Francis shook his head and said, "You do throw a fine fiesta, Chief, but I can't leave my new son alone or even with these fine people. He's just not quite ready for that, so I must humbly decline the rich offer being made to me."

The boy, Carl, did get as far as Cecilia's lap, as long as one of his hands still held tight to Francis' strong and soft hand at the same time. Cecilia, priest, and the judge promptly began to speak to the boy about science, law, and religion. Once again, the Salt Shack Dweller watched Cecilia with the two men and the child, who was comfortable in her presence.

He wondered what would become of their triad; what would become of the boy? Quietly to himself he spoke words that did not need to be heard by others, *Teach them well Cecilia. We will need their power. All of them, young, and not so young.*

He looked into the night sky. Though still fully dark, the Salt Shack Dweller knew there were only two or three hours left before dawn. He could feel and smell a soft and gentle rain coming to the valley from the southwest. He could feel the beauty and the patience of the woman next to him. The time had come. Quietly and unnoticed, he slipped into the darkness holding tightly to Patricia's hand, not pulling her with him but guiding her through unfamiliar territory.

They bypassed the shack and made their way to the flour pit. The Salt Shack Dweller removed the camouflage covering from the pit and set it aside. First, the Salt Shack Dweller entered the pit, standing on bags of flour. Patricia followed. They stood together, waist deep in the pit, the sky all around them. The Salt Shack Dweller took Patricia into his arms and held her tight. He could feel her body shaking.

He whispered to her, "Do you fear?"

She whispered back, "No, I am happy that this time has come."

The night air was mild and there was a gentle warm breeze upon them. The new lovers undressed each other. Still standing, they became familiar with each other's body. The virgin Patricia, with the most to see and feel for the first time, was guided carefully and slowly by the Salt Shack Dweller and by her own senses and intuition of things. She was a virgin but she had the ability to make him feel as though he was also a virgin, without the usual fear or lack of confidence.

She calmly fitted him with a condom he gave her. They stood together, holding each other's naked body, in the naked hours of early morning, as if they were the first lovers on a new, untouched Earth. Finally, they went down together onto a bed of flour sacks, a bed of red rose flowers.

Patricia took the man into herself and buried her cries and whispers deep into his ear, as he did with her, like two great rivers running together in a circle, the source was them, the course of flow was within them and the release of the river from its seemingly endless circular flow was back to the source in a varied and powerful new form.

Time was suspended for the new lovers. They spent the hours before dawn intertwined with one another and aware of nothing beyond each other. As dawn broke gray and subtle they were wrapped in each other's arms on the flour bed, in the afterglow of ecstasy. The finest mist descended upon them, from the sky, cleansing and purifying them; the Gods approved.

For 30 minutes, they continued to embrace each other under the mist and the silence of the morning. Finally, the silence was broken by voices and laughter from the area of the campfire, but the breach was far off and not offensive; the voices were proud, and the laughter was joyful—just the thing, besides a new lover, to wake to in the midst of a (mythical) desert morning.

As the new lovers returned to the campfire, Patricia held tightly to the arm of the Salt Shack Dweller. Her eyes were moist and fresh, her smile was perceptible and constant yet quiet and from within. She had nothing to say and even when Cecilia looked at her, she could not speak, she could only broaden her smile to reveal the new sense of herself.

The members of the clan were still around the fire, which had been kept burning, even though some were asleep. Empty bottles and jugs littered the sand. Raymond, the sorcerer, was awake but he acknowledged no one. He stared without blinking into the fire. There were dams to defeat, rivers to free and people to protect from extinction. There were people to protect.

Francis, the great orderly was asleep with the small boy Carl curled up on his chest. The voices that Patricia and the Salt Shack Dweller had heard came from the judge and the priest and the laughter came from Cecilia. With the fire ring symbolizing both the sacred altar and the judicial bench, the judge and the priest were independently but simultaneously, holding court and saying mass and Cecilia was spectator to both.

The judge was presiding over an imaginary civil trial concerning a man whose greyhound dog stood accused of mistaking a neighbor's Chihuahua for a rabbit and having killed and eaten it. He was being sued by the owner of the Chihuahua. The judge kept saying that the law knew no wrong too small to remedy. The judge acted out all of the parts, including the descriptive parts involving the greyhound and the Chihuahua in their short-lived battle. The judge barked quite well.

The priest was at the sermon portion of his mass. He railed against greed and selfishness and smallness of mind. He praised generosity and humility. He praised love, all kinds of love, mental love, love of a parent, and physical love (which caused him to pause and to glance at Cecilia).

He continued his sermon more in the nature of a philosophical debate with an invisible opponent than as a religious monotone, arguing that God was present everywhere in everything. He felt that this was an important point, necessary to be understood, but he felt that no one was understanding him, so he patiently continued to explain in a hundred different ways and with a hundred different analogies. God was, for example, present in the three-legged dog that hung around the shack, and also, at the same time, present in each and every particle of mist. The Priest went on and on as did the Judge.

Cecilia's interest wandered from those two-ring show to the Salt Shack Dweller and Patricia. She did not speak to either of them but after a minute, she rose from the now damp sand and walked past them in the direction of the flour pit. The priest and the judge continued with only each other as their audience.

Cecilia approached the flour pit and peered in; where there had been a single rose stitched into each of the three white flour sacks, there was now a fourth, a delicate, soft petal rose that had blossomed dark red next to the other roses, sometime during the dark and misty night. Cecilia returned to the camp fire.

She gently woke those who were asleep and then put a temporary stop to the babbling of the priest and the judge. When she had the clan's full attention, she came to Patricia and took her away from the Salt Shack Dweller to the center of the camp, holding her hand.

The soft mist continued, "This beautiful girl is now a beautiful woman. Please welcome her," announced Cecilia in both English and Spanish.

The clan clapped and cheered as one. They nodded their heads in approval, and they smiled. The pride was collective but was best seen in Patricia's smile.

The sleepers returned to sleep, with mist building up on them and covering them like a shroud of cobweb. The judge and the priest had found each other and engaged each other in debate, the subject being pre-destination. Patricia sat on a cottonwood tree trunk by the fire, next to Donella and spoke quietly with her. They were friends now.

Miguelito slept sitting up with his head resting against Donella's shoulder. Cecilia and the Salt Shack Dweller stood back a few feet from the fire surveying the growing clan.

Cecilia spoke first, "You've done well, Bones. You drew the first blood of love and made it good for the new woman."

The Salt Shack Dweller nodded without expression. Without taking his eyes from the clan he said, "It was done well by your advice."

Now the Salt Shack Dweller turned to look into the eyes of his old friend. "And you, Cecilia, how have you done?"

Cecilia's usual confidence showed in her face, "I also have drawn first blood from a virgin and also fresh blood from a veteran."

The meaning of his friend's words were clear to the Salt Shack Dweller, but still a surprise, "You took both of these men?"

Cecilia explained, "In silence, some time ago, it was decided that we could not make a duo from this threesome, so it was inevitable that we would consummate our decision to become a triad."

"This very night?" asked the Salt Shack Dweller.

"This very night," answered Cecilia. The mist turned to a light drizzle.

"Here in the Salt Riverbed?" asked the Salt Shack Dweller. "Yes," answered Cecilia.

The Salt Shack Dweller left Cecilia and went to the priest. He embraced the priest, kissing him on both cheeks, but saying nothing and then he did the same with the judge. He could feel the drizzles of the rain on his skin now.

The significance of things occurred to the Salt Shack Dweller as he walked back to where Cecilia stood. Power belonged to those who could call for the assistance of higher powers. To do so, one needed the talent to read the messages of the Gods. The Gods had spoken, once the night before through the scorpion and the black widow. Now, they were speaking again, with the rain and the Salt Shack Dweller was overwhelmed when the message became clear to him.

"Cecilia," he whispered, hardly able to control his excitement. "The Gods are responding to us."

"Right now?"

"Right now, with this rain."

"How?"

"All of our fecundity, all of our pollination, all of our intercourse between man and woman this night in this dry river has brought forth a response in kind from the Gods. This nurturing, life-giving rain is our product."

Cecilia saw it at once, "Surely something had to be created as a result of so much physical love."

"It was the rain, it was the rain!" said the Salt Shack Dweller, beside himself now. The drizzle came harder. "Do you know what this means?"

"I believe, I do."

The Salt Shack Dweller told her what it meant anyhow, "It means we can control the rain. We can bring water back to this river. We can flood this valley with love if we decide to wipe out our enemies."

"You would need legions of men and legions of women to get that much rain," said Cecilia.

"No, no," said the Salt Shack Dweller, as though he had already thought it through. "Once we get it started like this, it should be easy to keep it going. Patricia and I, or you and the judge and the priest, or Donella and Miguelito or for sure you and I or any of the others ought to be able to keep it going."

"We shall see," said Cecilia.

"Yes," said the Salt Shack Dweller, immensely satisfied. "We shall see glorious things."

The rain came hard now. The sleepers of the clan along with the rest took shelter in the shack. The Salt Shack Dweller stayed out in his loincloth to give thanks and to feel the rain on his skin. The clan bundled up at the shack's opening to have a look at their rain drenched leader. He kneeled in the sand facing the southwest, from where the rain came and he gave himself to the rain.

Perhaps, he thought, *even such a minor offering and sacrifice could keep the rain coming once it had started.* No one encouraged him to abandon his vigil. By late afternoon, when the rain stopped, the Salt Shack Dweller returned to the shack, cold and exhausted. Everyone was gone except for Patricia. She gave him hot tea again and a strip of dried meat. She undressed him and dried him and together they attempted to bring forth the rain once more.

18

During his time of sanctifying the rain the Salt Shack Dweller also meditated on the problem of the dam on the Verde River that would destroy the land of Raymond and his people. What fraud, what artifice could be successful enough to stop a dam?

Although he could see the growing strength of the clan by each day, he understood that they were not yet powerful enough to directly challenge their main enemies; tribes such as the Salt River Project that had incarcerated the river and Arizona Public Service, the maker of deadly rays constantly infecting the people. The only way to defeat them was to be cleverer than them, to employ trickery and cunning and deceit, to be like the coyote.

Yet even while he knelt in the sand promoting the rain, he could see the paradox of his actions. To encourage the rain and to be successful gave support to the dam builders; they could point to rising waters and cry out that flood control was needed.

Upon his realization of this, the Salt Shack Dweller could only sigh and say to himself, *This is how it is when there are major battles on every front. There are bound to be inconsistencies in the tactics but there is no time to slow down or retreat, only to press forward until the battle is won.*

With this in mind, the Salt Shack Dweller came out of the rain, with a plan to stop the damn dam builders. He was confident and proud of the plan; It combined oriental philosophy with Mark Twain folk psychology. The Salt Shack Dweller thought of his plan as would Miguel de Cervantes, John Kennedy Toole, Ken Kesey, and Edward Abbey and this was how it would work.

He and Raymond would perform an act that they alone were capable of carrying out. It would be an act purposely designed to have an effect on a large number of people who could do what the clan, small in number, could not do. This plan would bring sufficient public pressure to stop the dam. The act of

Raymond and the Salt Shack Dweller would be small and fraudulent, but the effect of their action would be broad and legitimate.

Raymond came the next day. There was no time to lose. He sat expressionless in the shack smoking the rough tobacco the Salt Shack Dweller offered him and listening to the plan. Raymond approved the plan; he thought it was good and it would work.

His only question was, "When do we begin?"

"Tonight," answered the Salt Shack Dweller.

In order to pass the time, from then until night, he opened a bottle of wine. They were alone. The last to leave the fiesta was Patricia. She did not want to return to her native tribe but there seemed to be no choice. The Salt Shack Dweller felt a longing and an emptiness when she was gone and the feeling lingered; not a good state of mind for a warrior to take into battle.

After dark and after the wine was gone, the Salt Shack Dweller and Raymond began. The Salt Shack Dweller did not like to be out at night exposed to the rays. The rays were thick and growing thicker each day. Yet a warrior needed to take risks and make sacrifices in battle. The hope was that the battles could be won before the rays eroded the structure of the body and left an empty, crusted shell without life, like the dancers, in its ever marching, insidious wake.

Upon departure, they crossed the Salt Riverbed and emerged on the opposite side of the river from the park. They walked in a northwesterly direction parallel to the highway. After walking for 30 minutes, they came directly across from the corporate headquarters of their main enemy, the Salt River Project.

Raymond took his time to recite a sorcerer's chant of general misfortune and then, he alone went across the street to the premises. Outside the main building was a fountain of water, illuminated by various colored lights and made supposedly entertaining by a clever little series of pumps; this was the enemy's bold but rude expression of their domination over God's gift of water to the (now mythical) desert.

Raymond poured a vial of javelina blood into the fountain. If this piece of magic was done correctly, the blood would coagulate the enemy's water system and then the massive reservoirs of coagulated blood water would slowly dry and harden into a bristling scab upon the Earth. Eventually, the scab would dry and blow away and underneath, the once scarred Earth would be healed.

Raymond returned. The sorcerers chant and the javelina blood was but a minor diversion from their main mission. Further, on a short distance, they came to a narrow road leading to north, to a place of unimaginable horror and suffering, a place of ruthlessness and incarceration, a place of repression, depression, and death, the Phoenix Zoo.

Raymond and the Salt Shack Dweller scaled the back fence to the zoo. They dropped into thick reeds and searched their way along the narrow side of a moat until they found a log spanning the water barrier. They walked gingerly, as if on a balance beam, and there were alligators below them, yes alligators in the mythical desert.

They passed through the elephants' domain, yes, elephants in the mythical desert. They were unmolested by the elephants and stopped for a minute of silent communication with the orangutans, yes, orangutans in the mythical desert. Their presence sent the hyenas screaming and there was a vicious verbal attack by the hyenas, but Raymond put a stop to it with ease by flashing the light of the moon into their eyes from a silver fetish he wore around his neck and also chanting some secret incantation to them at the same time.

The hyenas turned submissive at once, cowed and whimpering as they rolled over onto their backs. The Salt Shack Dweller and Raymond continued on, through the morbid jungle, Dante's Fourth Circle of the Animal Underworld.

Raymond reported that the animals were speaking to him through his animal ear, his left one, and they all cried out, "Free me, free me!"

Bald eagles were at risk of becoming a myth. Other than a few survivors in the finest hiding places that still existed (for the time being) eagles 'lived drugged in cages in zoos'. An eagle in a cage for the little children to stare at. Raymond and the Salt Shack Dweller were on a mission.

They had to ignore the desperate pleas from the untold disaster of captive, condemned animals that lived dead in the zoo. They made their way to the jail cell of the magnificent bald eagle, a symbol to the pride and power of countless people, crammed into a 16 by 18 feet enclosure.

There were two, a male and a female that had been reduced to accepting dead meat tossed into their cage, once per day by their handlers. Raymond spoke to them as the Salt Shack Dweller prepared a meal of sleep for them.

Raymond said to these eagles,

The Salt Shack Dweller gently slid two generous offerings of hamburger meat (laced with a properly calculated dose of sleeping powder made from native ingredients by an old and trusted herbalist) across the floor of the cruel cage, one for each eagle. To his surprise the raptors ate with great greed and without hesitation. They had listened to Raymond; they were anxious for their permanent freedom.

While waiting for the sleeping medicine to take effect, Raymond and the Salt Shack Dweller worked on picking the lock of the eagle's criminally tiny world. Neither could master picking the lock, so they brought out the hack saw, they had the wisdom to bring with them to use in just such a situation.

By the time they had gained entrance to the interior, the eagles were starting to nod off but simultaneously Raymond and the Salt Shack Dweller heard footsteps, surely it was the nighttime guards. The eagle poachers hid against the back shadows of the eagle prison. The guards stopped in front of the eagles' shame and watched the great birds struggle to stay on their feet. The guards laughed at the eagles, they asked the captive raptors if they were drunk or something.

"This will be the last time people laugh at you or gawk at you or pester you or fail to respect you," communicated Raymond to the eagles via telepathy. *"After tonight, people will praise your power and grace and freedom and not even this will matter to you. You will be far above it all."*

The guards drank from a flask shaped bottle and laughed again and then moved on, condemned for some harsh insult to the universe, forced to wander aimlessly in the animal underworld for eternity. Perhaps their sin had something to do with a sheep.

In a few more minutes, eagles were asleep. The Salt Shack Dweller had brought two burlap sacks. With untold care and respect, they placed the eagles in different sacks and made their escape from the jungle of terror, back across the highway, beyond the corporate sprawl of the Salt River Project. They were harassed by the enemy in blue, but the enemy did not question the contents of the sacks; he merely assumed that the sacks contained hobo essentials. He did not know that in the sacks were the main ingredient to a major, but God blessed, fraud.

When the eagles woke, daylight had come but they were confined in burlap sacks with their talons bound and their wings bound, and they were bouncing along a dirt road in the back of a pickup truck.

Raymond, who was driving the truck, was aware of the eagles having awakened and of their confusion, "What kind of freedom is this, anyway?" they were asking.

Out loud Raymond chuckled and answered, "Be patient great birds, our promise to you remains the same."

The Salt Shack Dweller, without the gift of the third ear that Raymond had been endowed with, looked into the back of the truck, and saw movement within the sacks. He silently praised the talents of the herbalist who had provided him with the sleeping powder. The dosage had been accurate to the hour.

Also, in the back of the truck with a blanket wrapped about him was Raymond's grandfather, an ancient sorcerer with the rings of decades written on his face. He had dark, moist eyes that seemed to be constantly gazing into another world; he never spoke to people, he only chanted and communicated with the spirit world.

Raymond's grandfather, known as dead-tongue, had stopped speaking to humans many years ago but Raymond knew that the old man understood perfectly when he was spoken to, even if he did fail to acknowledge. Dead-tongue would play an important role in the plan that had been conjured up by the Salt Shack Dweller and Raymond.

Raymond could communicate with the birds but that was not enough; someone had to communicate with those spirts that had the power over the natural world for such things, as watching over the zoo spoiled birds, finding a proper place for them to make their nest, and gaining cooperation from the river.

Many aspects went into an artifice as grand as the one conceived by these ambitious young men, conspired in by the great birds of freedom and carried out by all of them including a century old sorcerer. Soon the eagles would have only two duties; surviving and mating.

Raymond, his quiet grandfather, the Salt Shack Dweller, and their two eagle friends reached a lovely canyon by walking upriver from the road to a spot that Raymond and the Salt Shack Dweller had agreed upon from a series of detailed maps that included an outline of the parameters of the proposed (dead) lake that would bury ancient land and homes of Raymond's people as the best place to implement their plan.

It was a semi-remote spot of the sweet desert where the desert river cut though a small canyon of moderate rock walls. First, Raymond and the Salt Shack Dweller lifted grandfather from the back of the truck and set him on a flat stone; already the old man was chanting and naturally he declined to acknowledge a change in his location. Next the eagles were taken out and set on a large slab of flat stone near the river.

Both were removed from the burlap sacks but remained bound. The Salt Shack Dweller offered the raptors sustenance in the form of hamburger meat laced with nothing. Both eagles looked suspiciously at the meat. Where would they wake up next time? Raymond laughed.

He silently told them not to worry, as soon as they had their wits about them and their strength back that they would forever, thereafter be free to hunt and choose their own meals. Eventually, their hunger gave forth to trust and they ate what the Salt Shack Dweller offered. Night came and a sharp wind picked up all that could be heard was the snapping of the campfire and old dead-tongue chanting to the endless universe from his rock.

In the morning, after an early breakfast of jerky and boiled tea, Raymond spoke with the eagles and gave them their final instructions. Dead-tongue was fixed on his rock, still chanting away and may have been doing so all night long. The sequence of events had to be right.

It was necessary that this new world be prepared for the coming of the eagles. Until they were strong and confident they would have to be taken care of. Raymond went to his grandfather, spoke with him but received no verbal reply and then he removed a leather pouch from around his grandfather's neck. The pouch gave up two pinches of dried peyote powder which Raymond sprinkled onto the backs of the eagles to produce a combination of the real and the surreal that would be necessary for the success of the grand fraud.

Raymond then spoke to the eagles,

"Your freedom is at hand great raptors. Your charge is to engage your spirts soaring high and tirelessly through these canyons. Your responsibility is to yourselves and to your preservation and this will serve us all well."

"Your duty is to be seen by human beings as much as possible, to be seen here in your native habitat, but not to be captured or killed-under no circumstances are you to be killed."

"Your obligation is to find a cave above the river or a strong tree that overlooks the river and build a strong nest, and breed and multiply again and again for as long the river runs beneath you."

"Your twin birthrights, freedom, and dignity, have been restored to you, exercise them proudly and relentlessly and above all never relinquish them."

Raymond paused, taking two more pinches of the peyote dust from the pouch and this time sprinkling the magic onto the white heads of the eagles and then concluded his instructions to them:

"Dominate this place. It is yours. Let no person, take it from you."

Raymond then called out to his grandfather in the native tongue and his grandfather's chanting became frantic. Raymond had the Salt Shack Dweller hold the first eagle while he unbound it, and he held the second. The raptors were struggling to be free while dead-tongue brought the chant to such a pitch that it turned into a piercing scream.

That same scream was picked up, like a song, by Raymond and then by the Salt Shack Dweller and at once, when the three screamers had reached harmony, Raymond and the Salt Shack Dweller gave the eagles over to the sky above with the screams following until the scream was just an echo off the canyon's walls and the eagles were soaring high above the river, distinguishable as eagles only by their white heads like two small moons revolving around the canyon and the river.

Still the scheme was not complete. After returning Raymond's grandfather to the reservation, Raymond and the Salt Shack Dweller drove toward Scottsdale in Raymond's old truck. As soon as they left the brown and dusty world of clapboard shacks and broken-down automobiles, they crossed the line into beautiful Scottsdale.

Here were ornamental (useless) orange trees, lining the roads. The houses were estates with thick, rich grounds, with thick carpet like grass yards and trees imported from Ohio. In the back of the houses were swimming pools evaporating a percentage of the pool water every day in the 110 degree days of summer and gutters along the neighborhood roads where discarded car wash water could float away from clean cars.

The Salt Shack Dweller did not need a witching stick to locate the warm water running through sewer mains below him. It made him shiver and sweat to see what his river had been reduced to and it made him even more determined to get the river back and to disrupt the infrastructure that forced the water to serve aquifer sourced irrigated turf yards and clean cars and swimming pools.

He vowed to himself, that he and the clan would bring on a flood that would free the river from its incarceration, just as he and Raymond had freed the eagles.

Besides being home to great water abusers, Scottsdale was also home to the politically active environmental class who were so squeaky clean and who mingled with the rich and powerful, always extracting promises about water conservation that never came to pass. Ordinarily, the Salt Shack Dweller had no use for such naive behavior but on this occasion, they were just what he needed.

When the Salt Shack Dweller and Raymond entered the offices of the environmental activists, it was amusing to the Salt Shack Dweller to see the reaction. The scraggly haired Indian and the skin and bones man wearing nothing, but a loincloth were handled ever so gingerly, as if it was a handout that they were looking for and as if they would be dangerous, if they did not get it.

No blood (or dirt) in this office please, we believe in peaceful change, their eyes seemed to be saying.

"May we help you?" one of the staff dared while all eyes were tentative.

"There are eagles," said Raymond in his guttural dialect.

"Bald eagles," added the Salt Shack Dweller.

"Bald eagles?" repeated the one who had spoken first, a shiny faced youth with glasses.

Many other sets of eyes became alert at the sound of the magic words.

"There are eagles! Bald eagles!"

"We saw them. A lovely young woman named Patricia showed us where they were. She found them," said Raymond.

The Salt Shack Dweller looked at Raymond, caught completely off guard, thinking, *What is Raymond saying?* But he could not contradict Raymond, who would crash their credibility.

The apparent leader of the group came forward, as though he was approaching some sort of alien. He spoke slowly and emphasized each word as if he was speaking to aliens, "You've seen bald eagles in this valley?"

"Yes," answered the Salt Shack Dweller.

"And you've come here to report this information to us?"

"Yes."

"How many eagles did you see?"

"We saw two," said Raymond. "A breeding pair."

There was a murmur of excitement from those behind the leader of the group. The leader motioned for silence, perturbed that they permitted their emotions to interrupt the interrogation at such a critical point.

"When did you see these two eagles?" asked the leader.

"This morning."

"Did they both have white heads?"

The Salt Shack Dweller revealed a bit of frustration. "Of course they had white heads. We told you they were bald eagles. White heads like two little moons revolving round and round as they glided."

The group behind their leader would have sighed at the beauty of the Salt Shack Dweller's descriptive prose, had they not just been admonished to silence by their leader, who asked another question. "Where did you see them?"

"Got a map of the Verde River, up from the confluence with the Salt River?"

"Upriver from the confluence, right here," said someone sounding nearly orgasmic as he unrolled a map on a desk.

Raymond and the Salt Shack Dweller walked to the map and pointed to the exact spot where they had freed the zoo eagles.

"Right there." said Raymond.

"There aren't any bald eagles on that portion of the Verde," said one of the group member.

"At least not that we know of," commented another.

"Quiet," commanded the leader.

He turned once more to Raymond and the Salt Shack Dweller, "Are you both sure of what you saw?"

"Yes, we are," said Raymond.

"Did you see them close?"

"Very close. And another thing. Their location is right where the government plans to build a dam for the benefit of the Salt River Project that will back up water creating a dead lake destroying the ecosystem of the area and, of course, destroying the breeding grounds of these eagles. And worst of all displacing the Native Americans whose land and homes will be underwater."

"Of course," said the leader of the eco-fanatics.

This was sufficient for the leader. He could not ignore any reported sightings regardless of how bizarre the reporters were. He jumped into eco-action. He ordered his troops to take video equipment to the sight and to set up a blind in order to capture the eagles on film.

He cautioned the troops not to get too close so as to frighten or disturb the native habitat, "Leave only footprints, take only pictures," he said in summary.

To another of his troops, he ordered that, research on the bald eagles begin, so that a press release with proper historical information could be issued upon confirmation of the sighting with crystal clear photos. He, himself, was already gathering his gear; down sleeping bag and soft frame pack, freeze dried food, quick dry pants, and shirt, hiking boots without Vibram soles, and plenty of items that said Patagonia on them.

He would go to the vicinity of the sighting for a solo outing. His hope, his dream, was to catch a glimpse of the eagles with the naked eye but even if he didn't, he could report the more human side of the story; how it felt to camp under the stars for a night where eagles soared.

A group member, who had been studying the map in silence, since it was opened on the desk, spoke out excitedly. "Wait, wait a minute everybody, do you realize where this is? This reported sighting is right in the middle of the reservoir that would be created by the Verde River Dam. If the eagles are where these guys say they are, then the dam will destroy their native habitat."

Raymond looked at the Salt Shack Dweller. The Salt Shack Dweller looked at Raymond. At the same time, they said, "No shit, Kemosabe. Glad you're now listening to us. Time to get to work, right?"

An intense silence followed. All of the group looked at each other significantly. An important sighting had suddenly taken on major importance; Dams and bald eagles and Native Americans together were perfect environmental harmony, perfect music to their ears.

"Alright," said the leader with a deep breath and a touch of nervousness. "Let's get to work. All hands on deck."

As the members of the eco-freaks scrambled about to begin their assigned chores, Raymond and the Salt Shack Dweller also glanced at each other significantly. The script had been written and the stage set. Now, it was out of their hands; now it was in the hands of the actors who were able to take to the stage.

Now, it was time for Raymond and the Salt Shack Dweller to duck out unnoticed and to drop by the priest's Parish House (since they found themselves in Scottsdale), to see if the priest was at home and to see, if he had any holy wine laying around with which they could consecrate their fraud.

Indeed, the priest did have holy wine that he was more than willing to share with Raymond and the Salt Shack Dweller. He greeted them warmly and enthusiastically and introduced them to everyone who hung around the Parish House. Everyone who focused their eyes on these two friends of the priest, everyone who wondered where the two friends had been blown in from, no doubt another of heaven's endless jokes.

The Salt Shack Dweller could see in the priest's eyes a happy, fulfilled man. "Tell me, Padre, how is life?"

The priest looked about to see if he would be overheard in his confession.

When he had assured himself that he was at a safe distance from keen ears, he whispered loudly, "Life is wonderful…and love is the answer. Before I knew Cecilia, I did not know as much as I thought I did. A woman's outlook on life can enhance your vision of life. Thanks be to God that she has enhanced my life."

"You mean making you feel more fulfilled in your life's missions?"

"Precisely," answered the Priest.

Raymond grunted his disapproval and helped himself to more of the priest's holy wine, which, to him, was the only worthwhile product to come to the new world from the servants of Rome.

The Priest laughed with Raymond's grunt. They understood each other; they were cut from the same cloth.

"So, what brings you boys to Scottsdale?" the Priest asked.

"Your fine wine," answered Raymond.

"A good reason," said the Priest.

"And we were in the neighborhood," added the Salt Shack Dweller. "Bless us, Padre, for we have committed fraud—"

He laughed and Raymond joined him. The priest also laughed and said, "So long as it was committed in furtherance of some greater good, it is forgiven."

"We've been out viewing the diminished creatures of the Earth," said the Salt Shack Dweller.

"You must have gone early," said the Priest.

"Yesterday," said Raymond.

The priest's eyes widened. He looked from Raymond to the Salt Shack Dweller. "You haven't been to the river bottom since yesterday?"

"No. Why?"

"I'm sorry. I assumed you knew and that it was the reason you were gone. Someone came to your dwelling while you were gone. They killed the goat and the pig and the three-legged dog and left the lifeless bodies in your abode. It is an unholy sight."

"Who did this thing?" asked the Salt Shack Dweller, bewildered.

"No one knows," answered the Priest. "No one was around. The old brandy drinker was at the mill, drinking with his old friends. He discovered the massacre in the morning when he returned. Cecilia and I were there by afternoon to see you and that is when we found out about it."

The Salt Shack Dweller stood. He spoke to the Priest calmly, "Thank you for the wine, Padre. I must depart now."

Raymond drove him silently through the wealth and glitter of Scottsdale to the bone-dry Salt River bottom.

The Salt Shack Dweller was sickened by the carnage that had been brutally deposited in the shack he called home. He wondered who such an enemy could be. He wondered who could slaughter an innocent goat, an innocent pig, an innocent crippled dog.

The shack was a shack of blood and death now; it was no longer a good place and the Salt Shack Dweller never again stepped even one foot inside of the shack. He abandoned the shack to decay and destruction and took up residence in the far from complete pueblo.

He spent the following days, along with Raymond, building up one corner of the pueblo into an enclosed room using the usual building materials from the Salt River bottom. When it was done, it did not differ so much from the shack, but the shack remained untouched, nothing was removed, it would weather and ruin on its own. It was now a place of evil.

19

The mystery of the evil massacre and destruction at the salt shack was explained within the week. Cecilia was present with the Salt Shack Dweller when a very sad-eyed Patricia came to the river bottom, just before dark, with a bag of her possessions, crying so desperately that her entire body shuddered uncontrollably.

Both Cecilia and the Salt Shack Dweller embraced her into a single being. They tried to absorb her terrible sadness into themselves so that she could be released and able to speak to them but for nearly ten minutes she could not speak. Finally, she sputtered out her angst.

"It was my father who did this horrible thing. He forced our story from my lips, and it drove him crazy. I've seen him mad but nothing like this. He came here and killed the animals and left them in the shack."

"I screamed and begged him not to do it. I offered to do anything he asked if he would stop, but he wouldn't or couldn't. He is a coward, and he will be back, or he might send the authorities instead, I don't know."

"I have left the house, and I won't return. I will stay here, if you two will allow it. I'll work hard and make you proud and make you happy that I am here."

And she cried and cried until Cecilia feared she would choke on her tears.

Cecilia petted Patricia from the top of her head to the extension of her arms, from here forehead to her stomach, from the back of her neck to the small of her back. She embraced her as a mother held her child for the first time. She spoke softly to Patricia transferring all the love and peace from her soul to the distraught young woman.

The Salt Shack Dweller stayed close to the two women feeling no anger, no hate. The time had come to abandon the shack and move to the pueblo. The beauty and sincerity of Patricia filled him with calmness.

To Patricia, he spoke, while Cecilia continued to bring her under control in the softest way the universe knew, "You are welcome to stay, it would make us happy if you did. I know a man who says that the family you're born into is an accident of nature. But remember, while the slaughter of innocent animals is a terrible thing, your father probably believes he is protecting you."

"What's he protecting me from," Patricia managed to choke out, "a goat or a pig or a crippled dog?"

Cecilia and the Salt Shack Dweller smiled and laughed very lightly. "No," said the Salt Shack Dweller. "From us and from the life, we live here in the river bottom."

"I don't need to be protected from you and Cecilia and the other people who come here. I need to be around all of you and learn about life. I'm 18 years old now!" she proclaimed.

Cecilia and the Salt Shack Dweller smiled again. "Yes," said Cecilia. "You are 18 years old and that is a beautiful age."

To which the Salt Shack Dweller added, "Amen to that."

The Salt Shack Dweller paused and then spoke with strength to Patricia. "And just so you know how important you are to the clan, I want to tell you that, Raymond and I have appointed you the leader of an important operation we have initiated involving bald eagles, dams and the protection of the land where Raymond's people live."

Patricia looked into the eyes of the Salt Shack Dweller. She searched for sincerity and found it. She laughed nervously.

"That's a lot of responsibility for an 18 year old's first operation," she said, "but I promise you, I will do it, whatever you and Raymond are up to. What is it?"

"Well," said the Salt Shack Dweller sheepishly, "it involves a mating pair of bald eagles that have fortunately just moved into the same area where a dam has been proposed."

"There are powerful environmental groups who will want to see the eagles and obtain proof of their existence so as to organize some of the opposition to the dam. The bigger issue is that the dam will flood the land of Raymond's people and naturally they will be the most important factor in this battle."

"They are the most powerful opposition force, but the eagles will help invigorate some of the white world. You will show the people where the eagles live, so they can see for themselves and become involved. All the people you show must sign a legal document promising not to reveal the location of the eagles to anyone else."

Patricia took a deep breath, "I will do it. I can do it. We will stop this evil dam from being built. Thank you, for including me."

Patricia's prediction about her father was correct. He sent two forms of authority to the salt shack. First, officials from the health department came and put a sign up condemning the shack. They wore medical masks because they were concerned that they had wandered into a toxic zone and a previously unknown colony of sub-humans. As quickly as they had come, they were gone.

Next were from the child welfare department looking for Patricia. This had been anticipated and prepared for; the pit had been readied to hide Patricia and there was not a chance that anyone would find her.

Despite the fact that Patricia had turned 18, she had no proof of it and as a group they decided to hide her rather than allow her to be swooped up by the bureaucracy from which she might never escape. The child welfare officials were happy to depart and fill out their paper work by filling in the box that said, *No such person found at the designated area.*

Inside the perimeter of the half completed new abode at the pueblo, the Salt Shack Dweller, Cecilia, and Patricia consumed a small amount of wine and fell peacefully asleep, the Salt Shack Dweller on the left, Cecilia on the right and Patricia in the middle. No rain came that night, but the Salt Shack Dweller had a plan in which the rain played a very big part.

When the officials from the enemy camps had ceased coming to violate the Salt Clan's sovereignty, the Salt Shack Dweller and Patricia walked to the shack and read the condemnation notice. It was a small and relatively inconspicuous notice; perhaps potential buyers would not notice the condemnation or, perhaps, the Salt Shack Dweller would remove the notice once and for all because the Salt Shack Dweller had decided to sell the Shack.

He didn't need two dwellings and he could use the money that the sale of the shack would bring in. After all, there was a powerful real estate value surge and the shack, while somewhat smaller than most of the homes being sold or built, did have the tremendous benefit of being along the Salt River bank and a river front property that couldn't be matched.

Of course, he would want to be careful of who he sold it to. There was sure to be an attempt to infiltrate the property once word got out that the shack was for sale. He made a big *For Sale* sign and pounded it into the sand by the shack.

He walked to the phone and called a real estate agent chosen at random from the telephone book and set up an appointment for the next morning.

The Salt Shack Dweller planned to get what he could out of the shack. He'd worked long and hard to build such a prime living structure at such a desirable location.

The randomly selected real estate agent appeared at the appointed time and place the next morning. The agent was a man just over 30, wearing a black suit and shiny black shoes. To conceal the startled and confused look on his face, he started talking immediately upon arrival, telling Cecilia that he had once been a teacher in the Tempe Schools but had changed careers because there was much more money in real estate than teaching.

"Amen to that," said Cecilia, happy to hear that this dollar bill was out of the schools.

He carried a briefcase in his right hand and an increasingly dismayed look on his face, as Cecilia, who had met him on Mill Avenue, led him across the park and into the river bottom toward the shack but definitely not toward the desirable homes that sat above the river bank a safe distance back.

The Salt Shack Dweller met the real estate agent, named Bob, 20 yards from the shack. The agent's confusion and fear were evident from his eyes, but the Salt Shack Dweller tried to put him at ease.

"Welcome profiteer. Thank you for coming to my residence. As I told you on the telephone, I am interested in selling my previous home as I have outgrown its size and I have a new abode under construction, which will serve me well in the meantime."

The real estate agent wanted to turn and run but there was a problem. Quite a number of people surrounded him and watched him; there was a tall, slender man standing with the woman who had shown him to this place. There was an old man, obviously intoxicated, and there was an extremely good-looking young woman who stood back with her arms folded and then there was this madman he was speaking to, some mutant left over from days gone by dressed only in a loincloth and talking of selling a clapboard shack, made of wasted materials, on the open housing market.

Worst of all was that the madman talked casually and appeared to be completely serious. But Bob did not run, he did not want to provoke this mass of insanity. His strategy was to humor them until he could make his escape with life and limb intact. But there was a great and horrible stench carried by a mild breeze from the shack that forced him to breathe only through his mouth. It was unpleasant beyond words and made him gag.

"Now," continued the Salt Shack Dweller, "there are one or two requirements that I must insist upon as the seller. The first requirement is that the buyer must be someone who meets with my approval. This clan has built its pueblo here, so we will be neighbors with whoever buys and, as I am sure you can understand, we must assure ourselves of good relations with our neighbors."

"We could not tolerate someone who did not exhibit pride of ownership in their property; that of course would decrease the value and desirability of the entire area."

"Also, it would be an impossible situation if the buyers were associated in any way with the governing body of the so-called cities that surround our small clan, this too I'm sure you can understand."

"It would not be prudent for us to be infiltrated by representatives of our enemies and therefore, it would be necessary for us to have a political interview with all prospective buyers."

The Salt Shack Dweller paused and waited to see if the agent had any questions or comments concerning the first of the requirements. Apparently, he did not, he was not even taking notes. He was simply standing silently, breathing through the gaping hole in his mouth.

"The second requirement is price," continued the Salt Shack Dweller when the agent's silence went unbroken. "We must get our price for the residence, or we will not sell. We have determined the minimum should not be the asking price. You are the expert in these matters, and we will allow you to set the asking price after I have toured the property with you and have shown you the major features of the residence."

Again, the Salt Shack Dweller waited for a response from his agent but got none, only a mouth as wide open as the eyes but still no notes or comments or questions. Perhaps the random selection of real estate agents wasn't the best procedure.

"Are you ready for the tour then?" asked the Salt Shack Dweller. The agent nodded affirmatively but without much conviction.

So, the Salt Shack Dweller led the agent to the back of the shack to whet his appetite for the property's appurtenances.

He pointed to the garden, "This property comes with an established garden. The buyers would need to do nothing more than keep it up and reap its harvest. This is an essential feature for any buyer interested in avoiding the Armageddon. You might want to emphasize that in your first newspaper ad," said the Salt Shack Dweller, who, noting that notes on such features were not being taken, added, "Take a note on that," which the agent did quite promptly.

"The property has its own independent water system, another invaluable feature, as I'm sure you can appreciate, since we do live in an area that will soon be strangled by drought," said the Salt Shack Dweller, looking out of the corner of his eye to make sure another note was taken.

"This is an irrigation system direct from the Salt River aquifer, so, there is no cost for the water, and it can be used for gardens, animals and households. You can't find this feature anywhere else, can you?"

The agent seemed to jump a bit, finally stammering, "No, no, you can't."

"That will be worth something substantial in asking the price, don't you think?"

"Yes, yes, of course. Significant!"

Now the Salt Shack Dweller turned toward the shack but while still some distance away spread his arms to give the flavor of the expansiveness of the place.

"There's acreage here, no one crowds you in and that must be a good selling point…as well as the wonderful view from this property. Look around, you can see the Superstitions, the McDowells, the Estrella's, and the White Tanks…if there has been a gale force wind for a few days to clear the filthy air away."

"And South Mountain and the Tempe Buttes and Camelback Mountain shines like crystal. From here. you feel tucked securely within the valley and the rays aren't so bad as everywhere else."

"Yes, yes, I can see that," said the agent on cue, now knowing his cue.

"This should be an easy place to sell…everyone seems to want solar these days and the place is about as solar as you can get," said the Salt Shack Dweller as he approached the shack.

"The sun actually cools this place in cool weather, but don't take my word for it, step in and see for yourself."

He held the entrance blanket back for the agent as the warmed fresh stench rolled out in waves, pushing the agent back.

He gagged and turned away involuntarily, "It smells like something died in there."

The Salt Shack Dweller let the blanket drop and stepped out to where the agent had fallen back.

"Yes, there was but they seem to be gone now." He looked around and asked out loud, "Where did the carcasses go? They were still here last night. Did somebody dispose them off?"

Patricia stepped forward, "I did. Raymond helped me. It was my fault that they were dead in the house, so I got rid of them. Raymond said he could salvage some of the meat from the pig and the goat but not the dog."

And then she started crying again, but softly, quietly. Everyone stopped what they were doing (except the agent) to walk over to hug Patricia.

"I think it might still smell kind of bad. I couldn't get all the stench out. I tried."

The Salt Shack Dweller let the blanket door drop and turned to the agent, "Well, there you have it. All cleaned up. Problem solved. Thank you, Patricia."

The agent struggled to prevent himself from vomiting. He feared, he might have offended these crazy people but for sure everything about them offended him. But he was afraid to insult them. He searched for something to say.

He examined the list of features as this wild man of skin and bones called them. One feature that he knew was nonexistent would give him an excuse to decline the agency.

"Who provides electricity to your home? Salt River Project or Arizona Public Service?"

The Salt Shack Dweller turned to the agent with slow deliberation. If he had a sacrificial temple on top of a Pyramid of the Sun, he would have torn this man's heart out and held it, still beating, up to the sun as a token of man's struggle against ignorance. He might have done so in the hot sand and rock of the Salt River bottom if he'd had a knife in his hand. His anger was palpable.

"There is nothing on my property from Salt River Project or Arizona Public Service, you profiteer. There are no liquid lights. There are no black sky stoves. There is no gene-splitting, ray-piercing air conditioning here. Put that at the top of the list of features," said the Salt Shack Dweller. "It's the most important and valuable feature of all and ought to boost the price by a lot."

Having somewhat recovered a second time but still afraid and desperately praying for a peaceful means of escape, the agent said, "Speaking of price, what is the asking price to be?"

"You tell me agent. You're the expert."

"One question I forgot to ask. Do you hold a clear title in fee simple?"

The Salt Shack Dweller frowned and said. "What do you mean, fee simple?"

"I mean how did you acquire title to the property?"

"Oh, you mean how did I come to own it? You're right, it was simple. I got it by adverse possession. Do you know what that is?"

The agent paused. "Well, yes. It's where someone possess property without objection from the owner for a certain length of time."

"Right," nodded the Salt Shack Dweller. "That's what I did. Clever, huh?"

After another pause, the agent said, "Yes, very clever."

The agent knew he would buy peace or trouble by his response. A figure too low would insult and anger these people but this was his test. He had a narrow wire to walk; if he said a figure too high, they would know he was simply trying to humor and appease them.

His only clue was the Salt Shack Dweller's comment that the lack of electricity ought to increase the price by $10,000 (which revealed a severely warped sense of value if he had ever heard one).

The agent took a breath and gave them a number, "We should list the property for at least $105,000," all the while thinking that you would have to pay someone many thousands more to come to this place of delusion and insanity to haul the place away and then to sanitize the whole area.

There was a moment of silence before the Salt Shack Dweller made a small nod with his head and said, "We had thought more like $130,000, but you're the expert. We would accept $105,000 but the buyer will have to pay your fee."

The agent quickly agreed knowing there would never be a buyer or a sale. "Of course. The buyer pays all the costs of the sale. It makes it a bargain for a quick sale. Yes, yes."

The Salt Shack Dweller gave a slight smile, barely detectable. "Go then. Make the price $105,000 and accept nothing less. And bring back one of those metal *For Sale* signs that we can put in front of our dwelling."

"I will do that right away," said the agent as he took his leave, thinking as he quickly walked away, *Like hell I will, I'll never see you or this place again.*

I wouldn't be caught dead near here except, perhaps, to show the police or Salt River Project or both where these derelicts are squatting and taking up the valuable time of honest, hardworking citizens like me.

Cecilia and the priest returned to their chosen professions and were not seen for several days. Raymond remained at the Salt Camp, along with Brandy-breath, and each day, Raymond walked to the library to read the newspaper to learn whether or not the poached eagles had been spotted and if so, what impact it might have on the Verde Dam proposal.

Each day the newspaper was silent on such important matters, covering only murders, beatings, political corruption, very serious car accidents and advertising only cheap products that everyone had an abundance of already.

It was the peak of the citrus picking season; Octavio, Anastacio, Carlos, and Miguelito were hard at work. They needed money for their sick mothers and their newly acquired material needs and desires.

The judge had a time consuming jury trial in progress and very little was seen of him though he did come out one evening with Cecilia and consumed a small bottle of Irish whiskey with his friends, lamenting the state of judicial priorities that seemed to favor scheduling commercial trails over more serious issues like child molesters.

Silent, awkward eyes passed between the Salt Shack Dweller and Patricia who smiled discreetly and whispered, "I'm 18 now, remember."

It was a time of waiting. Patricia had not returned to her parents' house and she was classified as a runaway. Once every two days, at the same time, local child welfare authorities would make a routine stop at the Salt Camp, but Patricia was always invisible. She did not want to deal with them even if she was 18.

Health officials also paid a visit to make sure that the shack had not been rebuilt. The Salt Shack Dweller and Patricia had much time alone to pass. They discussed Patricia's education. She had, of course, ceased attending her public school and was only one semester from completing high school. Nonetheless, the Salt Shack Dweller thought she was ready for university.

As much as he despised the university, he knew that a person had to go through it to learn enough to determine if it would be a benefit for them. The Salt Shack Dweller and Patricia began to make plans for her entrance to university with the first step being her finishing high school or taking the GED.

It was a time of waiting but together the Salt Shack Dweller and Patricia had no trouble waiting. Together they made rain and kept the rain coming. Together they passed countless hours wrapped in each other's enthusiasm and peace, often not speaking but listening to the rain that they were making.

The rain that came was the soft, the nurturing and penetrating kind that came in winter and sometimes lasted for days at a time, saturating the (mythical) desert floor and releasing the fresh smell of an arid land infrequently moistened, bathed in thick creosote.

The rains were perfect preparation of the ground for a great flood that the Salt Shack Dweller was planning in his busy mind. The soft, ground-filling rains were the necessary prelude to massive runoff from major storms yet to come. In the mountains, there was snow accumulating and waiting. In the valley, the Salt Shack Dweller and the Salt River Clan were gentle and patient, passing time without fear.

The winter garden at the Salt Camp had been planted and with the rain plentiful, the produce had a good start along with the weeds.

One morning, while Patricia, Cecilia, and the Salt Shack Dweller were weeding the garden in bare feet with sand and mud between their toes, Patricia spoke, "I don't want to go to the university until I'm a little older, maybe a year or two."

The Salt Shack Dweller and Cecilia nodded their approval, so Patricia continued, "So what am I going to do in the meantime?"

"We'll study the Greek tragedies together," said Cecilia.

"We'll work on finishing the pueblo and you will help stop the dam," said the Salt Shack Dweller.

"That won't take up all my time, I'm so young. I might need more."

"Do you have something in mind?" asked Cecilia with a knowing look on her face.

Patricia blushed brightly. Cecilia focused on her with an encouraging smile.

"Go ahead," she whispered.

Now looking at the Salt Shack Dweller Patricia smiled a childish smile. "Well, maybe…you know…maybe I could have a baby."

Soft tears filled her eyes and her lips shivered, "Your baby. I mean our baby."

She shook her head all around. "You know. All of our baby; you and Cecilia and me."

The Salt Shack Dweller was silent for a minute. He looked at Cecilia who was calmly watching him, "Have you two been talking about this? Did you know about this."

Before Cecilia could answer, Patricia directed what appeared to be a flash of anger at the Salt Shack Dweller.

"You fool," she said, "of course she knows about it. I love Cecilia as much as I love you. I want her involved. I want her approval. I'm the luckiest girl in the world to know her. She probably knows more about it than either you or I do. I want all three of us to have a baby. It would be the best baby in the world."

The Salt Shack Dweller could not control his grin. He looked at Cecilia. "Did you hear her call me a fool? That might be the highest compliment I've ever had bestowed on me. A person has to be at least part fool to accomplish anything."

Then he turned to Patricia. "And I'd be a fool not to want to have a child with you."

"And with Cecilia," said Patricia. "She going to be one of the parents too because she's the smartest woman in the world and I asked her to help me, and she said she would."

"Marvelous," said the Salt Shack Dweller, smiling at both of them.

For the first time in years and for the first time ever, Cecilia spilled tears in front of the Salt Shack Dweller and Patricia. Once she sort of composed herself, she said, "Patricia and I are good friends. We do talk to each other when we can. When she asked me to be part of this parent trio, it felt like the highest honor of my life."

"You know, I was never able to have a child of my own. Now Patricia knows that too. I admit, I sort of like the plan, but I told Patricia that I'm not sure of the timing."

Cecilia turned lovingly to Patricia but also with a comforting frown. "You're so young. When you have a baby, your youth is over. As smart and wonderful as you are, you still have to learn how to live in this world. Don't be in too much of a rush. A baby cannot be undone."

Seldom used emotions encased the Salt Shack Dweller and prevented him from speaking for several minutes.

"The Gods have been more than good to me with you two in my life."

Then he turned directly to Patricia and looked deep into her eyes, "A child with you and Cecilia will be everything when the time comes. For now, you must continue to grow and learn, so the power you gain will serve you and those that you love, for all of your life."

"How long do I have to wait," asked Patricia with soft tears dropping from her eyes. "I've been waiting to start my life for all of my life. I'm tired of waiting."

"You have started it now that you live with the Salt Clan. You will have much freedom and much responsibility."

Cecilia smiled broadly and wrapped her arms around Patricia, and then pulled back and spoke with a glitter in her eyes. "For now, just remember my mantra—*no condom, no entrance*."

"Why don't I just take birth control pills," asked Patricia.

"Why should you?" said Cecilia. "Why send foreign chemicals to your perfect reproductive system when there are condoms to prevent pregnancy and they also keep your precious bodily fluids pure."

"Well," Patricia blushed, "I've heard that boys, and men I guess, don't like condoms."

"Well, tough luck for that fool. Simple as that. You're the one in control."

Patricia laughed through her tears while at the same time telling Cecilia how much she loved her.

"Harsh, but true," said the Salt Shack Dweller. "You can always trust Cecilia to tell it straight."

20

Several days later, Raymond showed up in the late afternoon. He brought with him a newspaper that he had borrowed from the library. On the front page, there was a photograph of two birds flying deep in the blue sky.

Beneath the photograph was a news story headlined: EAGLE HABITATION DISCOVERED ALONG THE VERDE RIVER.

The Salt Shack Dweller read the article and as he neared the end, a smile broke over his face. Though there was no official confirmation, it was strongly suggested that the discovery of eagle habitation, which would be wiped out by the building of the Verde River Dam, might be the death knell for the proposed dam, not because of two eagles but because two eagles would serve as the common denominator for the various grassroots groups that opposed the dam project.

As I thought, the Salt Shack Dweller allowed himself to think. Raymond appeared to be in a trance, dancing circles around the fire and chanting unintelligible but grateful songs of thanks for the great victory.

The Salt Shack Dweller turned to Patricia, "This call for a great celebration. Let's call the entire clan together. You have contributed greatly to this victory by guiding so many nature lovers and bird freaks to witness the existence of the eagles."

"As always, Raymond's people deserve the credit for protecting their land, their people and their homes. Just remember you were a part of that."

The only two, besides those who were already present, who could be summoned for a victory celebration that night were Cecilia and the judge. Because the judge came, the celebration included Irish whiskey. There was much to celebrate but only a handful to participate.

A major section of a river that flowed into the Salt River had been saved, the land of Raymond and his people would not become the bottom of a reservoir, twice uprooted eagles would not be uprooted again, and a dam would not be built. Everyone celebrated as hard as they could, and Raymond did not stop his dance of thanks or his native chant despite the torrential sweat that poured from his body into the sand.

Brandy-breath saw to it that the fire was always supplied with wood and Patricia's face glowed by the fire, happy, and beyond her face, the Salt Shack Dweller was watching the salt shack reflecting the flames. At midnight, he took a torch from the fire and tossed it inside the shack.

The shack (containing 0% humidity) exploded into flames while the Salt Shack Dweller called out, above the roar of the inferno, "We sacrifice our abandoned abode in thanks for the great victory you have given us."

The small clan cheered. All were happy to see the shack go. It had become a blight on the Salt Camp since it was given over to innocently executed animals. Also, it would mean the universally disliked real estate agent would have no reason to return.

Raymond, conscious of the larger fire, transferred his circular dance to a wide circle around the flaming shack. All the others stood, mesmerized by the flames. When, after a time, the flames died down and the shack collapsed in on itself, Raymond also collapsed in the sand. Cecilia made a quick check of him, determined it was nothing more than exhaustion and instructed that he should be put to bed in his sleeping bag. Brandy-breath stayed with Raymond to guard and protect him.

The Salt Shack Dweller and Patricia were left to complete the celebration. What celebration to the reprieve of an entire river could be full and final without the making of a little rain to the runoff that inspired the river to run faster and harder for a few hours bragging about its freedom?

In the pueblo, the Salt Shack Dweller and Patricia consummated the wonders that the clan enjoyed by making rain; yet when the rains did come, they came so hard that Salt Shack Dweller and Patricia observed that Cecilia and the judge must have been in on the act as well. All the better, they said to each other and no doubt that the Verde River was inspired as well to run hard and fast like a new river in a new world.

Life was good at the Salt Camp at the start of the new year. Jet airplanes, high-tension power lines, and the constant stream of filthy automobiles prevented complete peace and tranquility, but life was still good. Over the year, the clan had grown to include a variety of people. The pueblo was now inhabited, the garden produced bountiful crops, the rains came steadily in promise of a great flood. The Salt Shack Dweller had the girl-woman Patricia with him and the world's reigning and still the most fantastic woman, Cecilia, was expanding the clan with dedicated followers of many talents. There was a serenity to life that he had never known before.

Still there were nights when Salt Shack Dweller would leave the bed he shared with Patricia and sometimes with Cecilia and Patricia to sit in the opening of the pueblo to watch the night. Full moon nights were the best; a bright moon could light up the mountains all around (the Superstitions Mountains lit up pink under a new moon).

The jets would stop for a few hours in the early morning as would most of the cars and the tension would be nearly gone from the high-tension wires. Nights without a moon were good for hunting small game along the river bottom but not for star gazing since the sea of liquid light that filled the valley blotted out the stars.

The fruits of Salt Shack Dweller's hunts were released unharmed these days. He had no need for the game, and he knew if he didn't spare their lives there would soon be nothing left to hunt. He caught the same rabbit six times. It would come to him when he whistled.

It was not frequent for the Salt Shack Dweller to hunt at night. Usually, he felt compelled to sit in the pueblo's opening to watch the night. In the night, there were rays that came hard and fast, and he felt they were deadlier than ever before and sometimes he admitted to himself that the rays might have the power to overwhelm him.

Within the walls of the pueblo, he was safe from the devastating power of the rays but exposing himself to the naked night regularly, would be foolish with a constant river of rays as far as the night eye could see, up to the top of the sky and out to the farthest horizon-the night had been stolen by the rays.

"Let there be darkness, let there be life," the Salt Shack Dweller would find himself crying, in the pueblo's opening, until a hint of sunlight would appear in the eastern sky, forcing the rays into a temporary retreat until the next time of darkness when they would reappear in greater numbers and with greater force.

The ever increasing onslaught of rays gave the Salt Shack Dweller cause to contemplate darkness and death, birth and decay, resignation and inspiration, which he did in a sort of possessed state of mind, sitting cross-legged in the pueblo's womb, where he was safe, in the early hours of the

January nights, until Patricia or Cecilia or both would wake, find him gone, and join him or lead him like a sleepwalking child back to the bed of the (mythical) desert's morning cold.

But the time of waiting without acting was nearing its end. Despite the great victories and coups achieved by the clan, with him as their leader, he felt impotent and passive in the face of the constant aggression from every angle, every day. In his mind, he speaks, *That's how they work, that's how they defeat you.*

With one eye on the moon, the other on the rays, his mind-speak continued, *They attack you in silence and integrate themselves with the fibers and connectors of your body and your mind and then they segregate you from your manly instinct to do battle, to fight your own annihilation and genocide. They pervert your integrity.*

They ravage your potency and worm into your mind to sap your will to resist their imperialism and colonization. They get inside of you, they penetrate you, they are countless in number and relentless in pursuit, until they have filled your mind and your body with passiveness and weariness.

They put you to sleep and if you wake from sleep (unlike the dancers he'd seen frozen in time, a deadly monument, their souls and their eyes and their tongues gone) you awake a different person, not yourself, but one of them. So, waiting must end before it's too late, he said to himself with on eye still tracking the moon, *before the rays have succeeded in silencing me and reducing me and my clan to the status of a subjugated people. The ray machine must be stopped before a single ray penetrates the next generation.*

So, he left the pueblo's womb but not on the night of his resolve. It was 20 nights later, into February, when the month was short, and no one pays any attention.

He waited because it took that long, lying awake after an hour or two of Patricia's innocence and warmth in the not so quiet and the not so peaceful hours of the night, to develop a solitary plan, a plan he could implement himself without the assistance of any of his lieutenants because this act of sabotage would be of extreme danger and would require the maximum stealth that could only be realized when a warrior works solo and because the penalty for failure or capture must certainly be death by firing squad and *I, the leader of the Salt Clan, can only ask myself to take such a risk.*

We all came out of the corners and shadows of the bright night and accumulated ourselves in a group, on the perimeter of the Salt Camp after he'd started out that night by himself at 02:00 a.m. on a cold desert morning, in just his loincloth.

He chose the night of the full moon and therefore, we could see him walking alone, among the smoothed stones of the Salt River bottom, picking his way silently and carefully like a retreating figure in a dream. We remained quiet and still so as not to alarm him with our awareness of his furtive departure from the camp.

None of us, including Patricia or Cecilia, knew the nature of his mission but it was easy to guess that it was of the utmost importance. He had not discussed the matter with any of us and he had been pensive and contemplative for a month, he had been distant and preoccupied and had only nibbled at his food like some kind of a little rodent, say like a kangaroo rat.

We all noticed, until finally, without explanation, he fasted from food, taking water only these past three days and then we knew that something was up. We all knew that this night, the night of the super moon, would be his night of action.

I, Raymond, who had been with him on missions and campaigns of our history, wanted desperately to chase after him and join him in his secretive maneuver, whatever the danger, but the clan stopped me and prevented me from dashing into the muted light of the great moon to follow him.

Even young Patricia said, "Let him go. From the way he has been this last month, we must know that, this is something he must do alone and I hope he succeeds and gets it out of his mind, whatever grand scheme it might be."

It was a cold night and my loincloth did little to keep me warm and the moon reminded me of a frozen sun, encouraging me on my mission because a frozen sun is a dead sun and I imagined that this view I was experiencing of the Earth and the sky, this cold, quiet night of muted light was just as it would be in the not too distant future if the ray machine was not stopped.

A lifeless planet, once called Earth, but then called nothing because there would be no one to speak about it and no one to name names, leaving the ray machine spewing forth rays, surpassing all the rain drops that have fallen on Earth since time began.

His progress across the river bottom was slow because he departed the Salt Camp silently, without waking or disturbing any of the clan because he had decided that none of them should know of the mission until it was complete, and he could return to report to them that their greatest enemy had been neutralized.

But visions of success were not in the forefront of his mind when he stumbled among the stones, some nearly as big as basketballs, on the river's bottom. There was a time, he admitted to himself, when he would have floated across the river bottom, as blithely as a monarch butterfly on its migration from Mexico but this night his steps were difficult and awkward, the stones hurt his bare feet and it occurred to him for the first time that perhaps he was aging and the thought only concerned him in the sense that there were still battles to be fought before he could rest and enjoy living on the banks of the free flowing Salt River, when he would grow a long beard.

As I neared the bridge structure and then moved into its lower shadows, I awakened the sleeping pigeons but not the cooing mourning doves and once again, I reviewed my plans of attack on the ray machine.

Without my full army behind me, I knew, because I had contemplated my plan day and night these past 20 days, that a frontal attack on something as massive and water consuming as the ray machine was hopeless. Brute force was not the way, it could only lead to defeat.

No, I thought it would be necessary to outsmart them. Like a Zen master, I had to find a way to turn their power against them, of using the awful power that they have developed to destroy them. So, it was not necessary to even go to where the ray machine was, more than 50 miles to the west, all that was necessary was for me, to go to the enemy's corporate headquarters where the computers that operated their ray machines were. It was the brain of the machine that I was after.

So, I walked down the Salt Riverbed, turned right on Central Avenue, and made my way to Fifth Avenue and then to my goal, the home of Arizona Public Service.

Arizona Public Service, more like Arizona Death Service constantly zapping the people and the animals and the plants of the Earth with their wayward nuclear rays. Their arrogance to try to fool the people with the name Arizona PUBLIC Service sickened me.

Walking quietly in the quiet, dark night, I realized the beauty and simplicity of my plan. After figuring out how to gain access to the building, I would make my way to the computer room, identify those computers that controlled the ray machines and then instruct the computer to signal a ray machine malfunction and shut itself down.

And then code a repeat of the malfunction notification instruction over the next three months at random times. The enemy would search for a cause, not find one, decide it was a once in a lifetime error, until the code triggered the next shutdown, over and over again. A permanent spell, a good old-fashioned jinx, would eventually be the only explanation that the people would accept.

So much had the Salt Shack Dweller been concentrating on the reflective beauty of the Zen plan, reflecting back upon his enemy and the arrogance of their safeguards, their intelligence, their strength, their dominance, the fear of their customers to confront them, that he was only tangentially aware that he had completed his journey and was now standing before the dark side of the corporate building more than ready to gain entrance and execute the grand plan.

It was 03:00 a.m. the moon made the night like day and still the buildings and security grounds were lit up like a stupid Christmas tree. Arrogance knew no boundaries.

<h1 style="text-align:center">21</h1>

People come to stare through the interior windows. From the inside, you can see the look on their faces as they watched me. I never blinked. It is always as if they are looking into the cage of a wild animal at the zoo or as if they are staring at a lifer at the penitentiary. For more than eight days, they have had me locked up here for observation.

They took away my native clothing and replaced it with baggy white pajamas designed to humiliate and subjugate meeker souls than me. They serve plastic food, but it is refused and even the jail's medical advisor doesn't know what to do with the silent faster, whose identity is still unknown.

The medical advisor is considering force feeding because the strange man was skinny enough when he was brought in a week ago but now the man is an empty bag of skin and bones, who would not say what he wanted.

The medical advisor wasn't about to have the man die of starvation on his watch. There had been deaths before of course, by suicide and even murder. That was to be expected in a nuthouse for the jailed, but a death by self-starvation, a death from voluntary fasting was too much like a political statement, though the son-of-a-bitch won't tell us what he wants.

"He won't tell us a goddamn thing," the medical administrator yelled at his assistant, when his assistant dutifully informed him that the silent man had refused food for the third day and that the press was asking for photographs and a daily report on his deteriorating condition and asking what he was locked up for anyway and the medical administrator was not about to have that kind of death on his hands at his institution.

It was a trick, some kind of a communist trick, to put me in here, this looney bin, instead of in a normal jail with normal prisoners when they caught me fooling with the computers for their ray machine that night, a mere eight nights ago now. They caught me before I'd learned how to make the computers shut down the ray machines and sing out in a chorus of flashing lights and horrible, deafening emergency alarms, screaming, *Nuclear alert, nuclear alert, malfunction, malfunction.*

They say they hate the communists, but they are more than willing to employ their terror tactics against their most feared dissidents, in this case me, the leader of the potent and feared Salt Clan. They simply designated me insane rather than criminal and manipulated the system of their own design to put me in this crazy room rather than in a regular jail where I could have visitors, including the press.

This is much worse than when I was locked up by my so-called wife in civil detention to determine if I was a threat to myself or others. Not to myself for sure but for damn sure to others and the bigger they are the greater the threat I am to them.

This is much worse than a jail cell because here they can keep me forever, they can keep saying, *He's not recovered yet, he's still a danger, we have to keep him longer.* Yes, it was a communist trick, but I had a few tricks of my own, the first was clamming up from the very start so that not a word left my mouth and not a morsel of food entered my mouth, and the only exception were fluids and then let them explain starvation to my supporters and the press.

There were hospital officials and staff I came to recognize when they came to stare at me through the window, but I never blinked and never changed expression for any of them, there was nothing they could do to bring me around and they would learn that the only thing that would work would be unconditional release and an apology.

There was one man, however, who came to stare through the interior window at me and this was a man from the Salt River Project who was in charge of all the water resources, the most powerful man in three states. Or maybe he was from APS, or maybe from the zoo, or maybe from the airport, or maybe from the citrus fields.

They all look alike you know. They all travel together. One snarl is the same as all snarls. When he came to stare, when he was alone, then and only then, did I allow any show of expression. To this man I would raise my upper lip in all the viciousness I could muster and then snarl like a mad dog and to my surprise the man paused only a second before he mirrored my action by snarling back with primeval disdain and a taste for blood equal to my feelings for him and then I knew that I had an enemy to the death worthy of the great antagonist pairs of history; I promised that man, through my canine teeth, that I would be an adversary and an opponent worthy of his wildest dreams.

When Cecilia and judge finally arranged the release of the Salt Shack Dweller from the mental hospital on the 11th day of his fast, we were ready to receive him at the Salt Camp. Outside of the mental hospital, there were standing curious onlookers wanting to get an in-person look at him. The newspapers called him *undomesticated man*, and they analogized him to a wild animal that refuses to eat or mate in captivity.

His weakness was great and he should have been in a wheelchair but he refused, as we knew he would, so Raymond and Anastacio each helped him along, one of his arms draped over each of his comrades, with not enough strength to keep his head up and, of course, a newspaper man got a photo of him like that, hanging Christ; like between the Mexican and the Indian while a strange band of assorted well-wishers cheered him as he limped forward.

The only thing that caught his attention as we departed his incarceration was a well-dressed man snarling at him like a wild animal afflicted with rabies. The Salt Shack Dweller did not have the strength to respond.

At Salt Camp, we had obtained a real mattress for his bed in the pueblo, but he refused it and so I, Patricia, made him a new one out of dried leaves, left over flour, sand and pigeon feathers. Even the slightest contact with his emaciated body caused him extreme pain. Cecilia brought his meals for us to give him. They were all in liquid form, high in protein and nutrients and at first difficult for him to take.

He slept a great deal, but his sleep was fitful and pained and he frequently cried out, "I have failed. The rain of rays continues, I have failed."

When he was awake, he was morose. Healing him and loving him again as I wanted to do so badly seemed a long way off, but I was willing, and I was happy to care for this man who had awakened my mind and my body and who had changed my existence from instant oatmeal to smoked dove and squash.

My recovery was slow. Not only was my body empty, so was my mind and my voice. I felt wrapped in the pollen of lethargy and all I could think of was my failure to strike a blow against the ray machine and how easily I allowed myself to be captured by my enemy. I was unarmed and they were not but still I felt, I should have gone down biting and scratching and kicking, adding a little spit onto their computers for good measure as I was dragged off instead of going with them so calmly and silently upon my capture, as if there was some kind of pride in going gently into the night.

We all watched him mope around the Salt Camp, at this time a useless appendage to the clan instead of a leader to us. The days were again growing longer, and the sun grew warmer, slowly firing itself up for the burn of summer that was to come. He could be seen wandering in the river bottom to pass his days, slowly recovering the health to his body despite himself but without showing any evidence that his mind was on the mend from whatever affliction controlled him.

He spoke almost not at all, which broke my heart despite Cecilia telling me that time would heal him. I didn't really think of it as a personal rejection, mostly I saw it as a time of trial, and I only prayed that it would soon end. I was getting a little tired of it. Sometimes he could be seen standing idly in the middle of his neglected garden, staring off toward the mountains to the north and the east, truly not concerned with any of us or even himself as far as we could tell.

This is how he remained until one night at the campfire when he happened to join us in body if not in spirit, refusing to drink any of our wine or whiskey. The entire clan was present, though he hardly acknowledged anyone, he just continued to stare into the fire when Cecilia, who had been in active consultation with Donella for several days, announced that Donella was pregnant.

Miguelito blushed as crimson as the fire, while Cecilia went on to explain, diplomatically, that due to Donella's rather prodigious size of body in a non-pregnant state, that while pregnancy might have been suspected for quite some time, it hadn't been confirmed until just that day. Birth was expected within two months.

When Patricia heard Cecilia's words, they came into her mind slowly, like cool water through the hot water pipes of summer and suddenly she realized the meaning of it all and looked up from the fire, looked to Cecilia and to Donella for their eyes to be sure this was true and when she saw that it was true she asked for confirmation, "There's going to be a birth at Salt Camp? Can I help with the birth? Please? I'll do anything you ask me to do. I'll do anything!"

And finally, the Salt Shack Dweller smiled and spoke, "It is good, it is good. A birth in this place by one of our people will make this a real place with a history."

When everyone finally stopped smiling and laughing and congratulating Donella and Miguelito, Octavio stood up like a boy in school and addressed Cecilia.

He said, "What I want to ask is whether she was made pregnant before or after Miguelito lost his arm because I am curious to know if the child will have one arm or two?"

The clan laughed enough to fill the sky. Octavio laughed with them, then continued, addressing the Judge, "No, what I really want to know your honor is, whether the beautiful baby will be a citizen of this country so he or she won't have to worry about being kicked around so much?"

The Judge stood up. "The child will be a citizen of this country as long as Donella and Miguelito stay here and make sure that the baby is born here. And if the baby doesn't like it here, he or she can go to Mexico and be a citizen there. The baby will have many options and many opportunities."

The Priest stood up, "We will make this place a place of baptism for the child and we will use blessed salt water even if we must send an expedition 100 miles up steam to retrieve pure water from above all of the dams."

Finally, after much discussion and celebration about the magnificent news that would begin to insure the clan's future existence the Salt Shack Dweller stood up and said once more, "It is good. It is a sign. It is a gift from the Gods."

Then he took me by the hand and started for the pueblo. That night he made love with me like he hadn't since he went on his mission to destroy the deadly rays and I responded to him in kind. He was right. It was good. As we finished our love making the smell of rain came to our place and soon the rain started, to our delight, steady and penetrating and once again life seemed grand and eternal to me.

22

When the predicted date for the birth of the child of Donella and Miguelito came closer, preparations for the birth of a child at Salt Camp got under way. Anastacio was given $50 by Cecilia and the judge to buy a live pig that could be kept at Salt Camp until the first signs of labor in Donella occurred, at which time we would slit the pig's throat, save it's warm blood in a jug for the child, if it turned out to be a male child with two arms, then begin to pit-roast the pig then and there.

Anastacio was given his charge and the money on Tuesday but we did not see him again until Sunday afternoon and in the interim we suffered through rumors brought to our attention by Octavio that Anastacio drank, whored and gambled away $50 and the truth of these rumors was feared more than usual because not only would Cecilia and the judge have to be told by someone (certainly no one wanted that job) that Anastacio had squandered $50 but it would be an extremely superstitious omen for the unborn child, that funds to purchase his/her first meal had been wasted instead on wine, women and cards.

Worse yet, some of us posited, what if the rumors were true and the child turned out to be a one arm child. The auspiciousness of the omen would then turn dangerously threatening. But all of the angst proved to be unnecessary speculation as Anastacio returned with a fat and healthy pig in tow, stating that he and the pig had been to church that morning but refusing to say whether the rumors were true or whether the $50 he bought the pig with, was the same $50 he left the Salt Camp with five days before. Anastacio smiled and winked at his comrades.

The jealousy that once had infested and existed in Donella's soul had fully healed. Between the time when Cecilia first announced to us that Donella was pregnant and the time of her labor, Patricia and sometimes Cecilia, shared a sitting log in the Salt Camp where they spent their time sewing new shirts for each and every member of the clan, shirts they called birth-shirts, mandatory apparel for the time of birth.

Brandy-breath provided the material for the shirts by snatching yards of flour sack material. He washed the burlap five times to make it (sort of) soft and he helped Cecilia and Patricia design a pattern that would place the deep red rose of the flour sack over the heart of each shirt.

Patricia was especially pleased with the prominence of the rose, for it, reminded her of her first blissful night of love in the flour pit with the Salt Shack Dweller, laying gently and passionately on the three red roses of the three flour sacks, but she did not mention this to Donella.

The weather was ideal and not even the hottest part of the day was enough to drive Patricia and Donella in search of shade; they sat all day and sewed and ignored arriving and departing airplanes directly overhead, nearby rushing traffic and speeding electricity all around them.

Octavio had undertaken the duty to clean Salt Camp to make it immaculate and the best possible place to begin life at. One of the biggest jobs was the sweeping of the grounds with a brush-broom; a task that this patient man did grow weary of. Then he would call out to Miguelito, who spent his days as an expectant father sitting idly on the banks of the river staring into its emptiness, trying to understand its purpose and contemplating his future.

"Hey, Miguelito, my boy, soon to be a proud father, get your one-armed ass over here and do a little sweeping while I take a rest."

I was back in body and mind though I moved somewhat more slowly, somewhat more contemplative after the failure of my mission and my time of protest fasting while incarcerated. I felt these events had aged me. I thought that we bipeds should live shorter lives or else much longer lives so we could either spend our time in a flash of energy and then be gone with our youthful accomplishments or have a long time to methodically and carefully accomplish something worthwhile like abolishing plastic (plastic my boy, the future is plastic).

I dared not contemplate the rays. Each night I hid within the comfort and enthusiasm of Patricia's love allowing her to take me back to exuberant youth, to that happy mixture of ignorance and unquestioned certainty that measureless time lay quietly ahead to accomplish any goal the mind was capable of challenging. With my failure, I came to terms, but this meant abandonment of the helm, no longer could I legitimately consider myself a leader of this clan for I had failed to protect them from the deathly devastation of the rays.

Worse yet, now a child was to be born into this sad condition, the first of a generation that would never know a night without rays, who would never know whether his or her first (and possibly last) sickness was caused by the rays messing with its DNA.

A child who might rightly blame us for destroying the water, the air, a planet that depended on a basically steady climate when the only thing we really needed to be self-sustaining sent its love to us every day, Mother-Sol.

Even so, the Salt Shack Dweller was happy, even proud, that there was to be a birth coming to the Salt Camp, for the wonder of man and woman was that with every new birth came another opportunity that the greatest wonder of all would come forth. With this thought, the Salt Shack Dweller realized that he had now recognized the genius of Sophocles. He stood where he could see the moon and recited, quietly, inserting a mere two words of his own:

Wonders are many, and none is more wonderful than man (and woman). This power spans the sea, even when it surges white before the gales of the south wind and makes a path under swells that threatens to engulf him. Earth too, the eldest of the Gods, the immortal, the unwearied, he wears away to his own ends, turning the soil with the offspring of horses as the plow weaves to and from year after year.

The Salt Shack Dweller saw that there was all manner of necessary preparation under way around him. Some of the clan were gathering food for a feast to celebrate the birth and some were making common clothes for the baby. Some were making Salt Camp as clean as a maternity ward. Cecilia was in attendance for Donella and the priest was hand crafting a crib and a playpen from native woods gathered a day's journey away on the Mogollon Rim. The judge had enlisted the aid of his pocket book, spending his lunch hours shopping for infant care items and then carefully hiding them from his wife until they could be delivered to Donella.

For his part, the Salt Shack Dweller spent much time in the riverbed practicing his reed flute so that the child would come into the world greeted by harmony and order. He also began construction of a small drum, the skin of which came from a rabbit he had caught six times in the past, one that came now when he whistled. A rabbit that would, with sad eyes, sacrifice itself up to become a drum skin for the celebration of the first born at Salt Camp.

It seemed to the Salt Shack Dweller that with a new life, a new being about to surface from the underworld into the blue world where blue means water and water being the essence of life that he should start a movement to add an Eleventh Commandment to the never before updated Ten Commandments.

And what better time and place to reveal his proposed Eleventh Commandment than the once magical Salt River with the presence of the beautiful, brilliant clan, all of whom, along with every living creature needed water to survive this life.

When the time was right, the Salt Shack Dweller stood silently, until the clan members grew curious and one of them, perceptive Cecilia of course, said, "What's up, Bones?"

The Salt Shack Dweller took a deep breath, then spoke, "Before the birth of this wonderful child, I urge support and devotion from all living people in this world for the addition of an Eleventh Commandment to the original Ten Commandments to guide the lives of the men and women of this Earth."

Without doubt the Salt Shack Dweller most certainly had the attention of everyone present. Octavio translated for those who might not comprehend commandment-speak.

The Salt Shack Dweller nodded to each person present and then began.

"The Eleventh Commandment I propose shall read as follows:

Thou shalt not domesticate the rivers, nor

Convert them to the service of golf courses

Or flood irrigated grass lawns, or marry them

To nuclear plants, or pour them into a hole in

The ground for swimming, or any other such

Depravity that threatens the virginity and

Autonomy of such river."

A short silence followed the announcement of a new commandment. Then Patricia's hand went up into the air followed by all of the English speakers and then by the Spanish speakers for a show of unanimous approval and solidarity. Then there was cheering.

Waiting for a baby to be born can be tedious. As time passed everyone could see that both the priest and the judge were engaged in ardent contemplation following the Salt Shack Dweller's nomination of an Eleventh Commandment. Both seemed frozen in thought. Eventually they both started to speak at the same time and then they both attempted to encourage the other to speak first. It was only after the priest smiled and said that he had taken a vow of silence that the judge came forth with what was heavy on his mind.

"It is not only the Ten or Eleven Commandments that tugs at my soul. It is also the seven deadly sins: pride, envy, gluttony, lust, anger, greed, sloth. I don't know which of these sins I am guilty of but probably all."

"So here is my confession, to obtain the place that I had in this world, I am sure that I committed these sins many times by doing the bidding of the power brokers and ignoring my heart and soul which have ached for a very long time. And though I do not wish to say this publicly, I must also acknowledge, and yes, confess, that I have also failed my family."

"God willing, I will find a way to remedy that as well. So, I would like to offer up an eighth deadly sin, stupidity. And a ninth, willful ignorance. I sent people to prison for possession of an innocent weed, marijuana. I've signed orders evicting single mothers from their homes. I have denied my wife and children. The list goes on. I am guilty, but not, I hope, any longer. Thank you for listening."

Cecilia turned to the Judge with a concerned look on her face. "Did you lose your job as a Judge?" she asked.

"I did," answered the former Judge. "The judicial counsel removed me before I could quit. They discovered that I manipulated the case assignments so that I was the Judge every time Bones came to court and most recently on a case where I prevented the Child Protection Agency from taking Carl away from Francis. I just didn't think any other Judge could or ever would understand Bones or understand Francis and Carl."

"How did this effort to take Carl away from Francis come about," asked the Salt Shack Dweller, fearing that he already knew the answer.

"It doesn't matter," answered the Judge. "This is going to be good for me. The Legal Aid Society has already offered me a job."

"It was Harold, wasn't it," said the Salt Shack Dweller.

"It was. He recognized me from when he was here the other night. He made a report to the Child Protection Agency. When I rejected the petition to remove Carl from Francis, Harold researched how the case ended up in my court. Then the gig was up. I was removed as a Judge. I'll say it again. This is good for me."

The entire clan, one by one, started by Cecilia, walked over to the judge and shook his hand.

As the procession came to an end, the Priest spoke up, "Well, it turns out that the Judge and I have more in common than any one person would be able to guess."

And then he laughed deeply leaving no doubt that he was not being facetious but was equally as happy as the judge.

"I have been removed from my status as a priest by the bishop pending further training."

Even the Salt Shack Dweller was stunned by the dual confessions. He could see that the Priest had a sincere desire to include the clan in his confession.

"Please tell us what led to this, Father," said the Salt Shack Dweller.

"I will be happy to tell you. You all are my closest family. About a week ago, I was teaching a catechism class at my parish. The children were eight to twelve years of age. We were discussing the absolute requirement that for entry to heaven one must accept Jesus as their savior."

"One boy who had traveled a lot to third world countries with his family looked confused. I called on him to ask what his question was. You could see he was nervous but eventually he said, 'Well, what about people in Africa who never heard of Jesus before they died. What happens to them?' I knew in an instant that I was without an answer; I had wondered about the same thing many times."

"I dismissed the class without answering the boy. That very night at dinner with other priests and the bishop I told of the boy's question and my failure to have a proper answer. I was asking for help. A couple of the other priests were trying to make themselves invisible but certainly not the bishop."

"Without hesitation he told me that the answer was to tell the boy in very strong terms, to never speak blasphemy again and to follow it up by rolling up my shirt sleeve, making a fist and telling the boy that the next time he challenged church doctrine that your fist would be the answer."

The priest saw nothing but stunned faces. Patricia was silent but tears ran onto her cheeks.

The Priest started again, "The bishop asked me if I had any other disagreements with church doctrine. To my own amazement, I said yes, I did. I told him that I disagreed with the vow of Chastity. I said it was an obvious disaster that unnecessarily damaged the lives of countless priests and countless boys."

"I said the church might as well require a vow of fasting for life; it's not going to work. I told him that I disagreed with the way the church treated women and finally, I told him about that absolution via confession, to me, seemed too simple."

"I told him, some confessors, confessed to horrible things with a heavy dose of se la vie, now I'm free to run wild again. The bishop looked at me without speaking for a long time and when he did speak he told me that I was suspended from all priestly duties or privileges until I had been retrained and reset and been approved by him for resumption of the holy, infallible teachings."

Once again, each clan member stood up and walked to the priest to shake his hand. Like the judge, the priest said he was not unhappy about being relieved of his priestly duties. It gave him an opportunity to review his life.

The first to speak was Donella, "But who will give my baby the baptism rights, Father?"

The priest smiled like he felt capable of feeding the multitudes. To Donella he said, "I will, little sister. I will. Your child will be blessed tenfold."

The Salt Shack Dweller was truly stunned but not incapable of speech. In a slow, deliberative voice, he said, mostly to himself but also to us, "For how long have I been praying? Bring us Charlie Mingus, Linda Ronstadt Cochise, Geronimo, Stewart Udall, Zane Gray, Paolo Soleri, Sandra Day O'Connor, Cesar Estrada Chavez, Rose Mofford, Jeff Fake, Gabrielle Giffords, and Bill Ott."

"Where is the courage to dream? Where is the courage to listen to Spike Lee and do the right thing? Has it, by God's will, regenerated here and now with these Indian people, these Mexican people, these white men and women, a black man and his adopted white child? Tell me please. Send me a simple sign that a mere mortal can understand."

And then, for all of us to hear clearly, he said, "From this day forward, Harold, is no longer a person in our eyes. He no longer exists for us. He will never again be welcome to arrive at the salt shack. And that goes for the bishop too."

Cecilia, naturally, broke the silence following the edict of the Salt Shack Dweller, "Well, we win then. Thank God, it's not a zero-sum game. We get a new born baby, we get the judge, we get the priest. We lose Harold and the bishop. A terrific gain and nothing lost."

23

On 27 March, a fine day, Donella entered labor. Cecilia was summoned; members of the Salt Clan donned their red rose shirts, while Raymond jumped on the pig, slitting its throat with smooth dispatch, collecting the pig blood in a gourd. Three hours later Donella stopped her labor without giving birth.

"What happened?" everyone asked.

"A false labor," announced Cecilia.

"When will she start again?" asked a terrified Patricia.

Cecilia shrugged that it was a matter of nature, not science, she could not say, maybe hours, maybe days. Raymond said without humor that it must come again within hours because he had already killed the pig and the pig meat would spoil if not cooked and eaten soon and besides that the ceremonial events, he planned for the newborn called for fresh pig's blood and fresh meant less than 12 hours outside the body of a living pig, according to his grandfather.

Once more Cecilia shrugged without concern, there was nothing she could do about the matter, a false labor was a false labor, not uncommon and she hinted calmly, that perhaps Raymond should not have been so hasty, perhaps he should have heeded the orders of the great native war chiefs not to fire until he saw the reds of their eyes, which we all more or less agreed with but did not say.

Especially since Raymond was getting mad, mad enough to yell at his sister for fooling him with false labor. Accusing her of not caring whether or not her unborn child had the benefit of proper ceremonial birth rites, an accusation vehemently denied by Donella to the point of tears, leading Miguelito to comfort her with his one arm and defend her against Raymond.

Octavio instructed Miguelito to stay out of the matter, arguing that the dispute was a family dispute between brother and sister, besides he agreed with Raymond that women shouldn't fool men with false labors, especially with first born, and especially when questions of correct procedure for ceremonial birth rites hung in the balance.

Throughout the debate the Salt Shack Dweller played his flute for us, and Patricia sat close to him, somewhat timid in her youth but wide-eyed over the conflict evoked by poor Donella's false labor. A conflict which might have continued unabated into the night had not the judge, to our relief, exerted his authority of reasonableness by intervening and quieting everyone down.

He calmed the situation by revealing its prematurity. Perhaps Donella's true labor would soon begin (we all looked at Donella hopefully) and if so, then nothing was lost, the pig and the blood would be put to its intended use.

If, on the other hand, Donella's labor was delayed, then the only loss would be a $50 pig, no great loss in itself, since another pig just as useful as the dead one could be purchased with funds donated by himself. *Ah,* thought Cecilia, *money can salvage so many things.*

Labor was delayed. By the afternoon of 28 March, there was no doubt that the pig carcass and its blood would not be used. The Salt Shack Dweller and Octavio undertook to dispose of the useless pig. Anastacio was given a fresh $50 with instructions not to delay.

He promised to strictly adhere to his obligation. Raymond still showed signs of silent anger at Donella, but he also felt responsible for the $50 loss, so, he spent two days picking up aluminum cans along the river bottom, miles up and miles down, netting $9.24, which he turned over to the judge despite the judge's efforts to refuse Raymond's can money.

Meanwhile the Salt Shack Dweller and Octavio were busy hauling the dead pig far down the river bottom, far enough to prevent the foul stink from assaulting them but not so far that they wouldn't be able to listen to the song of the coyotes.

As they started back toward the Salt Camp the Salt Shack Dweller was aware of a man dressed in a suit standing on the far bank of the river, snarling at him like a mad dog, in the recently turned cool breeze, as if it was his personal property that was being defiled by the dead pig carcass. *This was the enemy,* thought the Salt Shack Dweller, the one he had seen the day he was released from the insanity cage. Octavio did not notice the man.

The man was ignored by the Salt Shack Dweller, for now, as he turned and started back up the river bottom, thinking, *This is not the time for confrontation. Confrontation will come. But now is the time for the celebration of the Salt Camp child, the beginning of our future.*

In time, he knew, that eagles, hawks, falcons, and other grand birds would spontaneously regenerate from the smelly mess and populate the empty skies with their presence. And in time, he and the snarling man would meet with dominance of the Salt River Valley at stake.

The 29 March was silent, and it found us all sitting around in the sand waiting for Donella who had started apologizing for being late. The wait did seem eternal but none of us used that word in front of Donella. That evening, however, the judge, the priest, and Cecilia gave up the vigil and departed, leaving instructions to send a runner when something important happened.

But they did not depart until the priest and Raymond came to a civilized agreement, that they would both have the opportunity to initiate the child into the world by their own chosen means. Raymond with pig blood and the priest with sanctified water from the Salt River.

It was agreed that Raymond would be first, since Donella was his sister, and the priest could follow. Donella and Miguelito, overwhelmed by the attention, assented to the arrangement at once.

The morning of the 30 March dawned cool without the sun. Rain teased but did not come. By noon, the Salt Shack Dweller completed his drum and we found that to be a good thing, perhaps prophetic, because several hours later, Donella went into labor. Those absent were summoned by a runner, a cousin of Miguelito, and Raymond killed the pig and set it in the mesquite filled fire pit to roast.

When Cecilia finished examining Donella in the temporary ramada, we had constructed she came out from the ramada, and she made the formal announcement, "Start the fire and the drum. Prepare the pig. This is not a false labor."

The Salt Shack Dweller started a soft drum beat on the rabbit skin drum that invited the chanting to begin. As darkness set in the smell and sound of mesquite wood grew as well as the moans of labor from inside the ramada. Patricia did not move a muscle but each time she heard a moan or a cry from Donella she voluntarily mimicked the sound until she was called to assist Cecilia in the delivery.

Along about full dark the judge and the priest arrived, bringing wine and whiskey and their ceremonial robes. Soon the full moon that had been promised scaled the Superstition Mountain peaks and conquered it. There was steam from the water kettles in the fire pit and there was mystery and real magic in the air. It seemed to all of us that this was a night for rebirth, and for new birth.

Throughout the night the Salt Shack Dweller alternated from the drum to the flute and there was a sense of nervousness in the clan, no doubt a reflection of the tension and nervous energy in the sky; speech and laughter were forced and somewhat artificial, frequently broken by cries of labor pain; we were all waiting for Donella.

Though the priest had been preoccupied with the general communion around the campfire, and with the whiskey, he suddenly jumped up as if he had been stung by a scorpion with a sense of panic in his voice.

"The sacrament of marriage! Oh, my God! The marriage must precede the birth. We are in danger of allowing an illegitimate child to be born!"

This ignited a wild debate, with the priest being severely outnumbered and loud voices pronouncing that there was no such thing as an illegitimate child regardless of the circumstances of the birth. Just when we had reached agreement that all children were sacred in the eyes of God, the Salt Shack Dweller spoke up and took exception by declaring, between flute and drum, that computer designed, laboratory manufactured children might be considered something different (he notably avoided the word illegitimate) in the eyes of natural born people, born of woman.

We all found this concept to be somewhat esoteric and we basically ignored his input on this subject, definitely outside his range of expertise, leaving the priest free to carry on with the obligatory marriage, somehow managing a prone Donella and a highly confused Miguelito while Cecilia and Patricia worked around them to bring the new child into the world.

In a minute of magic words and witnesses, the deed was done and the Priest was back on his log, sipping a bit more Irish, but inwardly in turmoil due to the strange look Cecilia had zapped him with, apparently as a result of his claim that the new child might be illegitimate without his intervention.

Old dogma designed to control women still held strong with the priest, thought Cecilia, but rules of celibacy for priests became as invisible as the Holy Ghost when offered access to a sweet honey pot or even a young boy.

Oh, my dear God, thought the Priest, *have I just lost the irreplaceable favors she bestows on me?* Sweat poured from his face.

Finally, in the last hour of the night, Donnella's cries of pain came more frequently, a good sign, until they were constant like the race of clouds across the sky, until, like the end of a long climb, there was a released silence. We too were silent, except for the flute, waiting.

Cecilia emerged from the darkness and the silence and appeared in the glow of the campfire with Patricia. We could see the fire in both of their eyes.

Cecilia nudged Patricia, who spoke with tears softly covering her face, "Donella has asked us to tell you that, a boy child has been born at Salt Camp"

There was an eruption of eight hours of pent-up excitement. Miguelito wept openly. Anastacio cried quietly. Octavio jumped up and down, slapping his arms against himself.

The judge and the priest had their arms around each other, each with a cup of Irish, each grinning and each saying back and forth to each other, "Aye, he's a fine lad, he'll go far."

Brandy-breath ran up to touch the infant and Patricia continued to cry silently next to me. When I looked up from the flute, I saw for the first time the beautiful firstborn child of Salt Camp, bloody from birth, silhouetted in front of the blood-red moon.

Cecilia, standing as still as stone except for the excitement in her chest, looked like a statue of life and continuity. The unearthly beauty of the event brought tiny tears to my eyes but when I saw, to my final unbearable distress, the snarling rays already licking and penetrating the unprotected child's brilliant brown skin, I wept openly, a gushing torrent of tears.

I wept in front of my family, and they thought the crying was joy, a joy that should infect all of us to the point where the entire Salt Clan, including the child, were soaked in tears. So much did we cry that we must have primed the opulent clouds that filled the sky with enough moisture to bring forth the rains because within a few minutes we had all taken shelter, huddled tightly together with the newborn, who was being fed at Donella's breast, in the tiny, covered portion in the corner of the pueblo.

This is where we stayed until the first light of dawn when there was a brief respite from the sweetly penetrating desert rain that had lasted all night. The Earth was rich in smell, deep brown in color, moist and fecund when we emerged from the pueblo to perform the child's birthright ceremonies.

Raymond went first, mixing animal blood with river sand. He applied a drop to each fingertip, a drop to each toe on the child, each time chanting an incantation in his native tongue, each time imbuing the boy with a different virtue or a different strength so that when he was done the boy had a reservoir of strengths and virtues: swiftness, alertness, judgment, courage, wisdom, compassion, Wiley senses, leather like skin, penis strength, Spartanism, coyote eyesight, resourcefulness and kindness along with some more obscure and primitive ones thought necessary by Raymond.

Now the boy had blood-red painted fingers and toes which Donella and Miguelito feared would create confusion in the boy as to his masculinity, so Raymond relented and said it only needed to stay on the boy for one hour to be effective and then he washed it off. The remainder of the pig blood was poured in a gourd and left under a bush for kangaroo rats, rattlesnakes, roadrunners and quails to consume as a means of thanking them, as a means of returning to the animal world a portion of what was taken from the animal world by humans.

Next came the priest to perform his ceremony on the child. From one hundred miles upriver, where the river still actually existed, he had obtained a vessel full of Salt River water that he had sanctified. He was dressed in his flowing robes of black and white with a gold sash. We watched as the priest, who looked more like a migrating bird than a person, let his colors billow in the wind to merge with the dark storm clouds of the sky like the opening of an ancient rap opera. The heavens were preparing to add another soul into the great, unfathomable mystery of life.

As an assistant the priest utilized the judge who wore his drab black robe but who, compared to the full ceremony dress of the priest, appeared to be just what he was, a secular helper. Like Raymond, the priest had his assistant hold the child into the sky, offering him and his innocence to the Gods above.

Also like Raymond, the priest spoke incantations (in Latin tongue) as he poured the holy salt water over the child's head to wash original sin into the sand, leaving it to filter through the crust of the Earth to accumulate and add to great pools of original sin sludge somewhere above hell but far below the surface of the Earth, the only danger being that it would trickle down further and flow into vast aquifers of underground water resources and contaminate that great body of pure water thereby, once again, infecting us with the disastrous condition of original sin, *Ahh, the circle of life.*

When the priest released the water from the elaborate and ornate challis, he also released the rain from the heavy clouds and down it came again, soaking us and doing battle with our discouraged campfire, but none of us moved until the priest's ceremony was completed and the poor, crying, twice ritualized child was returned to Donella and Miguelito.

And then we all commented, "What a beautiful day for a child to come into this world; what a year for the rains to come."

And we all knew of what we spoke because we were all native to Sonora. And we all knew enough to get out of the rain, except for the Salt Shack Dweller, who neither joined us in our comments concerning the wetness of the year or in our escape from the cold, continuous rain.

While the rest of the clan took cover from the rain, I remained standing under the dark sky. Yes, I shivered, it was a cold desert rain and I allowed myself to dream, once again, of a great flood, at least the possibility in this year of the great rains, and I vowed to do everything in my power to keep the rain coming, recalling those things done by us that had inspired the rain to fall in the past, such as lovemaking prayers to bring the great rains and our collective tears on this birth night and the priest's spilling and splashing of the holy water from the Salt River where it was still a free river.

I returned to the pueblo and crowded in with the rest of the clan in the small dry corner out of the rain behind both Cecilia and Patricia and prayed silently for the same strength of penis that Raymond had imbued the new born boy child with. I would send my warriors upriver a 100 miles to collect great vessels of Salt River water, vessels made from the ballooned intestines of javelinas.

I would find a way to generate collective weeping of the clan in the form of prayers to the rain Gods so we could bring forth a river of tears on a minute's notice. I would make love with Patricia and Cecilia and all the other males and females of the clan would make love all around in honor of the rain Gods so that the Gods might look favorably upon us and keep the desert rains pouring down.

From inside the pueblo, I could see the priest and Raymond. They both wore the smile of Saints and as if by miracle they both spoke at once, "There is life in this place, there is life all around us from the Earth to the sky."

Finally, from far off, I could hear the depth and the promise of this unusual and perhaps accommodating rain, and I was able to reach out and touch our continuity.

24

The rain stayed with us for a week. It seemed to depress each and every one of us except for the Salt Shack Dweller who seemed apart from us and driven by some new found inner spirit that none of us could quite penetrate. Each day he requested at least one of the clan to go miles upriver (using Cecilia's car) to gather and collect great volumes of Salt River water that he simply dumped into the sand when it arrived.

He brought us together each night and told us heartwarming stories of human tragedy until we wept collectively; only when he succeeded in making us weep was, he satisfied. And when he wasn't pouring water onto the Salt River bottom or telling us tragic stories, he asked us to make as much love as we could.

On Thursday of the week of rain, the Salt Shack Dweller began construction of a raft. His materials were pillaged from the neighboring villages and merchants or scavenged from the great piles of debris jammed against the massive concrete pilings of the Mill Avenue bridge. He worked for three days and nights and he refused to concern himself with the rays that were firing gene and chromosome poison at his body.

He worked throughout the night, taking time out only to dump the water filled intestine balloons into the sand and rock of the still dry river bottom. He did not eat, and his only drink was when he took one or two swallows from each delivery of Salt River water before dumping it.

His raft began to take a semblance of shape late on the second day. Its base was random sized timbers lashed together as tightly as possible with leather and dried coyote sinew and where necessary hemp rope. On the third day, the base of the raft was complete. The Salt Shack Dweller then started construction of a very small boat house with a peaked roof and shingles in the center of the raft using the most renegade and degenerate building materials imaginable.

The entire clan was intensely curious as to the Salt Shack Dweller's purpose, but he would not speak of it, he would say only that his mission was to act darkly and swiftly rather than spending his energy talking about his intended actions. Patricia had a stone of fear growing in her gut, knowing that the Salt Shack Dweller was most certainly on an insane mission and knowing only that whatever it was would be insane and dangerous.

Alone, I went among the orderly and subtle pestilence of the smug villages where all the houses looked alike and all the people were asleep while a doom that they could not see, appreciate or believe in grew like the universe's first three minutes. I went to find a weapon suitable for the destruction of the ray machine.

A solitary black butterfly accompanied me. Time was of the essence and only I was aware of it. No more would I permit myself to rely on seductive logic of a Zen-like attack, of turning power inward against itself; this was western technology, and it could only be eliminated by western power. The attack would be frontal and brutal, with no pretenses, an attack the unforgiving conquistadors themselves, mi padre, would have admiration for.

Alone at midnight, my black butterfly with me, I scoured the construction yards under a bright moon for dynamite to place at my enemies' doorstep. It was, in the end, my furtive butterfly friend that located a dozen cases of the powder for my use. I took them all. I carried them two at a time to a fine hiding place and then returned all night to carry two at a time back to the flour pit where I had captured the hawk and where I had first made love with Patricia, a well fertilized spot for the weapons of doom, for the destruction of the universally evil ray machine.

When the beautiful God given storm played itself out, it was followed by the warmest weather of the year. The sun again occupied the sky alone. Donella brought the salt child, named River Wind, out from the damp and dank corner of the pueblo into the sun to drive the wrinkles from his shriveled skin and return to him the rich chocolate brown color and skin texture his heritage promised him. Miguelito could not stay away, he was drawn to the child like a magnet; he was curious and proud, and he followed mother and child constantly like a lost puppy, stealing glances at the child, still mystified that credit for fathering the boy belonged to him.

Cecilia came frequently to attend to both mother and child. Octavio and Anastacio waited for the Earth to dry out so they could return to the fields to work. They insisted that Miguelito must accompany them and work twice as hard as before since now he had not only a wife and child but only one arm to do it with. His hard life was about to get harder than ever they told him. In Miguelito's eyes, one could see the burden of his responsibility at such an early age. Brandy-breath took pity and said he too would go to the fields and earn money to help buy food and clothing for the mother and child. In return, he wanted nothing more than to be an honorary uncle to the child.

More rain, a very warm rain, came after the sun had been with us for two days. The Salt Shack Dweller's silent delight was unrestrained. In the morning, he hunted the Salt Riverbed for the smallest scorpion he could find and when he found the one, he wanted to put it in a box in the boathouse on the raft.

In the middle of the day as a warm drizzle continued from the sky, the Salt Shack Dweller took me, Patricia, to the place of our wet campfire in the middle of the Salt Camp. He pointed to a man standing on the Mill Avenue bridge staring at our village with binoculars.

We returned to the man's stare with our own binoculars. The man wore an expensive suit and on his face was the mad snarl of a wild dog. He looked like a cruel person.

The Salt Shack Dweller accepted the look of the man without expression, saying quietly to me, "Remember that man. He is our enemy. He seeks to destroy us."

But I never did get the binoculars focused and did not see the man, just a blur.

That night, just after dark, the Judge came up at a furious pace, breathless and agitated like none of us had ever seen him before.

As soon as he had our ears, he spoke very fast. "They are going to flood the Salt River. They have already released water. The snowpack is melting fast, too fast, and the warm rain and temperatures have compounded the problem."

"The lakes upriver are at capacity, and they must release a torrent to protect the dams. We must move Salt Camp to higher ground. They've started with almost no public notice. Flood waters will be here before dawn."

We all looked to the Salt Shack Dweller to see what his reaction would be but he had turned and was staring up to the Mill Avenue bridge where the multitudes of cars were speeding by unconcerned, where overhead airplanes stayed the course without concern, where the high-tension lines continued buzzing life to the televisions and to the liquid lights illuminating the bridge and beyond, far beyond, to the mountains of Father Kino.

But the Salt Shack Dweller saw none of this. He could only see that man standing on the bridge, still in his modern uniform, also wearing the jackal's sense that the kill was imminent, his eyes burning like luminescent coal, waiting and watching for the dark and silent flood waters on the Salt River to violently swallow and devour, once and for all, the Salt Camp and its clan.

But the look of the Salt Shack Dweller was calm even though our homeland was about to be wiped out, along with our beloved pueblo. Serene and calm, he appeared at peace as much as the child River Wind was, suckling at his mother's breast. It made us wonder if the source of his serenity was his raft tied securely to a stout tree at the river's bank.

None of us said anything about the raft to him, afraid of giving him ideas. Most certainly it couldn't be his plan to pilot that heap of junk he called a raft down the flood filled Salt River, not even with Mark Twain. It would be simple suicide, and no one needed to say it to know it.

It did not take the Salt Clan any time at all to remove all of their material possessions up onto the bench of the dry Salt River and out of flood danger. Among them there was a somber atmosphere, waiting for the flood, waiting to be witness to the inevitable destruction of what they had built, the pueblo, the gardens, their waterworks.

But these were people who had already, in their mostly young lives, experienced disappointment and loss; they knew how to deal with it. Perhaps the judge and the priest were the most apprehensive. In their hearts lingered an unspoken fear of what would happen to the interesting, offbeat friends they had made at the Salt Camp. Would they lose all that they had come to love and cherish?

The clouds broke and the rain stopped at midnight. The night air was fresh and beautiful. Cecilia lounged in the collective arms of the priest and the judge. Donnella and Miguelito were like young lovers again with their child asleep on Miguelito's chest. Anastacio, Octavio, and Raymond were gambling and nibbling peyote on the grass on the bench above the dry river. Brandy-breath sipped brandy, secure to be with his adopted family, content to watch the sky.

Patricia sat between my legs with her back to me, my arms wrapped around her waist. She was the one among us who seemed uneasy. I came to think, she might have black butterflies in her stomach, for me, knowing as she must, despite my silence, that I would ride the impending flood waters at dawn on my great mission and her concern for my welfare and safety this night touched deeply and made me understand even more that I loved this innocent child of a woman, and I kissed the back of her neck gently and quietly.

Only because my back was toward him was I able to hide my thoughts from him and even then, it was not an easy thing to do. He was preoccupied with something, this business of the raft and his mission. I was afraid for him. He was stubborn. Sometimes, he was foolish. Sometimes, he frustrated me and made me mad.

Renegade and rebellious now, water always found its way back to the Salt Riverbed. We saw it before the sun at first light, coming swiftly like a huge snake down the middle of the riverbed all the while broadening, flattening and engulfing. This was free water that would not be humiliated into bringing forth liquid light to steal the night or sweet oranges for the breakfast table of Chicago or Carolina style turf lawns.

It was red and thick under the light of dawn, and it flowed proudly, extending itself for show in its march, like a conquering army that no enemy dares to oppose but simply submits amid a universe of white flags. We were all silent, listening to the growing music of the free River.

Anastacio, the young Mexican with gypsy cunning and luck in his eyes won a day's wages from Octavio because the river arrived before the first dance of sunlight pierced our position. Rapidly, the river was deepening at its middle and spreading toward its bank toward us, and toward the raft that sat dry and beached at a cockeyed angle only twenty feet from the river's flow path.

The Salt Shack Dweller stood and spoke as gently and as peacefully as any of us had ever heard him.

He said, "We have made this river, a river again and now it will join our cause."

He entered the river's bed, still dry two feet out but rising fast, asking none of us to accompany him. We watched him parade between the flour pit and the congress of defeated flotsam that he called a boat, which was crammed with boxes containing who knew what. None of us were naive.

We understood that he really did, after all, intend to ride that wild river on that ridiculous contraption to some silent purpose he no doubt saw as absolutely mandatory for the survival of the Earth. Still, we were not overly concerned when he finished stocking the raft and returned to our company on the river's bank to await the rising water as we passively watched the water run over our garden and backfill our waterworks and submerse the base of the thick mud wall of the pueblo to erode away so that it would eventually tumble of its own weight.

We were certain that the flood waters would simply wash over and drown his silly raft of old nothings. We were sure it is heavy as ironwood raft would never sit on the surface of the water. But his engineering skill surprised and horrified us.

Unknown to us he had lined the bottom of the raft with floats of old oil drums so when the water of the flood crept beneath it the raft rose to the surface like a heap of scrap somehow pumped full of air, creaking and straining all the way until it was, indeed, afloat, held in place only by the taught rope that secured it to a River bank cottonwood.

Only then did we become serious and highly concerned and we all expressed our sentiments.

The Priest said, "Do not do this thing, whatever is in your mind. To voluntarily enter danger where there is no hope is suicide, forbidden by the church. That river is now wild, it will swallow you before you reach 24th St."

Then the judge, intoxicated with too much fear, shook his head and asked with uncharacteristic sarcasm, "Do you have a will my friend because you are going to need one."

Miguelito and Donella accused the Salt Shack Dweller of wishing to deprive their newly born son of his godfather.

Cecilia sneered as she spoke, "Go ahead you fool, you'll never be happy until you've permitted your rebellion to kill you. You have a martyr complex begging to be released."

Anastacio and Octavio pleaded. It was all incomprehensible to them.

"Why do you want to do this thing, amigo? Stay with us and drink some wine and play some cards and watch the river from here, it would be much better, we think."

Raymond shrugged at the clan. "Go ahead mi compatriot, do what you must, there is no damage for I snuck aboard your vessel in the night and saw to it that you had as your guardian the tiny scorpion. I gave it the power to swim as well as to sting, so I believe you will be safe and protected on your secret mission."

Everyone had spoken except for I, Patricia, and I could find no words, my tears chocked in my throat, and I was afraid to look into my lover's face for fear that I would see the sign of death on his forehead and would still not be able to persuade him to abandon his madness?

Since I would not look up to him and since I could not speak and since my face was flooded with tears, he bent down next to me and kissed me on the ear and said, "Do not be afraid my love, I will return when I have destroyed the thief of the night, and I shall not fail again."

And just like that he was gone with the black butterfly in attendance, wading through the waist deep flood waters to board the raft as the sun, for the first time that day, overcame the clouds and pounded the Earth with heat. He gave Raymond the signal to cut the line between him and the river bank, setting him adrift to the west, slowly at first, into the mainstream of the now raging Salt River.

As we watched the raft drift into the mainstream until it was a mere dark spot far downstream, we were silent until silence was broken by the terrifying and elemental sound of a wall of flash flood water roaring forward without mercy. The vanguard of the increased water rushed by us in a vicious anger, hysterically chasing the Salt Shack Dweller.

We screamed for him to turn so that he could prepare himself for the surprise attack from the rear, all to no avail, and by that time he was so far downstream that we could no longer see him or the effect of the rushing wall of thick brown water upon him.

Everyone expressed their certainty of disastrous consequences but for one, Patricia, who was now silent and dry-eyed, her eyes fixed on the Mill Avenue bridge rather than downstream where her lover might well be ten feet under.

Her eyes through binoculars scoured the bridge, some magnetic force pulled her attention in that direction, and she saw, still on the bridge, the man the Salt Shack Dweller had identified as the enemy, the corporate king of the Salt River Project.

She could see the sneer the Salt Shack Dweller had pointed out. She could almost hear the snarl but when she focused the binoculars, she could see that the man was also using binoculars and was looking directly at her and she knew the man, she knew her father's sneer and his contempt. She had seen it many times before. With the powerful binoculars, she was able to see into her father's hate-filled eyes as if she was standing directly in front of him.

She was chilled, not knowing what else to do, she renewed her attention to the dark water that was turning and churning muddy brown and white, running free but also a cesspool transporting a universe of garbage and pestilence built up for years and miles, more than a mortal young woman could imagine.

The first of the clan finally departed, after two days had passed and by the end of the fourth day all of the clan members had dispersed but for Patricia who continued the vigil. The judge promised to find out what happened and to report back to everyone. Octavio and Anastacio went to the fields of yearlong vegetables courtesy of the great Salt River.

Miguelito and Donella went first to the reservation with River Wind but finding it barren and impoverished they traveled to Mexico, sneaking across the border ten miles east of Sasabe to no one's concern except a desert farmer's three-legged dog.

Brandy-breath hopped a train to visit a cousin in Milwaukee and to escape the summer heat. The priest returned to his unauthorized desert pulpit to hear the confessions of the unfaithful, the judge to his new desk to try to save the victims of capitalism, insurance companies and used car dealers.

Cecilia returned to the hospital where hospitalized citizens greatly needed her but not before asking Patricia to come with her somewhere to live. When Patricia declined, Cecilia promised that she would return early every morning before her work shift started to offer any assistance Patricia desired or requested.

Patricia waited. The river stayed full but flowed calmly day and night, much of its stink flushed downstream. The sun lingered longer each day and grew hotter, well into the nineties. When the child welfare officers came around asking her, if she knew of or had seen a teenager named Patricia, she calmly answered negative and when they asked if she was that person, she answered that she was not, that she was an emancipated 18 years old sovereign citizen of the Earth.

Transients and bums slept in their clothes with empty wine bottles for pillows all around her but none of them bothered her. Softball practice at the nearby baseball diamond started up in the early evenings when the temperature was perfect, and the blue pool was filling with water as midday heat under the all-consuming sun started to reach for the century mark. Patricia waited, always looking downstream.

She waited through hot days in June when the sun brought everything to a burned and silent standstill with a century and a tenth registering in the shade. The river was gone. It was once again tamed and that which had escaped in the flood had long since run to Yuma to meet the criminally castrated Colorado River where the joined rivers still failed to reach the Sea of Cortez and where the flood water soaked into the ground, finally falling in great cascades of dark, underground waterfalls through the abyss of cavernous space left blank by the rapidly depleting underground water table.

The Salt Riverbed was bone-dry, bleached white, and the smooth rocks the size of grapefruits could be heard as they cracked open at night like dried nuts when they failed to cool but no fruit juice or honey flowed from the broken rocks. Patricia no longer paid attention to the cars boiling over or the thunderous jets or the nervous buzzing of the high-tension power lines.

It was on the summer solstice, when the desert world is an inferno of blazing sun and heat, white and blinding, relieved only by a few dry hours of precious darkness, every other hour melted and welded into an eternity of fire, when she saw the Salt Shack Dweller walking toward her on the floor of the Riverbed from the west.

She first saw him an hour after sunset and she calmly watched him approach, shimmering and watery, mirage-like, in the flat distance. It seemed to her that he was no more than a few disjointed bones and sinew, with a bale of dusty, matted hair. His loincloth was filthy, and his skin was dark and crusty like dried up peyote. He came on, slowly, like a hungry, mangy, coyote passing through a season of heat and famine with never enough water to drink.

As he came closer, accompanied by a single orange butterfly, she could see that his high cheekbones were yet more pronounced by his sunken eyes and sallow cheeks. His lips were cracked, and bleeding and his feet were calloused to a hard shell. Cactus needles negligently protruded from his left calf. It was dusk when he came up to where she sat. The sky had taken on a beautiful color gradation from light pink, almost white, to a soft dark blue. A warm but welcome breeze appeared.

The Salt Shack Dweller squatted next to Patricia, and she spoke for the first time since Raymond had cut the rope to the raft.

Somewhat reserved she said, "I am glad you have returned. I have been mostly alone since you departed on the raft. I have learned to live alone when

I need to or want to. Sometimes, I like it, being alone. I learned a lot about myself. I like the decisions I have made. It is good that you have returned."

The Salt Shack Dweller smiled broadly, causing blood to run profusely from his broken and blistered lips down his chin, dripping into the sand between them.

He could not stop smiling, which continued the flow of blood, but he spoke for the first time, looking at her and nothing else, small tears welling in his parched eyes. "I've prayed to the Gods every day that I've been gone that you would still be here," he said.

"I'm very happy. I could not have been presented with better news. I do love you. Together we will start a great clan. This place is a good place to start a clan. I've explored this river valley from top to bottom. See the fresh water in this pristine river. It's cold and fresh and sweet and runs uninterrupted for more than a hundred miles, maybe more."

"There's plenty of game, see there; there's a small mule deer coming down to the far bank for a drink. The rabbits are fat and plentiful. The land along the river is fertile and we can build aquifers to irrigate our crops. The weather is never too cold, and the sky is always a beautiful blue. When the rains come, they are welcome relief, never oppression."

"See the mountains that surround us? They are only hours away. They are certainly close enough to be a good source from which to gather fuel for our fires in winter and solid wood for shelter construction and a variety of game and wild herbs and even medicine for our ceremonies."

"Yes," said Patricia. "I'm sure of all of that." She paused, then asked, "What have you done while you've been gone from our home, when you left on your raft?"

The Salt Shack Dweller smiled broadly, oblivious to the blood seeping from his sliced lips.

"Ah, I have eliminated the great threat to our land, to our life, to our children. Now I can rest."

"What did you do?"

"I rode the raft on that flooded night to the proximity of the nuclear plant that shoots the death rays at all of us at all times. I was crazy back then. I thought, I would use dynamite to stop their deadly onslaught, but thanks be to the Gods, I realized in time that if I used dynamite, I could possibly create a horrible catastrophe."

"So instead, I hauled a hundred gallons of deep red paint through the dark of night to their generating station. And I painted, in dripping, deep red paint, the entire structure in 15 feet tall letters."

"I painted the names of three places: Chernobyl, 3 Mile Island, Fukushima Daiichi. Everyone will get the message now. And there will be massive demonstrations. And they will force the corporate criminals to shut down the death plants before they explode or create terrible damage to the magical DNA that favors all of life."

Patricia was silent for a moment before she spoke.

"I don't really know what DNA is but I'm going to learn. I got a job at Chris Smith's bookstore on Mill Avenue. There is a lot I want to learn. And a lot I need to learn. He's a professor at the university. He is going to give me books to read. Like history books. And science books. And probably books about DNA."

The Salt Shack Dweller continued to smile and bleed and there was love in his eyes for Patricia.

"It will be a wonderful place for you to work and learn and further your education. Chris Smith is a wise and gentle man. He knows what is going on in the world. His bookstore is nearby. Everything we need is here. We will have the warm and gentle nights with no deadly rays to assault us."

"We will have tonight and every other night of our long lives to be together with the sensual air of the marvelous desert night for our blanket, the easy wind in these great river bank trees as our song, and the virgin stars and moon as our unblemished nightlight."

Patricia dabbed the blood dripping from the lips of the Salt Shack Dweller. Both of them felt a soft, cool breeze drift off of the river and when they turned to invite more of the soothing breeze, they saw Cecilia approaching quietly, softly, protectively. Walking with Cecilia was Francis carrying the silent boy, Carl. There was something somber in Cecilia's movement.

Nearing the Salt Shack Dweller and Patricia she spoke, "Francis would like to talk to us all together."

Francis stood facing the three. He did not hesitate. He spoke clearly with a solid demeanor.

He took a deep breath and said, "Within the next few days, I will be arrested and jailed."

Before he could continue, Patricia and Cecilia cried out at the same time, "But why?"

"Well," said Francis, "I once came upon a man beating up a woman outside a liquor store and I got a little rough with the man to stop the beating. Unfortunately, there were no witnesses."

"When it came to talking to the police, the man said I was the instigator. I tried to get the woman to tell the police what really happened, but she seemed to be too afraid to talk. She was bruised but she told the police that she injured herself early in the day, not from the man."

"They were white but I'm not white, so, I was arrested for assault and battery. I lost at the court. I was sentenced to two years in jail. But I couldn't leave Carl. I had no one to take care of him, so I hightailed it from Louisiana and ran out of money in Tempe."

"We'll get the judge to help you," said Cecilia as the Salt Shack Dweller and Patricia nodded.

"Yes, that would be helpful, but I still expect, I'll go to jail for some amount of time. Maybe, the judge can get my time cut down a bit, and I'm sure I'll get time off for good behavior," smiled Francis, trying very hard to lighten the disastrous event that was closing in on him.

He paused, then, composed himself and continued while the others were silent. He looked at Carl and brought the other three together in a circle around Carl with everyone connected with their arms over the shoulders of the others.

With Carl tucked comfortably in the sand at the bottom of the human tent, Francis continued, "I have come to ask you three collectively, if you would be willing to take care of Carl while I am gone. He has never reacted positively to anyone like he does with you all. I trust each of you. You are chiefs and healers and youth personified."

With a tear forming in Francis' left eye, he said, "I don't know what else to do. I know it's—"

Before anyone could speak, Patricia spoke calmly, leaving no doubt about her strength and sincerity. "I will care for Carl. I will protect him. I will teach him. I will make sure that he knows that you are coming back for him and that he is deeply loved."

"As will I," said Cecilia.

"As will I," said the Salt Shack Dweller.

Unable to speak any further, they all uttered a silent, collective cry, all looking down at Carl in the sand, encased in a human tent by Francis, by Patricia, by Cecilia, and by the Salt Shack Dweller. The tears of the four were warm and soft falling onto Carl's face as he looked up at the four without blinking.

Carl smiled, allowing the tears to sink into his skin, and said, "River" as the river started to rise again.